THE DEVIL'S GAMBLE

Lily DANES · *Eve* KINCAID

A LOST COAST HARBOR NOVEL

Dark & Stormy Books

To the gamblers.

Gamble everything for love, if you are a true human being.
If not, leave this gathering.
Half-heartedness doesn't reach into majesty.

Mevlana Rumi (1207 - 1273)

CHAPTER ONE

Bridget Donnelly navigated the dark, uneven parking lot that led to the dive bar. She hated this part of the job, but if Frank was going to dodge her calls, she had no choice.

These visits went much better when she had her brother standing behind her glaring at the client, though. Niall was out of town for the weekend and she couldn't wait any longer.

The tremor of excitement in her stomach increased as she approached the scarred door to the Vista del Mar and the muffled sounds from inside grew louder. Music from the aged jukebox. Yelling. Crashing. The muted sound of fist meeting flesh.

Bridget stepped aside seconds before the door burst open and two burly men tumbled out, propelled by the rotund bartender/owner/bouncer.

"Not inside!" he yelled, kicking one of the drunken patrons in the ass for emphasis. "You take that shit outside."

Bridget parked herself in the doorway so Frank couldn't miss her on his return trip. Hands on hip, feet shoulder-width apart. Her boots had a two-inch heel, low enough to run in if she had to, and giving her just enough extra height that she'd tower over most men. She pulled hers shoulders back, trying to take advantage of the few inches she now had on the bartender.

"Hello, Frank."

He nearly jumped. Would have, if his bulk could have left the ground.

"Jesus, Bridget," he said, his hand flying up to his heart, though Bridget had yet to see proof Frank had one. "Didn't see you there."

She raised her chin and looked down at him, letting a slow smile spread over her face. "Yes, I know."

Frank shifted and looked around nervously, but when he didn't spy Niall Donnelly, the desperation on his face faded.

"I was gonna call you back. It's busy tonight. I'll get you next week."

He started toward the door but she planted her feet in the doorway and stood firm.

"I'll get it tonight."

He laughed. "Whatcha gonna do, Bridget? I don't see your muscle around here."

She shook her head and crossed her arms. "Now, Frank, we've always had a good professional relationship. I'd sure hate for that to end over such a small matter. I'm sure you can hit up the till and pay your debts."

He snorted. "I'll get ya next week. I told you. You know I'm good for it."

A crash behind her warned that another brawl was about to break out and Frank took advantage of the distraction to push her to one side and get into the building.

Jerk. He owed her two thousand dollars and was a week late in settling up. If word got out that people didn't have to pay her, she'd be out of business in no time.

She stalked him to the bar, through the rough crowd, several of whom called out to her.

"Bridget girl, you slummin' tonight?" a man at the bar asked. "Why ain't you at your brother's? That's a better place for a girl like you."

"Hey, Lyle. Just doing a little work," she said. "You doing okay?"

Lyle, a dockworker and steady customer, shrugged. "Did all right on the last round. What's the line on the Villanova game?"

"Five points, Villanova."

Lyle smiled and showed off a gaping hole where a front tooth should have been. He ran a hand over his graying beard. "I'd take that. Say, a hundred."

"You got it, Lyle. A hundred on Villanova. Good luck."

Bridget turned her attention back to the bartender who was staying at the other end of the bar, even though everyone there had full beers. Frank was ignoring her. No one ignored Bridget Donnelly.

She made her way to the middle of the bar and leaned over. "You can at least buy me a beer, Frank."

His beady eyes squinted, nearly disappearing under his unruly eyebrows. "Since when do you drink here?"

Since you forced me to step into this creepy dive. But instead of speaking her mind, she smiled. He pushed a cold beer across the bar toward her.

"That's all you're getting tonight."

Bridget took a sip. It was ice cold, which was refreshing in the hot and humid bar. It also effectively hid the taste of the cheap brew. Frank watched her with a suspicious glare as she raised the glass.

"You're busy tonight," she said, keeping her voice casual.

He nodded. "Yeah, about time, too. Been a damn ghost town in here lately."

Not tonight. It was a Friday and there was nothing else to do in Lost Coast Harbor, so the locals went out to drink. The Vista del Mar was the watering hole for the dockworkers, timber fallers, and other rough crowds. You came here if you were looking for drugs or a fight or to make other regrettable decisions. There was a reason it was also known as the VD by the Sea.

"Looks like it's picking up," she said, and took another sip. Ugh. The temperature had risen a couple of degrees and it was enough to make the brew bitter. "Be a shame if the party had to shut down early."

She slid the mostly unfinished beer back to Frank, who frowned.

"See you tomorrow, Frank."

Frank's already beady eyes narrowed further. "What are you up to, girl?"

She gave him a knowing smile and then walked out of the door without looking back. The door slammed behind her and she gritted her teeth.

Son of a bitch.

Frank might think he could ignore her because she didn't have her brother with her, but he was wrong. She was more than capable of handling her problems. That bastard owed her money and damn it, she was getting it. She had plans for that money.

She hit the button on her key fob to open the trunk of the red convertible and then fished around for the lug nut wrench. She closed the trunk, and then she set her purse and jacket inside the car, and walked to the front bumper. The heavy metal tool was loose in her hand and she tested the weight while she looked around the parking lot. Mostly empty of people, but crowded with cars. And dark. There was not much security around the VD by the Sea.

Perfect.

She took a practice swing, then stepped up to the bumper, pulled the tool back and swung with all her strength at the headlight.

The light shattered with a minor explosion. She moved to the other one, reared back, and let go.

No one in the parking lot seemed the least bit interested in the woman destroying a car, so she continued her work. Focusing on the hood, she banged the wrench into the metal, leaving several large dents and scrapes in the paint.

Her breath came faster. Her heart thumped in her chest. She swung again, taking out the front quarter panel with a loud crunch.

When the car was sufficiently damaged, she straightened and admired her work. It was going to cost a few hundred dollars to fix, but that was the price of doing business. It would cost far more if her customers stopped paying their debts. With a satisfied nod, she examined the tool and saw some red paint scrapes on the metal. She walked down to the dock at the edge of the parking lot and tossed the wrench into the water. She took a deep breath, rolled her shoulders, and the tension in her neck eased. This was just what she needed. It was better than boxing at her brother's martial arts studio. It beat the hell out of yoga.

On the way back to the car, she took her phone out of the pocket of her jeans and tapped a number.

"9-1-1, what is your emergency?"

Bridget smiled. "Someone damaged my car down at the Vista del Mar. Can you send an officer to take a report?"

While waiting for the cops to arrive, she put her jacket back on, and sat on the trunk. The bar was nearing capacity. It was almost ten o'clock, and the party should be going full force for another few hours.

It took a whole six minutes for the Lost Coast Harbor police cruiser to turn down the sloped drive in front of the dive bar, lighting up the parking lot with the red and blue lights. Bridget stood and waved at Officer Sean Hollis, who returned the wave with a smile and parked behind her convertible. The driver door opened and the youngest and newest member of the police department stepped out, a fresh-faced recruit with an earnest smile.

"Hey, Sean."

"Hey, Bridget. What happened here?"

The passenger-side door opened and another man stepped out. Bridget's composure slipped for a moment.

Holy mother, who is that?

Tall, broad, with a short-trimmed beard, and hair that her fingers begged to run through. He walked around the car and stood next to Sean, emphasizing the officer's boyishness. This was a man.

A helluva man.

"Bridget, this is Ethan Ford. He's our new chief of police," Sean said. "Chief Ford, this is Bridget Donnelly."

The tremor of excitement she'd felt when she approached the bar that night, and the rush of adrenaline she'd experienced while beating the crap out of her own car—those paled next to the electricity in the police chief's touch as he shook her hand.

"Nice to meet you, Ms. Donnelly," he said, in a voice that was warm and deep.

She had to look up at him to meet his gaze and guessed he was at least six-four. His hair was a russet brown, and a bit too long for a police officer. He was wearing jeans and a heavy canvas jacket, not a regular police uniform.

He didn't look like any cop she'd ever seen before.

Eyes the color of whiskey stared back at her, and his lips quirked up at her deliberate study of him, as if curious as to whether he'd passed her inspection. He certainly had.

She smiled in return. "Welcome to Lost Coast Harbor."

He tilted his head slightly and his eyes crinkled up at the corners. In an instant, she knew—there was a spark there, a challenge, a puzzle to solve.

She'd always loved puzzles.

So this was Lost Coast Harbor.

Ethan took in the scene in front of him—the red and blue lights reflected off the puddles in the rutted parking lot and the dirty siding of the bar. A steady stream of patrons exited the bar, pulling caps down low over their faces, and averting their eyes as they scurried into the shadows and away from the Lost Coast Harbor police cruiser. Like cockroaches running for cover when a light was turned on.

It was a rough crowd, and if the rookie officer would look up from his inspection of Bridget Donnelly's front end, he might actually see a few patrons who were wanted on outstanding warrants. As yet, Ethan was too new to the department and the town to be that familiar with the warrants or the residents.

This was his first chance to do a ride-along with his officers and get to know his new town. Lost Coast Harbor was worlds away from Bakersfield in every way. His former home was flat, dry, and sprawling. Lost Coast Harbor was a quaint town on a remote stretch of the Northern California coast that drew tourists with its charm and the chance to experience the unspoiled landscape.

And while Bakersfield had its share of crime, Lost Coast Harbor had a slightly different crime problem—the small town had recently lost its police chief and a senior detective to a corruption scandal. It was ugly, and the town council wanted it cleaned up fast. Lost Coast Harbor depended on its tourism season, and this was bad news.

The town needed someone to come in and make a clean sweep, and the timing couldn't have been better for Ethan. It was time for a fresh start for him as well.

Despite the town's recent history, Lost Coast Harbor was exactly what he was looking for—a small town, with small problems. The cancer of corruption had been excised, and now the new police chief could make a difference, set things back on track. Make the picturesque town everything it should be. Safe. Secure. Mayberry by the Sea.

The young woman at his side looked pleased as she watched the crowd walking away from the tavern. Ethan studied her in the dim light. A hint of a smile hovered around her full lips, and she didn't seem to be the least bit upset about her car being bashed in. He had a hard time imagining that this was her usual hang-out.

"Wouldn't Donnelly's Pub be more your speed?" he asked.

She flashed him a smile that made his heart stop—wide and bright and charming. "Sure, if I wanted to hang out with my brother. But I don't."

Of course. Lost Coast Harbor was a small town, far smaller than Bakersfield. Two people here with the same last name were very likely related.

"This doesn't seem like your crowd," he said, watching still more people vacate the building like it was on fire.

"I just stopped by for a beer," she said.

Ethan leaned back on the cruiser's hood and crossed his arms. He'd been suspicious before, but this was a flat out lie. "Really?"

Bridget Donnelly returned his direct and suspicious gaze without blinking. She was tall, not as tall as her boots made her out to be, but tall nonetheless. And she was fucking gorgeous, with a long mane of dark hair, pale skin, and large blue eyes. Her lips were full and pouty, almost looking bruised. And she didn't apologize for her beauty or hide behind false modesty. This was a confident woman.

And there was no way in hell she was stopping in at the Vista del Mar for a drink after work.

"Wow, Bridget, you must have really pissed someone off," Sean said from the front of the car where he was cataloguing the damage. "I'm afraid you can't drive this home tonight. Need me to call you a tow?"

"Thanks, Sean, that would be great," she said, then turned those spectacular eyes back to Ethan. "So, Sheriff, how long have you been in town?"

"Just a couple of weeks," he said. "And it's chief. Not sheriff. The sheriff's office patrols the county."

From the teasing tone in her voice, he had no doubt that Bridget Donnelly knew the difference.

She shrugged. "Sure. Where did you come from?"

"Bakersfield."

"Guess I don't need to ask why you left, then," she said with that wide smile.

"It's not as bad as its reputation," he said. "And what do you do, Ms. Donnelly?"

"It's Bridget. And I work at Donnelly Lumber."

Another Donnelly business, and one he knew more about. Donnelly Lumber was one of the largest employers in Lost Coast Harbor. The family also owned a construction company. Gavin Donnelly had the pub on the town square, where Ethan had already enjoyed a couple of pints. And another brother had a bookstore, he recalled.

"And what do you do there, Bridget?"

"I'm the controller."

His eyebrows shot up in surprise. "You are?"

Bridget's lips turned up. "Yes," she said, leaning forward as if to tell him a secret. "I'm actually quite intelligent."

He laughed and held up a hand. "I meant no offense. You seemed a little young for that title."

"And I am," she said. "But I also have a master's degree in

finance."

And her father owned the company. How much did that help her in her career?

A stout man in a stained white shirt emerged from the knot of bar patrons who were still exiting the building like it was on fire. He stomped across the parking lot toward them, gave Ethan a murderous glare, and then shoved a paper bag into Bridget's hands. Without a word, he waddled back to the bar, closed the door, and a second later the neon "open" sign went dark. Ethan had never seen a single police cruiser clear out a party so fast.

"What's that?" Ethan asked, nodding at the bag in her hands.

Bridget smirked. "To-go order."

He raised an eyebrow at her words and got a sly smile in return. While it had a reputation for being the dregs of the dive bars, he doubted the bartender would be bold enough to hand over a bag of drugs right in front of the police car with flashing red lights. And Bridget Donnelly didn't look like a drug dealer.

She looked like trouble—just not that kind. She looked like the kind of trouble that ended with a hangover in Vegas and a cheap gold band and a lot of blank spaces leading up to that. And Ethan Ford's new mantra was to stay away from trouble, of all kinds.

Bridget tucked the brown paper sack into her purse with a satisfied smile on her face.

"Any idea who would want to beat your car up?" he asked.

She shook her head and her long hair fell about her face. "No idea."

"Are you a regular here?"

"Here? No. I try and avoid this place."

"But you stopped in for a beer?"

She shrugged at being caught in her own lie. "It was convenient."

He tilted his head and watched her. She was lying, but he had no idea why. Someone had taken a crowbar to her sweet little convertible and she was acting like it was no big deal. Insurance would cover it. A minor inconvenience.

And he supposed that was true, but the privilege she had wrapped around herself rankled. Growing up poor, bouncing between foster families and various juvenile facilities, that little red sports car would have been an unattainable dream. To have someone damage it would have been devastating. Even now, as an adult with a solid career and retirement plan, that cavalier attitude rubbed him the wrong way.

"You can come down to the office on Monday to pick up a police report for the insurance claim," he said.

She nodded, watching him. "Why did you come here?"

"You called 9-1-1."

She shook her head, sending a ripple through the long black waves of hair. "Why did you come here, to Lost Coast Harbor?"

"They hired me to be the police chief."

Bridget continued to study him openly and the intense scrutiny made him feel as if he were naked. And then he thought about being naked with her and was uncomfortable in a whole new way.

"What time on Monday?"

Her question ripped his thoughts out of the gutter. "Pardon?"

"What time on Monday should I come by your office and pick up the report?"

He didn't bother to say that she could pick it up at the public counter. He wouldn't mind seeing her again. Maybe a view of Bridget Donnelly in the bright light of day would dispel the inappropriate thoughts gathering in his mind.

"Anytime after eight o'clock."

A dark, sleek sedan pulled up and idled near them and Bridget threw her purse over her shoulder.

"That's my ride," she said, meeting his gaze. "See you around, Sheriff."

He grinned at her and walked her to the car.

"See you around," he said, helping her into the car, which was driven by a young man whose jacket indicated he was a security guard for Donnelly Lumber. "You stay out of trouble."

She winked, communicating what both of them knew— that wasn't going to happen.

CHAPTER TWO

Bridget staggered out of bed when her alarm sounded, barely opening her eyes as she stumbled to the bathroom. The cold tile floor under her bare feet woke her better than any coffee could, but coffee would be needed to get her through the reports she had to do every Monday. She reached into the shower to turn on the water and heard the old pipes groan.

"That's new," she said, her voice echoing in the enclosure. The pipes had done funny things before. Burst in unusually cold weather. Leaked, ruining the ceiling in the guest bedroom. Shot out a thick, rust-colored slurry to let her know it was time to invest in new pipes.

A weak stream of icy water trickled from the shower head and splashed on the tile.

"Oh, for fuck's sake," she muttered. She twisted the knob all the way open, but the water pressure remained just above zero.

She loved her old farmhouse in the hills east of Lost Coast Harbor. It had been her grandmother's house and she'd been thrilled that she'd been able to buy it from the estate. Many of her happiest childhood memories had been forged here.

She was looking forward to building her future on this land. But damn if the place wasn't a money pit.

Bridget threw her work clothes and make-up into a tote bag, dressed in gym gear, and headed downstairs. She'd have to shower at the gym this morning and get ready for work there. She walked out of the house and threw her bag into the passenger seat of the company car she'd borrowed until her own was repaired. Then she made the short walk to the small wooden building that housed the well. She'd call someone to come look at this, and the first thing they'd ask her was if she'd checked the well. Not that she knew what she was looking for, but she'd check the damn well.

The first thing she saw when she opened the door was that a board from the back of the little square building was missing and she could look straight through to the other side, like a tall narrow window.

The shaft of light illuminated a new white PVC pipe that led out the back of the pump house.

"Son of a bitch."

Bridget walked around the back and started to follow the pipe, which headed east toward the property line. At least she knew what the problem was now, even if she didn't yet know *who* the problem was.

The rage inside her bubbled over and she went back inside the wooden structure and studied the new connection. It was crude and she quickly disconnected it, filling her shoes with cold water before she got the house water reconnected.

Sloshing out of the shed, she stared into the woods that bordered her property, separating it from the neighboring undeveloped parcel. Some asshole was stealing her water.

And she had plans for that water. The discovery was enough to wake her fully and she stormed back to her car, then sped out of the driveway, sending gravel spraying behind her.

A little more than an hour later, she pulled into the employee parking lot at Donnelly Lumber's corporate office—a simple two-story building across a two-lane street from the lumber mill. She took the stairs and walked to the end of the hall to her office, throwing her gym bag on a chair in the corner. She was the only person in the executive offices upstairs, and it was as quiet as possible. A steady hum from the mill always filled the air, along with the near-constant rumble from trucks delivering the massive logs, or taking away the hewn lumber.

Bridget frowned at her calendar and noted the deadlines for several reports, then jumped into her work. She may have looked calm as she double-checked entries and saved the files, but inside she was mad as hell. She emailed the file to her coworker, copied her father, and plotted how to protect her water from thieving neighbors.

It was too early on a Monday to already be fighting off a headache. Today, she couldn't really blame the job, like she normally did. It wasn't hard work, just tedious, and she really didn't care about the Donnelly Lumber financials. It was her family's business, and she was glad it was successful. It had paid for her college degrees, gave her a cushy upbringing, and meant her parents and siblings were secure. She took pride in doing a good job.

But the company was her father's passion, not hers. It was Richard Donnelly's drive that kept the family's legacy growing—from timber to milling to construction to rental properties, and more recently an investment into the Hastings shipping business. It was a legacy that would make her ancestors proud, if a little confused about how the family was doing it all completely within the law. That hadn't always been the Donnelly style.

A knock at the door drew her attention and she looked up to see Grace Ransom, the in-house counsel for Donnelly Lumber and the family's other assorted businesses, standing in her doorway, holding two large coffees. Her light-brown hair, always perfectly cut in a precise A-line bob, was mussed from the wind. She'd been Bridget's best friend since grade school, even though they had never had much in common. Grace, bookish and serious, balanced out Bridget's temper and impulse-control issues. They'd even gone off to college together at the University of California, Davis. They shared an apartment for four years until Grace went off to law school in Oregon and Bridget headed to UCLA for her Master's degree.

"For me?" Bridget asked with hopeful smile.

"It's nine o'clock on a Monday and I'm already done with this week," Grace said, setting one of the cups on Bridget's desk and then sinking into the upholstered chair across from her.

"Tell me about it," Bridget said with a nod.

Grace shook her head. "I just had to go confront the plant supervisor at the mill about allowing his men to use their work email to trade porn. How's your day?"

Chastising idiots who sent porn through the company server seemed to be a large portion of Grace's work as an in-house attorney for the company. Bridget raised an eyebrow. "Not nearly as interesting as yours."

"Yeah, well, I find porn's less interesting when I'm discussing it with a sixty-year-old man sporting a beer gut, who worked with my dad. We have to install that monitoring software," she said. She took a sip of her coffee and took a deep breath. "Tell me why your day is off to a bad start."

Bridget considered diving into the water theft, but thought she'd start with the good news first.

"I met the new police chief."

"Oh, God. Bridget, what did you do?"

She laughed at Grace's worried expression. "I didn't get arrested, if that's what you're asking. He was with Sean Hollis, who took a report on my car getting banged up Friday night."

Grace frowned. "What happened to your car? Are you okay?"

She waved her hand dismissively. "It's fine. Just a few dents. I had one of the security guys pick me up, and then borrowed a company car for a few days until I get mine back," she said. "But what have you heard about Chief Ford? What's his story?"

Grace tilted her head. As of very recently, she was the newest member of the town council, which had hired Ethan Ford. Up to now, Bridget hadn't seen why being on the council was worth the hassle. Now, though, she saw an up-side, since her friend would have the inside scoop on the chief.

"I haven't met him yet, but I've heard only good things. Mayor Strong says he's going to be a great chief," she said. "He has a sterling reputation and he's going to get the department cleaned up."

Someone needed to do that. The former chief had seemed to run a good department—right up to the moment he'd been arrested and charged with corruption.

"Chief Ford is going to have his work cut out for him," Bridget said.

"I suppose I'll get an introduction next week at the town council meeting. We're voting on his contract then," Grace said, then glanced at the thin gold watch on her wrist and stood up. "Oh, damn it. I've got to meet with your dad about the succession plans for the business. Let me know if you're going out for lunch."

"Wait, Grace," Bridget said, and Grace turned in the doorway.

"He's not planning to retire, is he? I mean, I know he will someday, but not in the immediate future, right?" Bridget asked.

Grace stepped back into the office and lowered her voice. "No, this is just to update some paperwork. As far as I know, Richard is not making imminent plans to step down."

Bridget nodded and breathed a sigh of relief. She was the most likely choice to take over the family's lumber and construction businesses—she was the controller, knew the business inside and out, and was the only one of the six Donnelly children who worked for the company.

"You really do need to tell him, Bridget," Grace said.

"I will."

Grace raised an eyebrow.

"I mean it. I will tell him. But just not right now," Bridget said.

Her friend gave an exasperated sigh and a wave as she

returned to her office across the hall. Bridget understood why Grace was frustrated. She was caught in the middle, knowing that Richard planned on having Bridget take over—and that Bridget had other plans. That wasn't fair and Bridget was going to talk with her dad. Soon.

But she'd been saying that for more than six months.

She took a sip of the coffee and returned to her spreadsheets, reviewing the end of the month reports from February, and other assorted accounting tasks that she had to grit her teeth to get through. Her strategy was to do it as quickly as possible. By late-morning, she had completed the most pressing tasks.

That meant she had plenty of time to run over to the police department to pick up the report. Bridget ran a hand over her pencil skirt, and checked her lipstick in the mirror on her bookshelf. She straightened her collar, then undid the top button, just enough to hint at what was beneath.

With a toss of her hair, she headed down to the parking lot. She made a quick stop on the short drive to the Lost Coast Harbor police department, and walked into the station with a large pink box of donuts, which she set directly in front of Sean Hollis.

"Good morning, Sean," she said with a friendly smile. "Where's the new sheriff?"

The young officer's eyes widened at the sight of the box.

"Oh, donuts. Thank you, Bridget. And it's chief, not sheriff," he corrected, giving her a grin as he opened the box. "I think he's back in his office. I can call him."

"No need, I'll find him," she said, walking past the end of the counter toward the closed office door in the back of the room. "Make sure those donuts get to the break room."

She waved to a few familiar faces as she walked back toward the chief's office. She knew most of the people who worked for the police department—either as a result of growing up in a small town, or because at some point, many of them had worked for her family. Or arrested one of them. Despite the fact that Bridget didn't belong in the police station, no one stopped her. In her experience, a confident walk and a friendly smile could get you into just about anywhere.

Halfway across the long room, she heard her name called out.

"Hey there, Bridget," Sgt. Carl Spatz said, meeting her in the middle of the main office. "How ya been?"

"Hi, Carl," she said, shaking the sergeant's hand. "Haven't seen you in a while. What have you been doing?"

Carl shrugged, ran a hand over his thick graying hair, and made a vague motion toward the rest of the room. "Lots of overtime in the last month, since we were, uh, understaffed."

Bridget nodded with a sympathetic smile. It couldn't have been easy for the rest of the police force to learn that two of their own were corrupt. Rumors swept through the small town like wild fire—who had known, who else was involved, and who would be the next officer fired or arrested? And Carl, a veteran of the force, had surely been one of those scrutinized in the wake of the scandal.

"Things settling down now?" she asked.

Carl nodded. "Yeah, the new chief seems like a good guy," he said, then leaned a little closer to her and dropped his voice. "Hey, uh, the Purdue game—what's it look like?"

She edged toward him and kept her voice low. "Six points,

Kentucky."

The sergeant nodded thoughtfully while he considered the odds, and then gave her a smile. "Put me down for five on Kentucky?"

The overtime may have been a hassle for Carl and his coworkers, but it also meant that her law enforcement customers would have extra money to play with. And with the college championship tournament starting, it could be a very profitable season. Just in time, too. She had plans for the money she'd make this month.

Bridget gave him a wink and a grin. "You got it."

Carl coughed and looked down, and Bridget turned to find Ethan Ford standing directly behind her.

"Good morning, Ms. Donnelly," he said. His voice was low and rich and she wanted to wrap herself in it. "Is there something I can help you with?"

She smiled and motioned to the pink box on the counter, now surrounded by the officers and support staff. "I brought donuts."

Carl's face lit up. "Donuts? Thanks, Bridget. You're a dear."

He hurried toward the counter to fight over the last of the maple bars. While the sergeant seemed happy to have breakfast, Chief Ford frowned and gave her a stern look.

"You didn't have to do that," he said. His tone said she shouldn't do that.

"Cops like donuts. And it's not like the Lost Coast Harbor police force can be bought by a box of pastries," Bridget said. Everyone knew damn well that the going rate for this department was a lot more than fried dough.

The chief was trying to keep a serious expression, but his

amber eyes sparkled with amusement and his lips twitched. "Still, we have a policy against taking gifts, however well intentioned. And it will be strictly enforced."

In the light of day, Ethan Ford was just as handsome as he'd been in the dark parking lot. His hair was still a shade too long for a cop, and that neatly trimmed beard gave her all sorts of thoughts about how that would feel…everywhere.

"Enforce your rules after lunch," Bridget said. "Your police force is hungry. Anyway, I'm here to pick up the report on my car."

He nodded toward his office door. "It's in my office. Come with me."

She followed him the rest of the way through the main room, admiring the view as she went. He was tall, and even though she'd worn heels, she'd had to look up to make eye contact with him. No small feat, since she was five-nine in her bare feet. His shoulders were broad and now that he was wearing a shirt and tie, but no jacket, she could see the outline of the muscles in his arms and shoulders under the fabric.

Too soon, they were in his office and she found herself seated across his desk from him. She was trying to stem the flood of very inappropriate thoughts she was having about the police chief. It wasn't working.

"Officer Hollis couldn't find anyone who witnessed the vandalism of your car," he said, sliding a piece of paper across the desk to her.

Bridget took the paper without reading it, folded it and stuck in the outside pocket of her purse. "I'm sure he tried."

Ethan leaned back in his chair and studied her carefully.

"You don't seem very upset about this."

Was she supposed to be crying over it? Even if she hadn't caused the damage herself, it was just a car. And a ten-year-old, used car, at that. No reason to get upset.

"Well, these things happen," she said.

"No. They don't happen," he said. "Usually, if a car gets damaged in a parking lot, it's because someone was trying to steal it or break into it for the stereo. Clearly, that wasn't the case here."

Bridget leaned back in the chair and crossed her legs, watching his eyes follow the movement.

"I'm sure you'll get your man," Bridget said, and her heart skipped at the twitch in his lips. He was trying so hard to be stern. "I mean, if that's your goal."

Ethan bit his lip and looked down, a slow smile spreading across his face. When he looked up and met her gaze, her nerves jumped at the heat there. A dangerous banked heat, hidden behind the professional facade.

It was in her best interests to stay on the police chief's good side. Chief Grady had left her alone, perhaps out of professional courtesy since he, too, was breaking the law. She ran a low-key business and never gave customers any reason to turn on her. If there were problems, like with Frank, they were handled quietly and quickly. Never in any way that would require law enforcement to get involved. And she was fairly confident that there wasn't anyone on the police force who cared to shut down her operation, even the few who weren't regular customers.

The last thing she needed was to get off on the wrong foot with Ethan Ford. Not now. March and April were usually her most profitable months, so she really needed to focus on the college basketball series and not on the lovely police chief with the broad shoulders, eyes the color of whiskey, and a troublesome grin.

"Is there anything else I can do for you, Ms. Donnelly?" he asked.

Had the door behind her been closed, she might have taken him up on the offer in his eyes. But the chatter and ringing phones in the other room reminded her that they weren't alone.

Yet.

And her mind started working on how to fix that.

IN THE TWO DAYS SINCE HE'D FIRST LAID EYES ON HER, Ethan had nearly convinced himself that once he saw Bridget Donnelly in the bright fluorescent light, he'd find some flaw to fixate on and that would get the haunting, dark-haired woman out of his mind.

He was wrong. As she sat across from him in his office, Ethan couldn't think of a single thing to improve. She had classic black Irish coloring. The long, nearly black hair had been tamed, pulled back from her face, but hanging down her back in soft waves. Her bright blue eyes were framed by the thickest, darkest eyelashes he'd ever seen, and her full lips were a distraction he didn't need right now in his life.

"There may be something else you can do for me," she said, and his heart rate picked up at the idea. "I recently moved out to my grandmother's house and it appears that my neighbors might be tapping into my well."

Ethan picked up a pen and found a fresh notepad. "When

did you notice this? What did you see?"

"This morning, there was no water pressure in the house, and there's a new white pipe going out the back of the well house toward the trees."

"Who lives next door?"

"No one. It's undeveloped."

That meant growers. It was a common problem on the North Coast. Some of the marijuana growers had gone legit, attempting to comply with state laws that regulated medical marijuana. Others didn't bother. None of it was legal under the federal law. But even the legal grow sites could be magnets for trouble—home invasions, theft, and Lord knows what pesticides they threw down on their crops.

"What's your address?"

Bridget gave him the address, an unfamiliar street. "Where is this?"

"It's about twenty minutes outside of town, you go east on Old Stage Road, and then go south on Townes Valley Road."

He set the pen down. "You're outside of my jurisdiction. Have you talked to the sheriff's department yet?"

She shook her head. "Of course. I'll call them."

"I'll call over there and get a deputy to look into it. Give me your phone number and I'll let you know what they say."

"Are you asking for my number, Chief Ford?"

He wasn't so far out of the game that he couldn't charm a pretty woman with a smile. Though the stakes felt higher with Bridget. Like she'd see through any forced grin and call him on it.

"Call me Ethan."

Her eyes darted down and she bit her lower lip, then

she pulled a card from her purse and took his pen, writing her number on the back. When she stood, he followed and walked with her to the door of his office.

At the door, she stopped and turned back, handing him the card and looking him straight in the eye. "That's my cell phone. Call me if anything…comes up."

His eyes widened at her saucy grin and then she walked away with a long-limbed, hip-swinging swagger.

Damn. That woman was trouble. As he was intimately familiar with trouble himself, he should know. But Bridget Donnelly should come with a warning label, and maybe flashing orange lights.

He shook his head and went back to his desk, but Bridget's absence made the room feel far more empty and far less interesting. He looked through the small phone directory for a sheriff's substation phone number, but couldn't figure out from the listing which one would be closest to Bridget's house. He walked back into the large main room and found Valerie Childs at her desk.

Valerie, the only female officer in Lost Coast Harbor's police department, had been appointed interim chief until Ethan's arrival. She'd been instrumental in uncovering the corruption that led to the last chief's arrest, and her reward was a temporary appointment to lead the office. The fact that she'd been so eager to hand the title to Ethan should have been a clue about the department he was taking over.

Ethan knocked on Valerie's desk and she looked up from her computer.

"Good morning, Chief," she said. "Can I help you with something?"

"Yeah, I need a sheriff's substation number to give Bridget Donnelly. She's on Townes Valley Road," he said, taking the seat across from Valerie.

Like him, Valerie was a transplant to Lost Coast Harbor. He didn't know too much about her, except that she'd been working in San Jose until her transfer to the small town department. That raised a bit of a red flag for him—what would prompt a young up-and-coming police officer to move from a large city department to a small town police force? And then he remembered that was exactly what he had done.

Valerie reached for a map from her desk drawer and smoothed it out on the blotter. "This is Townes Valley Road, here," she said, running a finger over a road that led into a valley east of Lost Coast Harbor. "The nearest sheriff's office is here in Lost Coast Harbor, but just call Curt McBride on his cell phone. It's easier than trying to catch him in the office. He's got about four deputies patrolling the area outside of LCH."

She wrote a phone number on a scrap of paper and slid it across the counter. "What sort of problem does Bridget Donnelly have?"

"Someone's stealing her water. Tapped into her well," Ethan said, tucking the paper into his pocket. "The parcel next door is undeveloped."

Valerie nodded, her face serious. "Growers."

"Yeah, probably so."

She tilted her head and gave him a curious look. "And she reported it to us?"

Ethan shrugged. "No, not really. I mean, it came up in

our discussion. Why would that be unusual?"

Valerie smiled. "The Donnellys aren't usually the ones reporting the crimes. They're more often the ones committing them."

"What?" Ethan asked, trying to reconcile that with the image he'd had of the family as one of the town's founders.

"Well, maybe committing is too strong a word. Suspected of them," Valerie said. "They're just troublemakers. The Donnelly Devils didn't get that nickname by accident."

"What the hell kind of nickname is that?"

"A well-earned one, I hear. Apparently, they were quite a handful during the teenage years, though I guess most of them have outgrown that," Valerie said. "Don't get me wrong, they're very nice people. Just used to having things go their way. Whether or not the law permits it. But don't worry about it. Make friends with them, and you'll be fine. They're connected politically, and that's what you need for your job."

Whatever trouble the Donnelly family was, it couldn't be worse than what Ethan had left behind. And as if to drive that point home, his cell phone buzzed, and he saw his brother's phone number on the screen. He silenced the phone and shoved it into pocket. Whatever Trevor had gotten himself into this time, it was nothing that Ethan could fix for him. His younger brother was on his own, and it was about time.

"Anyway, you've got bigger fish to fry, Chief. Sounds like you've got an illegal grow on private property, maybe theft of resources."

"It's outside our jurisdiction," he said.

"Call Curt McBride. He'll handle it," Valerie said. "We do work together on these things, so if you need me to help out, let me know."

"Thanks, Valerie," Ethan said, standing.

"So, uh, how are things going with the town council?" she asked, and Ethan paused.

"They're fine, I guess. I still haven't met some of them in person, but the council meeting is next week and I'm sure I'll see the rest then."

Valerie nodded, her face thoughtful. "Are they behaving themselves?"

Ethan sat back down. "What are you talking about?"

"Well, it's just that this is a small town and they're the big fish. Sometimes they like to hold up votes to squeeze favors out of the new hires. I figured you might have run into this. But if not, that's great. Maybe they're trying to impress you."

Ethan frowned. "No, nothing like that is going on. They approved my temporary contract for ninety days, and they're voting on my permanent contract at the meeting this month."

Valerie paused, and then pressed her lips together, as if she didn't want to deliver bad news. "You might want to keep an eye on the council agenda, make sure it doesn't get tabled for a month."

"Did they do that to you?"

Valerie laughed. "No, but that's because they needed someone to act as interim chief who wasn't under investigation. That left me and Sean Hollis, and Hollis is like, twelve years old. They needed me."

The young detective hadn't held the chief's job long—just under a month—and had handed over the job and all its perks and obligations to Ethan with great enthusiasm. Not that he blamed her, since it hadn't been her choice to head up the police department.

"Thanks for the tip. I'll watch the agenda."

He walked back to the claustrophobic office, and went straight to his computer. He was still a little surprised that he'd gotten the job as chief of police, since he'd only been a detective sergeant at Bakersfield, and had little political experience that would have let him climb into the upper ranks there. Knowing his resume was thin, he'd worked the interview with everything he'd had, and it had paid off. At the time, he figured that getting the job was the biggest hurdle. Lost Coast Harbor was a small town, and Ethan hadn't worried about his ability to work with the elected officials who hired him.

He pulled up the Lost Coast Harbor website and clicked on the town council's agenda for the meeting the following week.

An addendum had been added to the schedule of items the five-person council would be taking up. The vote on his permanent contract, scheduled for the March meeting, was moved to April.

Son of a bitch.

CHAPTER THREE

The sun was just setting behind her as Bridget headed east out of Lost Coast Harbor. It was only a twenty-minute drive to her house, but once she got home it felt a world away from work. Her grandmother's century-old farmhouse had always been a refuge from the chaos of the Donnelly household. Some of her fondest childhood memories were of working in the garden with her grandmother, and learning to cook in the rustic kitchen. Now Kathleen Flynn's house was one-hundred-percent Bridget's, and each time she took the turnoff that led her home she felt that warm glow of arriving somewhere she belonged.

Bridget slowed the sedan as the road curved around the west-facing hillside. With luck, and a lot more cash, that hillside would be covered in pinot noir grapevines by this time next year. All she needed was a really good end to the basketball season and she'd have enough set aside to pay for fifteen acres of vines and the labor to plant them. The wine wouldn't be ready for several years at least, but this was a long-term strategy and she was willing to be patient.

Not that she had a lot of experience being patient, but

she'd made a plan to start her own business—literally from the ground up. While that would take time, at the end, she'd have something of her own. Not something handed to her because of her family, but something she built with her own hands.

And if it failed—well, that was something she didn't want to think about. Too many nights she was kept awake by the fear that if she didn't escape Donnelly Lumber, she'd be stuck there, taking over the business from her father and never able to walk away.

She pulled up to the mailbox and left the car running as she walked around to open the box. She pulled the envelopes out and heard the clink of metal hitting metal. Leaning down, she peered into the opening and saw a cylinder in the back. She reached in and pulled out a .223 round.

"Son of a bitch."

No need to wonder who was threatening her. She glared eastward at the dark row of trees as the gravel crunched under her tires.

She unlocked the door and went inside, leaving the mail and the message from the neighbors on the worn wooden table that her grandfather had built. Its benches could easily accommodate ten hungry people elbowing each other for another helping of her grandmother's Irish stew. The kitchen itself was generous, too, with wide wooden counters and lots of cabinets. Bridget's own addition—a commercial range—had replaced the wood-burning stove that Grandma Kathleen had used, but it was still as warm and welcoming as it had always been.

Acting on a hunch, Bridget turned the sink faucet. The

water was down to a trickle again.

"Fuckers."

So much for her plans of relaxing in a hot bath with a glass of wine and a good book. Bridget kicked off her shoes and walked barefoot up the stairs to her bedroom, the stairs creaking as she went. She might as well head to Donnelly's Pub for dinner. At least she could get some work done while she watched the scores for tonight's games. Thankfully, she didn't have to be dressed up for this part of her job, and she quickly changed into jeans and a black sweater and pulled on a pair of black ankle boots. Her black leather tote was traded for a canvas messenger bag, and she tossed in a sleek laptop, a thin black ledger, and a couple of extra pens.

Going out in the dusky evening to fix the water connection again did not appeal to her. So she checked the doors and windows, then locked up behind her as she left the house.

When she'd moved in six months earlier, she had never bothered locking her doors. The house was too remote and her grandmother didn't even have keys to the doors. But then her nearest neighbor, a couple who lived about a mile from her, warned that they'd lost some equipment from their unlocked garage. Bridget had invested in new locks for the house, and was careful about locking up when she left. Now with someone bold enough to install their own irrigation system out of her well, she wasn't likely to forget.

Maybe it was time to get an alarm system, she thought, as she drove back down the hill toward Lost Coast Harbor. But the response time to any intruder would be at least ten minutes, likely more. A dog might deter anyone who set out to frighten her, and that seemed to be what the neighbors wanted to do. She thought about the round ball of fluff that her sister Elizabeth had brought home on her last visit—yapping, shedding, leaving land mines all over their parents' manicured lawn. Definitely not that kind of dog, at least.

It was dark by the time she parked behind Donnelly's Pub. She let herself in the backdoor, walked past the pool tables and the crowd enjoying the basketball game on the large-screen TVs, and made her way to the pub's quieter main room. Gavin wouldn't allow a TV in that area, preferring that his customers talk to each other.

Her brother waved to her from behind the bar and she saw that he'd reserved her favorite small booth for her at the end of the room, the only table where she could catch a glimpse of the TV so she could check the score.

She sat with her back to the rest of the bar, which had the added advantage of letting her work unobserved in the booth. She pulled out her ledger and a stack of small slips of paper she'd collected over the course of the weekend and started entering figures into the book. She had only made a couple entries when a glass of red wine slid into her view.

"I'll thank you to keep a low profile here tonight," Gavin said, sliding into the booth opposite her.

She grinned. "Of course."

"No money changes hands here," he said, his face serious.

"Nope."

"I mean it."

She took a sip of the pinot noir. "Does that mean my wine is free?"

"It means I'll kick you out before I risk my liquor license," Gavin said.

"You like this bar better than your own sister?"

"I have three sisters. I only have one pub."

"You won't even know I'm here," she said. With any luck, neither would any of her customers. Her presence could remind them of the stakes they had on the game. And if they thought too much about that, they might stop gambling.

The noise from the back room spilled into the bar and she looked up to see a replay of a three-point play. As predicted, the game was close, within a few points. She supposed she should get a satellite dish set up at her house. And buy a television. But until she got around to that, she enjoyed the atmosphere at Gavin's pub. Watching the games could be stressful, too, so she preferred to wait and see the scores after the buzzer.

"I'll get you something to eat," Gavin said and returned to the bar.

Bridget returned to her book, entering the bets along with initials of the bettors. It was a system that she'd developed in the ten years she'd been in the business. She'd learned from the best—Oscar Pimentel, her dad's old bookie. She'd known him as Uncle Oscar when she was growing up. She knew he loved sports, and she liked to hang out with her dad when he watched the games, so she'd spent a lot of time with Oscar.

Eventually, she'd figured out how he made his living and when she'd asked about it, he'd been more than willing to teach her about odds and payouts and splits and how to protect your business from poachers. By the time her dad had figured out what they were discussing, Bridget had discovered a new world full of opportunity for a mathematically gifted individual.

In college, she'd refined her skills and made enough to boost her standard of living at the University of California, Davis. She switched her major to finance, which allowed her to explore the advanced math courses that honed her skills. It was a highly successful venture. When she'd graduated, she'd sold her business to an incoming junior with concentrations in sports medicine and statistics. That seed money had helped her buy into Oscar's business, then take over when he retired and moved to Las Vegas, where he was working in a legit sports book for extra money.

Gavin set a plate of fish and chips in front of her, then sat down again.

"Next weekend is St. Patrick's Day."

"Your busiest night of the year," Bridget said, biting into a crisp fry.

"Especially since Mom decided to make it some sort of town-wide bash."

"You don't have to remind me. I'm the one stuck organizing most of this event. And in the middle of the college championship series, which couldn't be worse timing."

Molly Donnelly had proposed a St. Patrick's Day celebration for the whole town and now the entire square in the center of town was going to be transformed into an outdoor party with activities for kids, live music, local restaurants showing off their specialties, and of course, a lot of beer. Molly had immediately roped in every available Donnelly offspring to help, and Bridget had been tasked with overseeing the entire event.

"Do you have everything you need for the Irish coffees?" she asked.

"It's under control. We'll set up the booth right outside the pub and that way I can keep the bar open, too," he said. "With you and Mom in charge, I'm sure everything will go smoothly."

Gavin returned to the bar and Bridget finished her dinner while updating her ledger. As she tallied her year-to-date profits, she frowned at the figures. Business was slightly down from last year. She suspected it wasn't due to anything but a change in how people bet on sports. The bulk of her customers were leftovers from Oscar's business—the old timers who liked the personal touch of betting cash. A few of the younger clients thought it was cool to have a bookie. But it was hard to recruit new clients when they could just as easily go online and put some money down on a fantasy sports league. Bookmaking was becoming a relic, and unless she wanted to expand to online betting, her business was going to eventually fade away.

Not that she expected to make a career of it. This was simply a short-term plan to make some extra money while the industry still existed. She only needed the extra income for another three years, five max. She hoped the business could hold on that long.

Bridget kept an eye on the point spread while entering the last of the bets into the book. As she added the last figures, a fresh glass of wine was set down in front of her.

"I hope you don't expect me to pay for that, Gavin," she said, focusing on the book.

When she didn't get an immediate reply, she looked up and saw Ethan Ford standing at the end of the booth. Her stomach did a slow roll at the mere sight of him. He was still wearing a coat that was dotted from the rain, and his hair was mussed.

"You're not my brother."

"No, I'm definitely not your brother," he said. "And the wine's on me."

She smiled and slid the papers off the table, closing them in the ledger book and setting it on the seat beside her.

"Evening, Sheriff," she said with a grin.

"Hello, Ms. Donnelly," he said, flashing her a smile that made her melt inside.

"Call me Bridget."

"And you can call me Ethan."

"Are you here to watch the game, Ethan?" she asked.

He shook his head. "No, thought I'd stop in for a beer. What are you doing?"

"Same," she said. "Won't you join me?"

His eyes flickered in the direction of her ledger, but when he looked back she met his gaze without offering any explanation. If he was a good cop, he'd figure it out eventually. And if he was a bad cop, that might work to her advantage. And if he was a really bad cop, he might just become her best customer.

But when she studied the man across the table from her, she got the impression he was a good cop—in all ways. And that might be a problem if he was serious about cleaning up Lost Coast Harbor.

Ethan shrugged out of his coat, hanging it on the hook at the end of the booth, and she got a better look at the way the cotton shirt clung to his shoulders and chest, the muscles well-defined, even through the fabric. A rush of heat surged through her, settling in all the right places and pushing away any concerns she might have.

As he slid back into the booth, a tall and rangy young man approached the table with a wide grin, one hand already reaching for his wallet.

"Bridget! Hey, there you are. I've been looking for you."

"Hey, Owen," Bridget said, greeting one of her favorite customers. Owen played the long shots, which meant he lost almost every single bet. They weren't called long shots for nothing. "Have you met the new police chief? This is Ethan Ford."

Owen's face went pale and he stammered a greeting and shook Ethan's hand, then skedaddled into the back room. She wouldn't have accepted a bet from him in the bar since she'd promised Gavin, but saving Owen in front of the police chief had probably cost her. She hoped the young idiot appreciated that.

At least Ethan didn't seem to notice the quick backpedal. Maybe she should stay close to the new police chief. What was the old adage? Keep your friends close, but your enemies closer. Ethan Ford wasn't exactly the enemy, but he could cause problems for her.

And she wouldn't mind keeping him close. Very, very close.

BRIDGET DONNELLY WAS DEFINITELY UP TO SOMETHING. It was something she didn't want to share with him. But at least she was hanging out at her brother's pub and not at the dive bar.

At Bridget's invitation, Ethan ordered the special and

savored the perfectly poured stout.

"That's your brother?" he asked, nodding toward the dark-haired bartender with the blue eyes. Except for the age difference, they could be twins.

Bridget nodded. "That's Gavin. It's his pub."

"So how many siblings do you have?"

"There are six of us. Gavin is the oldest. Then Niall and Neve. They're twins. And then Declan," she said. "Then me and my younger sister, Elizabeth."

"And which ones are the Donnelly Devils?" he asked.

Bridget laughed and the sound warmed him. "I suppose all of us, at one point or another. Maybe Elizabeth could skate on that, but only because she's the baby and learned how not to get caught by watching the rest of us. Where did you hear that?"

"From a good source," he said with a smile. She didn't seem the least bit offended by the title.

He'd been amused by the nickname himself. Whatever mischief Bridget and her siblings got into, it couldn't have been too bad. She had no criminal record, and Ethan hadn't found anything on her siblings, but there were plenty of rumors in the police department. Reckless driving, some minor vandalism and destructive behavior. The sort of things that Ethan and his brother had done when they were children—before they'd graduated to the serious stuff.

"Do you have any brothers or sisters?" she asked.

His stomach churned. Such an innocuous question, but it never failed to make him tense up. It led to other questions—where was his brother, what did he do. And those were topics that Ethan would prefer not to talk about.

"Yes, one brother," he said. "He's a few years younger than me."

Gavin appeared with a plate full of fish and chips before Bridget could probe further.

She introduced Ethan to her brother. Gavin nodded to his sister. "You may have missed it, but Kentucky pulled ahead by six."

He walked away and Bridget leaned over to see the TV, then focused her attention back on him with those piercing blue eyes.

"You follow basketball?" he asked.

"A little," she said, then sipped the wine he'd bought her. "How goes the crime fighting?"

He smiled. "I suppose it's going well."

So far, his job had consisted of a lot of paperwork—vacation requests and overtime approvals, signing off on police reports by his officers, and learning the ins and outs of the budget process so he could ensure enough funds to keep the lights on in the small department. It felt a long way from crime fighting.

"Is it hard, coming into the department after Chief Grady's arrest?"

The direct question took him by surprise. With few exceptions, no one had yet addressed the ousted chief's departure except in hushed and oblique ways. He'd only discussed the details with Valerie Childs. Even the town council had glossed over the criminal conduct going on within the department.

"A little. I think the fact that it happened so fast threw the department for a loop. They had an idea of who Grady was, and now they have to figure out who he really was, and come to terms with that."

The entire town was going through that adjustment, from what he could tell. Chief Grady had led the police force for sixteen years and had been a respected member of the community. His arrest, along with that of his chief detective, had rocked Lost Coast Harbor.

"At least the town council acted fast to get a new chief of police," Bridget said.

"Yes, though they've delayed the vote on my contract for another month," he said.

Bridget laughed. The musical sound warmed him. "You've got to be kidding me. What have they asked you to do for them?"

He shook his head. "Nothing. But Valerie Childs warned me that they might seek favors until the permanent contract was approved. What do you think? Is that what's going on?"

She nodded, then her eyes went to an approaching figure and she forced a smile.

"Mayor Strong," she said with a wide smile. "How nice to see you here."

Lost Coast Harbor's council was a part-time governing body, meeting once a month unless a special session was called. All five members, including the mayor, had outside jobs because the position paid only a few hundred dollars a month. But in return for a paltry paycheck, the town council members had outsized influence over zoning decisions, business licenses, and all sorts of regulations. And from what little Ethan had learned so far, Dale Strong, an insurance broker who had been mayor for more than eight years, seemed to have the most influence.

"Chief Ford, I'm really glad I ran into you. I don't know if you saw, but the vote on your contract was delayed to April," he said.

"Yes, I saw that. Is there a problem?" The delay wouldn't have annoyed him except for Valerie's warning about the council members. As long as it was just one month, he didn't care too much.

The mayor shrugged his thin shoulders. "No, not at all. These things happen. We have a new council member and need to make sure that Ms. Ransom is up to speed on everything before she votes on something so important."

At that excuse, Bridget's eyes narrowed slightly and her lips tightened. "Grace is highly intelligent and she's a lawyer. She knows how to read a contract."

The mayor flashed Bridget an annoyed glance, then looked at Ethan. "In the meantime, your temporary contract is in place. The vote is merely a formality."

It was a formality that he wanted behind him, Ethan thought. He didn't move to Lost Coast Harbor for a temporary job. This was where he planned to settle down, get a fresh start, and build a career.

"If you say so," Ethan said.

"How are you enjoying our little town?" Mayor Strong asked, clapping Ethan on the shoulder.

"It's very nice, thank you," he said.

"You're from Bakersfield, right?"

Ethan nodded. "Yes, that's right. I was with the Bakersfield Police Department for twelve years."

"Is that where you grew up?"

"I grew up in the Central Valley," Ethan said, hedging

his answer. The Central Valley covered a lot of territory, and so had he and his brother. Bakersfield was supposed to be a place to start over, and for many years, that had worked out. Until it didn't.

"Is your family in law enforcement?" Strong asked.

"No, I'm the first one," he said. He supposed his family had worked in the criminal justice system, just not as cops, attorneys, or judges. But someone had to make the trouble that those players were paid to deal with. So in that respect, they were an integral part of the criminal justice system.

"What do they do?"

Ethan took a sip of his beer before answering. "Various things, mostly small business owners, like yourself. How is the insurance business these days?"

His answers seemed to satisfy the mayor, who was quickly distracted by the chance to talk about himself. But a quick glance at Bridget told him that she caught his dodge. She watched him with a bit of a smile on her full lips as the mayor droned on about the exciting world of commercial insurance.

"Well, I'll let you get back to your dinner. I'm sure you'll find our little stretch of the Lost Coast a friendly place," the mayor said, then wished them a good evening and departed.

Bridget rolled her eyes as the mayor walked away. "You just wait. You'll be dismissing his wife's parking tickets before the end of the week."

Ethan laughed. "No, I won't be. The mayor will be disappointed if he asks me to do that."

It would be easier to stand up to the council with some allies, though. Like the Donnelly family. They had influence and their stamp of approval would carry some weight. And if that meant spending time with the lovely Bridget Donnelly, well, that was a sacrifice he was more than willing to make.

"What are you doing this weekend?" he asked. "Would you like to get dinner?"

"We're getting dinner now."

"Yes, but like a date."

"*Like* a date?" Her blue eyes were teasing, sparkling in the low light of the bar and he knew that his reason for getting close to Bridget had nothing to do with her family's social status.

"A date."

She smiled. "Sure, Sheriff. That sounds nice."

"Friday night?"

She shook her head. "I can't Friday. There's a game."

He studied her with a curious expression. "You're really into basketball."

"I am."

"Saturday?"

"Oh. Saturday." She hesitated, glanced at the bar where her brother was working and then looked back at Ethan. "Why don't you come to the St. Patrick's Day party with me? Donnelly Lumber is sponsoring it. It should be a good time. You can shake hands and kiss babies."

"And meet the Donnelly family."

She laughed and slid out of the booth. "Yeah, that too," she said. "You might as well meet all the criminals. Gonna make your job a lot easier."

CHAPTER FOUR

B ridget pulled her wool coat around her, hurrying to the town square. She was late, but it couldn't be helped. The crew from Donnelly Construction was finishing the repairs to the well and erecting a small chain-link enclosure around the building. She couldn't leave for the St. Patrick's Day party until they were finished with the last-minute job.

But at least now she could relax, knowing that her obnoxious neighbors couldn't drain her well while she was gone.

Don't fuck with the woman who owns a construction firm. And especially don't fuck with her ability to take a shower.

The security was a start, but it was still playing defense. It was bad enough that her neighbors were trespassing onto her property, with all its precious and personal history. But water was the lifeblood of a vineyard. Bridget was angry enough to play offense with the unknown neighbors. But later. Now she had a date with the tall, dark, and sexy police chief.

She had debated whether to tell Ethan about the rifle round in her mailbox, but inviting the police into her life would make things complicated. The deputy she'd spoken to seemed to be angling for information on her "business associates." They'd ended the conversation with an impasse. He wanted to come out and see the property, but she put him off for now. Hopefully, securing the well would put an end to the theft. Then the neighbors, and the cops, would turn their attention elsewhere.

As she turned the corner, the town square came into view, but the familiar landmark looked completely different than she'd seen it before. Strung with lights, with two large white tents open at the sides on one side of the park. The band was set up in the gazebo. The streets bordering the town square had been closed for the event, and crowds milled around booths selling hot drinks and food.

Bridget nodded and smiled at familiar faces and greeted friends as she wove through the crowd. Her mother would be thrilled with the turnout, and no doubt this would become an annual affair. She suppressed a sigh at the thought of this becoming her annual chore. She loved a good party, but planning this one had stretched her thin with juggling her duties at Donnelly Lumber. Add in the fact that the party fell smack in the middle of the college basketball championships and she was seriously at her breaking point.

A blast of warm air hit her as she walked into Donnelly's Pub, and the heavy wool coat instantly became too warm. She shrugged out of the coat and scanned the bar for Ethan. She'd suggested they meet here, rather than have him pick her up. Her house could be hard for a local to find in the daylight. It would be cruel to send the new chief up into the hills when she was just as capable of driving herself to town.

Ethan was at the end of the bar, chatting with Gavin. His hair was slightly neater, as if he'd finally located a barber, but was still longer than usual for a cop. She was pleased that he hadn't gone full military crew-cut. The thick waves suited him.

As if sensing her, he looked up and directly at her. His eyes were the shade of whiskey, and warmed her the same way—spreading slowly through her body, with an unsettling side effect of making her a little lightheaded.

He stood as she approached and pulled out a barstool for her.

"I'm sorry to be late," Bridget said. Her cheeks felt flushed from the warmth of the bar.

"It's not a problem," Ethan said, taking her coat and purse and hanging them over the back of his chair. "You look lovely."

"Bridget, get you a glass of wine?" Gavin asked.

She shook her head.

"No, not right now, thanks," she said, catching her brother's raised eyebrow. "The new sheriff has babies to kiss, hands to shake, and backs to slap, right?"

She ignored Gavin's doubtful expression and flashed Ethan a smile. "Want to go meet your constituents?"

As they walked to the door, Ethan placed his hand on the small of her back and the heat penetrated the fabric of her dress, warming her. His fingers brushed her skin as he helped her into her coat and left a tingle in their wake. When the brief contact ended, the absence of his touch left her off-kilter and momentarily stunned at his effect on her.

When the door opened, the cold air brought her back to her senses and she saw Ethan watching her closely. Too closely. She pasted on a smile, buried her lust-filled thoughts, and hurried out into the cool night air.

Before they'd gone thirty feet from the pub, Bridget saw a client wave at her, trying to get her attention. And unfortunately, it was Rowdy Pritchard, who could not be trusted not to place a bet in front of a cop. She waved back with a cheerful smile and pulled Ethan in the opposite direction.

"Friend of yours?" he asked.

"I grew up in Lost Coast Harbor. I think I know everyone here," she said. No need to introduce him to Rowdy. They'd probably meet soon enough, if Rowdy's past was any indication of his future.

The crowd was growing, but especially around two booths on the square—Gavin's tent featuring Irish coffees, and the booth outside The Sweet Spot bakery, where Annabel had probably already sold out of her éclairs. And wherever Annabel was, Declan couldn't be far away.

Sure enough, while she placed her order for a coffee, heavy on the Irish, Bridget spotted her brother standing at the edge of bakery's booth, chatting with Councilwoman Marlene Dewey. As soon as Marlene walked away, Declan's gaze returned the booth, seeking out Annabel.

While she wasn't hiding from them, Bridget wasn't going out of her way to introduce Ethan to her family members. Declan was the exception to that, so she steered Ethan in that direction. Declan owned Lost in a Book, the town's only bookstore, and was the family's good seed. And he was, at that moment, so distracted by Annabel that he didn't even notice when Bridget sidled up next to him.

"Look at you, being social," Bridget teased, sliding an arm around her brother's waist. His love for the pretty baker was on display in the way he looked at Annabel. It made her happy that he'd found someone who didn't mind that Declan could be bit stuffy, at least by Donnelly standards. Annabel seemed to be just as in love as Declan. That he was even at the St. Patrick's Day party was proof that Annabel was a good influence on him.

Declan returned the hug and extended his hand to Ethan.

"Chief Ford, it's a pleasure," he said. "Welcome to Lost Coast Harbor."

"Dec, what did Annabel have to promise you to get you to stay out past dark?" she asked.

He shook his head with an exasperated smile.

"It's the weekend, so I can stay up past my bedtime," he said, and then a wicked glint crept into his blue eyes. "Will I be seeing you two at dinner tomorrow night?"

Her eyes widened at her brother's nerve, suggesting that she subject Ethan to the Donnelly family's mandatory Sunday night dinner. Their mother had been bemoaning the lack of grandchildren in her life, and bringing a date to a family dinner would be like drawing a bullseye on her own back. And it would be unconscionable to put Ethan under that pressure. Declan was probably trying to use her to draw fire from himself and Annabel. Which was smart, but really sneaky.

"Oh, look at the time," she said, grabbing Ethan's arm. "We should let Declan toddle off to bed."

She grabbed Ethan's arm and led him away, then looked back and gave her brother a glare. He smiled and returned to mooning over his new love.

Ethan laughed as she took his arm. "Dinner?"

She shook her head. "Every Sunday, dinner with the family. It's like a forced march, but with pot roast."

"Doesn't sound so bad," he said.

"My mother is on a rampage to get grandchildren, so it can be an ordeal," she said. "It's not for rookies."

She could have gone into the other reasons to be wary of an invitation to dinner with her family, but Mayor Strong interrupted them with a hearty greeting.

"Chief Ford, I'm so happy you could make our celebration," the mayor said, clapping Ethan on the back.

The Irish coffee was making her warm inside, and more than a little reckless. Bridget leaned closer to Ethan while the mayor was jawing at him, brushing her breast against his arm. He was a rock, though, and couldn't be sidetracked from the discussion. But up close, she caught a hint of Ethan's scent—deep, woodsy, and clean—and was so distracted that she missed the mayor's question to her.

She gave him a nod and a smile and Mayor Strong looked pleased. Ethan gave her an incredulous look, which he covered up quickly. Her mind raced for a clue as to what they were talking about so she could figure out what she'd just agreed to.

The mayor shook Ethan's hand. "I guess I'll see you next week then. I sure appreciate your help with this," he said, then melted into the crowd.

Ethan led her away and took her mug from her and sipped her Irish coffee. "So why did you think I should help the mayor out with his property boundary dispute?"

She hadn't been paying attention to Mayor Strong's tale of woe, but if that's all it was, that wasn't too bad. She met his gaze and smiled. "It's good politics."

"I don't do politics."

"Yes, you do, Sheriff. You need those votes."

He shook his head. "I thought you'd have my back, Irish."

She laughed. "And I do. This minor chore will help you in the long run."

"I play by the rules," he said.

"What rules?"

"The ones that everyone must abide by. Play fair. Do the right thing. Never hurt a woman or a child," he said. "And you get a job based on merit, not on favors."

She studied him under the light of the streetlamp. Though she rarely needed liquid courage, the whiskey loosened her tongue a little.

"Is that what you think of me? That I got my job because my daddy owns the company?" Bridget asked, tilting her head. She wouldn't be offended if he did. Everyone probably thought that. They'd be wrong, but it was a reasonable assumption.

"I did not say that," he said.

She shrugged. "You'd be correct. He had a controller retire a few years ago and right after, he found out that the man had embezzled a small fortune over his career. I came in and cleaned it up. He asked me to help because he trusted me. But I've stayed because I do a good job."

"Would he fire you if you didn't?" he asked with a hint of a smile.

"No, he'd have Grace fire me," Bridget said with a laugh. "Grace has to do all his dirty work."

"Is that Grace Ransom, the new council member?"

"Yes, she just won the special election," Bridget said.

"And you two work together?"

"Yes, and we've been best friends since we were five years old," she said. "And before you even think it, no, she didn't get her job because of our connection. She's very good at what she does."

"I'm sure she is. And I'm sure you are, as well," he said. "But I didn't have a family business to fall back on. And I thought I got this job on merit, but now I'm finding out that it's conditional."

Bridget tugged his arm, pulling him away from the square and dodging another insistent wave by Rowdy Pritchard. Of all her clients, he was one she most wanted to drop. But he paid up regularly, so she kept taking his bets. Tonight, though, he was insistent about talking to her and no matter how often she brushed him off, he kept trying to get her alone. It would be hard to pass Rowdy off as a friend when she barely tolerated him, and if he didn't blurt out his bet in front of Ethan, he'd probably tell some story from when they were in high school—which was the peak of Rowdy's personal development. Bridget pretended not to see another urgent wave and kept her eyes on Ethan.

"It has nothing to do with your ability to do the job," she said, as they skirted the outside of the crowds gathering to listen to the band. "They're used to being kowtowed to. They don't have a whole lot of power, but what they do have they like to wield."

Ethan snorted. "Yeah, well, they have the power to reject my contract."

She squeezed his arm. "You'll be fine." Another wave

caught her attention and she sighed. "Speaking of which…"

"Chief Ford," Councilwoman Lynn Fitzgerald said, elbowing Bridget to the side to get to Ethan.

"Ms. Fitzgerald," Ethan said, tugging Bridget back to his side and keeping an arm loosely around her waist.

If he was concerned that Lynn was hitting on him, he needn't be, but Bridget couldn't say anything. The security of being snug against his body flooded her body with heat and her mind with very naughty thoughts. It may not have been a too-familiar feeling, but she certainly liked it.

"I've been wanting to talk with you about the police station renovation project," Lynn said.

Ethan glanced at Bridget and then back to Lynn. "I'm really not familiar with the details of it."

"That office needs to be gutted and rebuilt and we have the funds set aside for it," Lynn said. "And of course, my partner Karen is the ideal person to do the work. She's very reputable. She owns Merz Construction. Very competitive. She'd do the work for almost cost. I'll have her come by the office this week."

"I look forward to meeting her," he said.

Bridget grinned at his cautious foray into politics, held up her empty cup, and excused herself for a refill. Ethan shot her a panicked look as she backed away. She winked and then wove through the crowd. Bringing Ethan to the St. Patrick's Day party was good for him, and staying close to him was good for her. She could keep an eye on whether he was going to butt into her business. And he was good company. Not to mention damn easy on the eyes.

It was a slow crawl through the party to get to the booth,

and Bridget stopped several times to greet people on her way. After what seemed like an eternity, she was within reach of her goal and could get back to the police chief before he'd been besieged by the rest of the local politicians. Looking back, she caught a glimpse of him, trapped with Lynn Fitzgerald and now joined by Mayor Strong. He stood a head above the rest of the crowd, and looked down on the council members with a patient expression.

Bridget turned away and started back to the table to refill her drink, still dwelling on the memory of how it had felt to be tucked under his arm.

So she was unprepared when a strong hand gripped her forearm and yanked her around the corner of a building into a dark alley.

As soon as Bridget left his side, Ethan missed her presence. She was an expert tour guide to Lost Coast Harbor's politics and history, happy to point out the people who he might need to suck up to, and the ones he'd be likely to arrest in the future.

He watched her walk away, then glance back at him and toss him a wink that made his cock stir. Hell, his cock had been on alert since she'd walk into the bar and shrugged off her heavy wool coat to reveal a form-fitting dark green dress. Even now, bundled up again in her coat, his body reacted, knowing what was underneath.

Ethan turned back to the councilwoman in front of him, who was too busy badmouthing all the other construction firms in town to notice that Bridget had left, or that Ethan's attention was diverted. He nodded and smiled, taking a cue from Bridget, and let Lynn Fitzgerald do most of the talking.

"Karen can start work right away. She has a very competent crew and it doesn't hurt for the city to hire women-owned businesses, either. Sends a very positive message supporting diversity," she said.

Ethan nodded and glanced around for Bridget. Gavin Donnelly's booth selling the Irish coffees was doing a brisk business, but it was close by and he could see it from where he was trapped with Lynn Fitzgerald. Bridget should have been back. He scanned the crowd, but couldn't see her.

After another minute, which dragged on for an eternity, Ethan politely excused himself to go look for Bridget. She wasn't on the sidewalk, and he was sure he'd see her in the crowd because she was taller than most of the women in attendance, and a good portion of the men, too. And his height, he should have a good view.

He was almost to the booth when a flash of movement in a narrow space between two buildings caught his eye. It was a dark passage, barely wide enough to be called an alley, and Ethan moved closer. A man, young and broad-shouldered, gripping a woman's arm—a pale, thin hand twisting to get away.

Ethan reacted without thought, pure instinct driving him into the dark. It was as if he were twelve years old again, barreling into the room to save his foster mother from her abusive boyfriend. He had gotten flattened by the man's fist for his trouble, and then got up and charged him again. He'd had far too much practice playing that role.

With a growl, Ethan yanked the man away, and Bridget stumbled backward out of his grip. Ethan slammed the man against the brick wall.

"The fuck?" the man sputtered, but Ethan's fist cut off any further questions.

It felt good. It always felt good to punch a bully. But never more so than when it was a man who thought he could throw his size around with a woman. He pinned the man to the wall by his throat, then turned to Bridget.

"You okay?"

Her nod said yes, but her eyes were wide and confused. Behind her a heavily muscled man barreled into the alley.

"What's going on?" he demanded, took in Ethan, and then his eyes fixed on the man with the blood flowing freely from his nose.

"It's fine, Niall," Bridget said, recovering from the shock. "Rowdy, meet the new police chief."

Ethan let up on the man's throat and he gasped for breath.

"Chief Ford, meet Rowdy Pritchard," Bridget said.

"What do you want to do, Bridget?" Ethan asked. "File a complaint?"

She paused, then shook her head. "No. Just let him go. I'm fine."

He narrowed his eyes. "Let him go?"

"I'll take care of him, Chief," Niall said, a wide grin lighting up his face. He was tall and broad with gingery red hair. He looked like he knew his way around a boxing ring.

"No!" Bridget said, stepping between Niall and Rowdy. "Niall, it's fine."

Ethan let go of Rowdy Pritchard and the man hit the ground running.

"Yeah, you better run, you son of a bitch," Niall called

after him, but his tone was more mocking than threatening. He immediately turned his attention back to Bridget with a grin. "You forget everything I taught you?"

She shook her head and rolled her eyes. "Ethan, this is my brother, Niall."

Another Donnelly brother. They were everywhere. But this brother he'd heard of. He owned the martial arts studio, and Ethan had heard he still competed in MMA tournaments. He was surprised that Rowdy Pritchard was stupid enough to harass Bridget, knowing who her brother was.

"What was going on with that guy?" Ethan asked Bridget and saw that some of Rowdy's blood had gotten on the cuff of his shirt. Bridget pulled a napkin from her pocket and tried to dab it away, but the stain wasn't going anywhere.

"Nothing. He's just a jerk," she said quietly.

"You'll let me know if you need anything, Bridge?" Niall said. "Nice meeting you, Chief. See you around."

Niall disappeared into the crowd that seemed completely unaware of the brief altercation in the alley. Bridget kept working the napkin against the fabric of Ethan's shirt with hands that trembled slightly. Enclosing both her hands in his, he waited until she looked up at him.

"What did that guy want?"

"Can we get out of here?" she asked.

He nodded and led her out of the alley, keeping her hand tight in his, and leading her back to Donnelly's. It was quieter inside the pub than outside, where all the festivities were, and Bridget's confidence seemed to return once she was on familiar ground. She took their coats and hung them on pegs in the hallway that led to the backdoor. Then she stepped behind the bar and grabbed a towel and a glass, which she filled from the nozzle, and led him to a corner of the room where a tall table was open.

She dipped the towel into the glass. "Club soda. Takes out any stain."

He let her focus on the small stain on his cuff while he watched her. She really didn't want to talk about what Rowdy Pritchard was doing, and he didn't want to push. But at the same time, he needed to know. A man had just put his hands on Bridget. He wasn't going to get away with that.

"Is Rowdy his given name, or just a well-earned nickname?" Ethan asked.

She looked up and smiled and this time, the expression reached her eyes. "Unfortunately for him, it's his real name."

"A self-fulfilling prophecy?"

She laughed. "Probably so. Though genetics didn't help. You probably have ledgers in your archives going back generations, detailing the many arrests of the Pritchard family."

"What would I find about the Donnelly family there?" he asked.

She grinned. "Well, going back a few generations, you'd find quite a bit. My great-great-grandfather stole his business partner's gold, which is how he founded this town, along with the Hastings family," she said. "But more recently, just lots of little things. Pranks gone wrong. Reckless driving. A few instances of various Donnelly children being escorted home by officers."

He raised an eyebrow. "Including you?"

"You have to ask?"

He laughed. "I guess I don't."

She took the dry end of the towel and used that to absorb some of the wetness from his shirt, and the stain which had lightened to a barely noticeable discoloration.

"Thank you," he said. "You want to go back out to the party?"

She glanced toward the door. "I suppose so."

"We don't have to," he said.

She sighed. "Yeah, I do. My mother organized this event. I need to make sure I'm seen."

She forced a smile and headed for the hall to get their coats. Ethan followed, and held her coat for her, his fingers brushing the back of her neck as he helped her with the collar, and he felt her shiver.

Good. He wasn't the only one affected by that contact.

Bridget turned and faced him, just inches away, and he could smell a hint of perfume. He wanted to lean in, inhale it, run his hands through that mane of black hair and across her porcelain skin. Her eyes locked on his and his breath caught in his chest. Damn, she was beautiful.

He reached up, cupping a hand behind her head, his fingers stroking the skin on her neck. Her lips parted and he leaned down and brushed his lips across hers.

He just wanted a taste. To see if those lips would taste as good as they looked. Something chaste, to get this relationship off to a nice, respectable start.

And then her hands were in his hair, pulling him closer. Her mouth opened and his tongue swept in, gliding against hers. The muted sounds of the party were gone, there was just the two of them and all he could hear was his heart beating in his ear and Bridget's sweet, soft moan when his kiss grew more demanding. His hands slid under the coat, settling on her waist, and he pulled her against him.

Bridget groped the wall behind them, found a doorknob and they nearly fell into a room that smelled of detergents. He pressed her against the wall, his hands still on her body, as if trying to memorize the shape of her hips, the span of her waist, the swell of her breasts. As if he could forget.

Her hands ran over his chest, then lower, and his body jerked when she brushed the bulge in his pants. He groaned into her mouth, his body eager for more. He grasped her leg, pulling her close to him, his hand searching under the fabric, meeting thick winter tights that frustrated both of them.

"Jesus, Bridget, are we in a janitor's closet?" he gasped, the heavy perfume scent finally getting to him.

"It was that or the parking lot," she said, biting his neck.

He growled and his hand cupped her sweet ass. She arched and ground herself against his leg.

"I was picturing something more romantic," he said, coming up for air after another deep kiss.

The door rattled behind them and Ethan yanked Bridget's dress back into place. They stumbled as a sharp wedge of light illuminated them, and then both froze as Gavin stepped into the supply room.

He looked them over, and nodded to Bridget. "Hand me the mop."

She unfroze and grabbed the mop, tossing it to him.

"Thanks," he said, backing out of the closet. Then he stuck his head back in. "Mom's looking for you."

The door shut and Ethan expelled a breath.

"We just got caught making out. By your brother," he

said.

"Yeah, that hasn't happened in, like, at least a month," Bridget said.

He pulled her close again, taking his time with the kiss, tracing her full bottom lip with his tongue until she gasped, then sliding his tongue along hers.

"Next time, let's find a place that's a little more private," he said.

"You're assuming there's going to be a next time," she said.

He ran his thumb along her pout and smiled.

"There's going to be a next time, Bridget."

CHAPTER FIVE

The only sound in the Lost Coast Harbor Police Department was the slow drip of the coffee pot. Ethan's impatient sigh echoed in the quiet break room. It was still dark outside and the only other staff around was the overnight dispatcher, Georgie, who was knitting in small glassed-in office off the main room. As he walked by, he raised his coffee and she waved.

"Morning, Chief Ford. Here are your messages," Georgie said, setting down her knitting needles and handing him a small stack of pink message slips.

He returned to his office alone with the coffee. He enjoyed this time of the day, before the chaos of the police department really got going. It was a time to collect his thoughts, plan the day in peace.

He idly flipped through the stack of pink message slips and his stomach tightened at the familiar names on two messages taken several hours apart. It must be important for his brother to call him at the police department. He imagined Trevor handling the phone like a vampire holding a vial of holy water. For Trevor to pull out two old aliases meant something, too. But it wasn't anything Ethan was ready to deal with yet.

Lost Coast Harbor was supposed to be his safe haven from the chaos of his complicated past. He intended to keep it that way. Pure and free from those associations. Not only would it be difficult to explain certain things in his past to the town council, but it wouldn't help with the bruised image the town now had.

He put his brother's two messages on the bottom of the stack of calls to return and started with the one from Deputy Curt McBride.

"Good morning, Chief Ford," McBride said.

His title still felt unfamiliar. Borrowed, or stolen. Not quite his yet.

"Hey, McBride. Got a message that you had something about Bridget Donnelly's complaint."

"Yeah, she's got some bad neighbors."

The hair on the back of his neck stood on end. "How bad?"

"Not sure who they are yet, but it's not the first time we've had this problem up there. There's been a run of thefts in the area," he said. "This is the first time someone has tapped into a well. At least up there. We've seen it before. This one is bold, though."

"How did they do it?"

"Don't know. She wouldn't let me come up there," McBride said.

Ethan sat up in his chair and leaned back from the desk. "She wouldn't let you go there?"

"Yeah, you know. Probably wary of inviting the cops in,

what with her business and all," McBride said.

Ethan's mind ran back to his few prior encounters with Bridget. She'd been hiding something from the first moment he saw her. And then there was that encounter with Rowdy Pritchard on Saturday night. She never did tell him what that was about.

"What business?"

McBride exhaled. "Sorry, Chief. Thought you knew. Bridget Donnelly's a bookie."

He pressed two fingers against his forehead, where a dull pain throbbed. Of course she was. He couldn't be attracted to a schoolteacher. Maybe a nurse. A secretary. Or just a regular controller of a family business.

"Why hasn't she been arrested?"

McBride's laugh was partly embarrassed, partly amused. "Probably because she'd take down the town's elite with her. Also, she doesn't cause any trouble. It's not a big operation, but she's probably taken bets from a fair share of law enforcement officers over the last few years."

Ethan cursed under his breath. "My officers, too?"

"Well, now, I have no first-hand information on that, Chief," McBride said, and Ethan saw the problem with prosecuting Bridget. No one wanted to rat out their friends, and that's what would happen if they arrested the town's bookie.

"What's the scope of her operation?"

McBride's exhale carried over the phone. "Small, she doesn't do business with anyone who doesn't pay up."

"How does she enforce that?"

"Have you met her brother Niall?"

The big redheaded guy who'd barreled into the alley a

few minutes too late to deal with Rowdy Pritchard. Ethan closed his eyes as the pieces fell into place. "Yeah, met him this weekend."

"He's some MMA champ," McBride said. "No one wants to tangle with that guy."

"Who'd he beat up?"

"No one yet. He doesn't have to. And everyone wants to keep it that way," the deputy said with a laugh.

Ethan ran a hand through his hair and heard the sound of his staff arriving at work. How many of them had made illegal wagers with Bridget this weekend? He recalled her stop at Carl's desk when she'd stopped in to pick up her police report.

And suddenly he knew why she'd been down at the VD by the Sea when he'd met her.

He closed his eyes. Christ, no wonder he'd felt an instant attraction to her. He'd recognized a kindred spirit when they'd first met, but had denied what his soul had instantly recognized. He nearly laughed at the irony. That chemistry he'd felt when they'd kissed Saturday, that force of nature awakened with a touch—it was not simply lust. It was recognizing another crooked being, another criminal, and that attraction was simply the familiar finding its way home.

"Look, I'm not trying to get Bridget Donnelly's operation shut down. I do want to take care of her problem with the neighbors. I'm sure they're tapping her well to water a crop. I don't have their names yet, but it's never good to provoke these guys. She shouldn't be handling this on her own," McBride said.

Ethan pinched the bridge of his nose and let out a long

breath. "Is that what she said? That she would handle this on her own?"

"Yeah. She put me off, said she'd take care of it."

"Let me know if you hear anything about who the neighbors are," Ethan said, and then hung up the phone.

The muffled sounds from the main office grew louder and he wondered why Chief Grady hadn't put in a window, at least in the door to the office, so he could see what was going on from his desk. Ethan flipped through the messages again and put the two from his brother in his desk drawer, where he could forget about them for a couple of hours.

Then he added one from Councilwoman Fitzgerald about setting up a meeting with her partner about the renovation job. On top of that, he added one from Councilman Kenneth Snell, who had an urgent matter to discuss with the chief of police.

He'd get to those petty tyrants later. First, he needed to deal with his own staff.

Ethan walked out into the main room to find his weekday staff already at work, and he waved them all to the conference room. As they trickled in, he studied them. It was a small staff of just over a dozen sworn officers. They were down two officers, with a recent retirement and a senior detective who was arrested along with the last chief. Those remaining were suffering—overworked and with low morale. But damn it, he couldn't allow them to participate in the crimes they were supposed to be preventing.

"Good morning," he said and got a weak chorus in return. "I'll be brief and let you all get back to work."

He picked up the local paper, which was already opened

to the sports section. "As I'm sure you all know, it's basketball season. The college finals are going on. Championship's just around the corner."

Ethan saw a few heads nod, including Carl.

"I want to make it clear that I won't tolerate illegal betting among my police force," he said, looking around the room. "Everyone understand that?"

He made eye contact with each of the eight officers and detectives who were present and got a nod of assent from all.

"Thank you. That's all."

"Uh, Chief, are we cracking down on illegal gambling?" Valerie Childs asked, her brows knitted in confusion.

"I'm not trying to sweep up every tournament bracket in town," Ethan said. "But if I find that my own officers are taking part in illegal activity, I will fire and prosecute them."

He gave them a tight smile and walked back to his office to deal with the rest of his problems—such as fending off the council members who wanted special favors for their votes. Ethan's jaw tightened as he pulled open the desk drawer and withdrew those messages. That may be the way that Lost Coast Harbor was used to handling official business, but that was not the path Ethan intended to follow. He'd just have to figure out a way to placate them until they voted on his contract.

And he'd also need to head off Trevor, before his brother showed up on his doorstep and unleashed the chaos that usually followed him. That sort of trouble wouldn't help his bid for a permanent contract.

He leaned back in the antique chair and felt his shoulders tense. The entire reason he was here was to clean up the police department. That meant leading the office, not merely directing it. And so far, within weeks of arriving, he'd located the town's bookie. And attempted to seduce her.

Way to go, Ford.

It was not exactly the fresh start he'd imagined. But then he remembered the way Bridget's lips felt against his, and how her body fit against him, and he realized that she was the most difficult problem of all.

BRIDGET WATCHED THE SUNSET FROM HER OFFICE, THE bright orange and red clouds deepening to a dark purple, until all she could see in the glass was her own reflection staring at the window with a frown. Mondays sucked, but they sucked even more when she was stuck reconciling the numbers for the company's new investment in Hastings Enterprises' transportation arm.

There was no game tonight, so she was finally going to spend her evening with a nice glass of pinot noir, a bath, and a book. A perfect evening, messed up by the fact that the new bookkeeper at Hastings sent over the necessary documents just an hour before Bridget should have gone home. It might be a long night, and it probably wouldn't include any wine.

The cell phone on her desk buzzed, as it had been all day. This was the time of year when her phone never stopped ringing, which was a good thing. Every call meant money. And every dime meant eventually she would grow her own winery from the ground up, and be able to quit her job at Donnelly Lumber.

"Hi Carl," she said, greeting the police sergeant. Carl Spatz had been a longtime customer of Oscar's when Bridget took over, and he loved basketball. "What can I do for you tonight?"

"Nothing, kiddo. That's why I'm calling," Carl said with a resigned sigh. "The new chief is cracking down on illegal wagering and I wanted to let you know why you're not gonna be hearing from me or any of the other guys from the station for a while."

Bridget's stomach had done a slow somersault at the mention of the police chief, then dropped like a stone at the rest of Carl's announcement.

That toe-curling kiss at the party Saturday had kept Ethan at the front of her mind. He was still that puzzle she hadn't figured out, but now there was something else, too. He'd played the role of police chief very well, but when he'd kissed her, pinned her against the wall, there was a wildness in his eyes, in his touch, that belied his professional veneer. She'd been worrying that memory over in her mind since then, and it was driving her crazy. Not just because she wanted him to do that again. She definitely wanted that. But she wanted to know what was beyond that badge.

"Does he know about me?" she asked.

"I don't know, Bridget. But I think he knows about me," Carl said with a laugh.

"Oh, hell. Are you in trouble?"

"Nah, Ford's just cracking down going forward. I guess my wife gets her wish and I'll spend my overtime money on a vacation with the grandkids instead of basketball games. I hear Disneyland is nice." His sigh said he'd rather be anywhere than shepherding his grandchildren around an amusement park.

"Maybe he'll relax by next year," Bridget said.

"I don't know. This guy's a straight shooter. That's a good thing. After everything with Grady, you know, we need that. But I'm only a couple years from retirement, so I can't risk it," Carl said.

"I understand completely," she said. "I appreciate the call."

"Well, I just thought, you know, in case he is looking to crack down on you. Maybe you should lay low for a while, too. I'd sure hate for you to get caught up in something ugly."

She'd hate that, too. Sure the last police chief was corrupt, but at least he'd left her alone.

Bridget sighed. "Well, thanks for letting me know. You want to pull that money you rolled over to the Duke game?"

"Well, let's not get too hasty. I'd already placed that bet," Carl said. "And Duke's looking pretty good coming off that last game. That center's got a three-pointer that won't quit."

"Okay, then. I'll miss seeing you around," she said, and meant it. Carl was a friendly and reliable client. The kind she preferred. In fact, a good half-dozen police officers were among her regular customers. "Am I going to be getting a bunch of these calls tonight?"

"No, but only because the rest of the guys wanted me to pass on their regrets for the rest of the season."

Damn it. There went the about two acres of the drip irrigation system that she would have bought with those proceeds. And she was losing her most reliable customers, too. The cops always paid up, never caused trouble.

She wished Carl well and hung up with an uneasy feeling settling in her stomach. If Ethan knew it was her, would he try and shut her down? She couldn't imagine that Rowdy's behavior at the St. Patrick's Day party had tipped him off. Lucky for her, Rowdy had a certain sexual-predator vibe that hid his true intent when he'd grabbed her. He'd been insisting that they needed to talk, but he hadn't had the opportunity to explain himself before Ethan had punched him in the mouth.

Bridget frowned at the memory of Ethan's reaction. It seemed like the right thing would have been to arrest the man, read him his rights, and haul him off to be charged with assault. Not cold-cock him and shove him up against a wall out of view of the rest of the crowd.

And then there was his reluctance to talk about his past. He mentioned his prior job in Bakersfield, but skirted every attempt to learn more about his life before he was a cop.

She tilted her head and leaned back in her chair. The punch that broke Rowdy's nose had been a reflex, and not one trained into him in the police academy. It was more like how her brothers, who had trained in martial arts since they were old enough to kick each other, knew exactly how to take someone down to the mat. It was efficient, practiced, and yet brutal.

A soft knock sounded on her open door and she looked up.

"Hey, Bridget, I'm done with the security upgrades to your network."

Bree Rogers stood in the doorway, a canvas messenger bag slung across her body. She was wearing a pair of ripped jeans and a black, long-sleeved T-shirt, and heavy black eye makeup. She looked more hacker than computer security, but she was the best at what she did.

"Great, Bree. Thanks for doing this. I know it's below your pay-scale. Everything went okay?"

"Yes, you're secure. And I've installed the monitoring software on the email server that Grace wanted. Now you'll know pretty much instantly which of those boys in the lumberyard are the real sick fucks."

Bridget grinned. "Want me to send you a list?"

"I'll find my own sick fucks, thank you very much," Bree returned with a laugh. "If you don't need anything else, I'll get out of here."

"Thanks, Bree. Appreciate your help," Bridget said, then realized that she was looking at a great resource. "Hey, wait. There is one more thing you might be able to help me with. Do you have a minute?"

Bree stepped into the office and Bridget stood, walking to the door and shutting it. She leaned back against her desk and crossed her arms. She could trust Bree not to let her request go any farther than the office. Still, she hesitated another moment before making the request.

"If I wanted to do a background check on someone, can you do that?"

"Like the basic criminal and driving checks that you guys do when you hire? I quit doing that for you guys years ago."

Bree's skills were far too much in demand to still be handling small jobs like that. But she wouldn't run to Richard Donnelly for approval first, unlike the Bay Area firm that handled the company's routine background checks.

"I know. But I can't ask the new guys to do this," Bridget said. "This would be off the books."

Bree raised an eyebrow. "Go on."

"The new police chief, Ethan Ford. Can you dig into him?"

"I can. What do you want?"

She bit her lip. Was she really doing this?

Then she thought of the hillside below her house, bare for another year. Another year of putting off her own business venture, of working for her father. She loved her family, but she craved being independent of them. Though she had insisted to Ethan that she didn't care if people thought that her career was due to nepotism, she did care. Her work for Donnelly Lumber was precise and kept the company on sound financial ground. She did good work, and it ate at her when someone doubted that she got her position on merit. Those doubts would be there, as long as she remained as controller for the family's company.

But it was so much more than a need to prove herself that drove her to buy her grandmother's house and property. It had been impulsive, but nothing had ever felt so right. She had a connection to the valley, the land, the house, and all the family history there. It mattered to her in a way that the mill never would.

Just a few more years and she would be able to stand on her own. Build something of her own. That desire was what fueled her. It was so strong that she could taste the wine that wouldn't exist for years. So strong that even as she leaned back against her desk in her cool corporate office, she could feel the warm soil in her fingers.

Yes. She was doing this.

"Anything you can find."

"How soon do you want it?"

She loved Bree for not asking any other questions. "As soon as you can get it."

"I'll be in touch." Bree gave her a nod and headed out of the office, leaving Bridget alone.

She was not comfortable with what she'd just done. Not at all. But at the same time, she knew Ethan was hiding something. If the town council wasn't going to dig into it, someone had to. And if he figured out what she did for extra money, maybe she'd be able to convince him to leave her alone if she knew his secrets.

CHAPTER SIX

The road to Bridget Donnelly's house wound up a hill, twisting around trees that seemed to grow out of the hillside. During the day, it probably offered up a spectacular view of the sloping foothills below. At night, the single-lane road was a nightmare of unexpected curves and soft shoulders that washed out to steep drops.

Ethan kept his truck at a slow pace and gritted his teeth. It was remote, and this road would slow any emergency response if Bridget's fight with her neighbor escalated. He tensed even more at that thought. God, she was stubborn. She might be able to handle a difficult client, but she wasn't dealing with a dentist who refused to pay his tab, or some jerk-off like Rowdy Pritchard. They didn't yet know who they were dealing with, but someone brazen enough to tap into his neighbor's well was bad news.

The truck's high-beams lit up a mailbox labeled "Flynn" at the end of a driveway and he slowed to a stop. Flipping on the overhead light, he checked the map and confirmed the address. This was the house, no matter what the name on the mailbox said. The road curved toward the left, and the driveway to the right, down a slight slope. Wheels crunched on gravel as he turned off the road.

It was another minute before the house came into view—a white two-story farmhouse with a porch that stretched across the front. The driveway curved in front of the house, then past a detached garage and into the darkness. He parked in front of the house and climbed out. The downstairs windows were lit up, with warm light spilling out. He started toward the steps to the front door, when he heard the sound of footsteps from the side.

Bridget Donnelly emerged from the darkness between the house and the garage, a determined look on her face and a shotgun in her hands.

"Jesus, Bridget!" Ethan exclaimed, jumping at the sight of the gun.

"Oh, it's you," she said, lowering the barrel.

"Who the hell were you expecting?" His voice rose with each word and his heart thumped in his chest.

She shrugged, then exhaled. "No one you know."

"Maybe it's someone I should meet."

Bridget let out another long breath.

"Aren't you outside your jurisdiction, Sheriff?" she said, raising her chin and giving him a defiant look that almost made him overlook the slight tremble in her hands.

"I'm not here to arrest you," he said. "Yet."

Her smile spread slowly across her face. "In that case, you can come in."

He followed her around to the back of the house, up the stairs to a deck and into the inviting living room of the farmhouse. A fire crackled in the corner hearth. Two soft couches sat at an angle to each other, facing the fireplace. Beyond that was a weathered dining room table with two long benches and then the kitchen, set off by a counter with two barstools.

Bridget set the shotgun near the staircase, and waved him toward the sofas, but he followed her through the open living area to the kitchen.

"Can I get you something to drink?"

"Whatever you're having."

She held up a glass of red wine and he nodded.

"How long have you lived up here?" Ethan asked, taking in the decor. Warm and worn, the living room welcomed visitors to stay and relax.

"About six months. It was my grandmother's house. She died a little over a year ago," Bridget said, taking a glass out of the cabinet and pouring the wine. She handed him the glass, making eye contact with him over the rim. When he took the glass, his fingers brushed hers. A warm glow filled him at the touch, and Bridget's blue eyes widened.

"She left it to you?" The concept of being given a huge house in the country was as foreign as being given the ability to fly.

Bridget shook her head. "I bought it from the estate. My brothers and sisters weren't interested. Now I know why."

She grinned and pointed at the ceiling. He followed the motion and saw the newly patched plaster. And when he looked closer around the room, he saw the unmistakable signs of renovations—a ladder peeked out behind a half-opened door, a folded tarp over the steps. By the back door that he'd entered sat a bucket of paint and plastic wrapped paintbrushes.

"Are you doing the work yourself?"

"Some of it. The painting, I can handle. I'm learning how to do other things as they come up. I'm getting pretty good with mud and tape."

"I'm impressed," he said. "How much work is there to do?"

She ran a hand through her hair. "It's a hundred-year-old house, so I imagine everything will have to be replaced eventually. Honestly, I had no idea what I was getting into."

The house was old, but it was well-built. The windows looked new, the framing not yet painted. Wool rugs covered the hardwood floor in the living area and under the dining room table. Under the slight scent of smoke from the fireplace, he detected a hint of sawdust, freshly cut lumber. Turning, he saw the outline of a sawhorse in the darkened room through the half-opened door.

"Are you having regrets?" he asked.

Bridget's eyes softened. "No, not at all. I love this house. It's on twenty-two acres, with natural springs and a good water table."

"Is that important?"

She looked down at the wine in her glass and swirled it. "It may be. Someday."

When she looked up, her expression was back to the bravura, the front. A sassy smile that his body reacted to like nothing else. There was something there. No denying it. But what to do about it was a question he wasn't ready to confront yet.

Bridget picked up her wine glass and raised it, keeping eye contact with him.

"*Sláinte.*"

He touched his glass to hers, then sipped the wine. She led him to the couch and sat down. "Have a seat. If you're not here to arrest me, you can relax."

Ethan sat on the same couch as Bridget, and she turned toward him, her head tilted. "What are you doing here, outside of Lost Coast Harbor, at night?"

He grinned. "Maybe I needed to put some money on a game."

Her eyes sparkled and her full lips turned up. "Why, that would be illegal, Sheriff."

She tossed her hair and stared him straight in the eye. No denial, just a flirty response. He hadn't expected anything less.

"Actually, I wanted to see if you needed any help with your neighbors. And since you greeted me with a twelve gauge, I'm guessing you could use some backup."

Bridget's lips hovered over the rim of her wine glass, her expression giving nothing away. Damn, he would not want to play poker with this woman. Still, he knew she needed the help, just didn't want to ask for it.

"Do you know who they are?" he asked.

Bridget frowned and then shook her head. "No, I don't know them. I haven't seen anyone. The first I knew that anyone was using that property was when my water stopped running."

Ethan reached over and took her hand, his fingers loosely encircling her wrist, and then he stroked the soft skin on the inside of her wrist.

"Why didn't you let Deputy McBride come up here and

investigate what's going on?"

She tensed, but didn't withdraw her hand from his. Her eyes were focused on his hand, wrapped around hers.

"I didn't refuse to let him come up. I just told him I thought it was under control," she said, raising her eyes to his. "And it is."

"You took care of it?" he asked.

She nodded. "Haven't had any problems in the last few days."

"How?"

"Want to see?" she asked.

He nodded slowly and she stood, taking his hand and leading him to the door. Then she grabbed a flashlight from a basket on the table and picked up his coat from the peg behind the door. She slipped her coat on and waited for him to put his coat on before she opened the door, then took his hand again and led him around the house and back toward his truck. Ethan tipped his head back and looked at the clear skies, the stars so close it felt like you could reach up and touch them. The cold damp air penetrated his clothing and he was glad for the heavy weight of the coat, but it was Bridget's warm hand in his that was heating him up.

She led him past the garage, their footsteps crunching on the gravel path with only the weak flashlight beam to illuminate the way. They were a few dozen yards past the building when Bridget pointed the flashlight's beam straight ahead and he saw the old weathered shack at the end of the path. It had been completely enclosed with a new chain link fence and the gate in the front was padlocked.

"How's that working so far?"

"Like a charm," she said, turning to look at him in the moonlight. "I used the tools at my disposal. My father owns a lumberyard and construction company."

The fence wasn't huge, but it still would have been expensive. The message it sent was clear—she was serious about keeping someone out. Also, that she'd rather pay for this security than call the cops.

"I think I underestimated you, Ms. Donnelly," he said with a laugh. A determined thief could cut through the fence, but he admired her ingenuity.

"Not every problem requires a gun and a badge, Sheriff," she said lightly. "Let's go back inside."

He kept her hand in his while they walked down the trail toward the house, enjoying the feeling of her warm skin against his, the buzz that the contact sent throughout his body. The walk ended too soon, and he stepped into the living room again. Bridget hung up their coats again, then she moved to the fireplace to warm her hands and shake off the chill.

She was wearing a pair of worn jeans that fit her like a soft glove, showing off long, lean legs. A deep grey sweater hugged her curves and ended at her hip. When she bent to pick up a piece of firewood to throw it on the fire, his cock stiffened and his mind flooded with images that he'd been fighting since Saturday night when they'd kissed. Hell, since the week prior to that when they'd met.

"Let me get that," he said, his voice sounding rougher than normal. He took the small log and added it to the fire, then stacked a second piece of wood.

"Thank you," she said. "I'm glad you came by tonight."

"Are you?" He straightened up and found her close to him, a faint hint of vanilla and something floral surrounded her.

She nodded, her blue eyes crinkled up at the edges with a suppressed smile. "You did say there was going to be a next time."

Standing on her toes she reached up and brushed her lips across his, the feathering touch of her full lips firing a full load of adrenaline into his body. He stood still, letting her take the lead, but when her mouth slanted over his, his control snapped. He wrapped an arm around her waist, pinning her close, and deepening the kiss, sinking into her, tongues gliding against each other. There was no sound in the room but the soft sigh from Bridget when he pulled away.

Her cheeks were flushed pink and her lips even more swollen. He ran a thumb across that incredible pout.

"I've been thinking of these lips all week," he murmured and her eyes darkened at his words. "The things I want to do with them, to them."

And he kissed her again, falling into the heat and the deep moan that escaped her. Her hands tangled in his hair and urged him on.

Christ, he should get in his truck and go before he did something stupid. By all rights, he should be investigating her for illegal gambling. He should be arresting her. But he wouldn't do any of that.

He was going to stay until she kicked him out.

THIS WAS WHAT HEAVEN FELT LIKE. IT WAS HOT AND SWEET and delicious. It caused one's body to vibrate and brain to shut off. It triggered an avalanche of emotions and needs.

One need really. Just this one man.

His mouth was hot on hers. His close-trimmed beard, barely more than a few days' growth, rasped lightly against her skin and her nerves fired and snapped in response. Her entire body flushed hot and need settled at the juncture of her thighs, throbbing, aching for more.

This was dangerous. She didn't lose control like this. Not over a man she'd only just met. A man who held her future in the palm of his hand.

Then that hand brushed over her breast, cupping the weight, and her body arched on its own accord and a moan slipped from her mouth.

Good Lord, she'd lost it. And she didn't care.

Ethan's tongue traced her bottom lip, sending a shiver through her that made her knees weak. Her hands gripped his back, as much for support as to get closer to him. His lips moved to her neck and she tilted her head back, her eyes closed.

Fuck. That rough scrape of his beard across her skin was driving her wild. Her pulse surged and the only sound she could hear was the blood rushing through her veins, his breathing, and her own soft cries of desperation.

"God, you taste so good," he whispered and even the breath across her skin set her afire.

Abruptly, he jerked back and she nearly fell from the sudden movement.

"Did you hear—"

It was the unmistakable sound of wheels on gravel, a car making its way down her driveway.

Ethan's jaw clenched. "You expecting company?"

Bridget shook her head and blinked to clear her head. Her family would call first to make sure she was home before making the trek out to the hills. Her friends would have summoned her to town.

That left the visit she'd been expecting. And dreading.

"Goddamn it."

The anger rising up was fueled now by more than the neighbors and their theft and vandalism. They'd just interrupted the best kiss of her life and someone was going to pay for that. She whirled away from Ethan, grabbing her coat and stuffing her arms into the sleeves. At least things hadn't progressed so far that she had to completely dress herself before confronting the jackass. That was both a blessing and a curse, she supposed.

"Where are you—"

She grabbed the shotgun and threw open the door. He was going to follow her and she couldn't stop that. But she could get out there first. No fuck-nut water thief was going to intimidate her.

"Bridget, no—"

She ignored Ethan's command and stalked across the back deck, heard him swear and follow her. "Get back here."

"No, this is my problem."

At the corner of the house, she saw a familiar Bronco idling behind Ethan's truck and the sight brought her up short. Before stepping out of the shadows, she turned, pushed Ethan's chest, and looked up at him. His jaw was set and he shook his head.

"Hell no," he said.

"You can't be seen here," she said. "Just stay back."

Then she walked briskly out to the driveway, racking the shotgun as she went.

Two men stepped out of the Bronco, only one of whom she recognized. Rowdy Pritchard walked around from the driver's side and leaned against the hood of the car, his face obscured by shadow.

"What's going on, Rowdy?"

"We didn't get a chance to talk Saturday," he said.

Bridget's jaw clenched and she tightened her grip on the shotgun at the memory of being hauled into the alley. It wasn't even the shock at being manhandled that still made her angry. It was the fact that she'd been so blissfully unaware that the attack was coming. She was calm, relaxed, and among friends and family, and this jackhole had managed to catch her unaware.

"I see you hired muscle. Should've hired brains, too," she said, glancing at the scowling block of a man who stood by the passenger side. He was halfway behind the open door and she couldn't see if he was armed, but assumed he was. The man was a solid cube of muscle. Shooting him would be easy, she thought. Literally like hitting the broad side of a barn.

"I wanted to introduce you to my new business partner," Rowdy said, stepping forward and into the light so she could see his wide, slimy smile. "Thought you'd want to hear about a business opportunity that could affect—"

The cocky smile slipped and Rowdy squinted at her, then behind her as she heard Ethan's footsteps approaching.

"Chief Ford, how are you this evening?" Rowdy asked. The business partner straightened up and adjusted his belt, tucking something into the back of his pants—likely some overly dramatic handgun designed to compensate for the steroids' theft of his testicles.

Bridget kept the shotgun at the ready and stared at the man's face, committing it to memory. Thick neck, ruddy cheeks, flattened nose, dead dark eyes, and a thick hairline that started low on his forehead, too close to his dark and bushy eyebrows.

"Mr. Pritchard," Ethan said, his voice steady and strong behind her. "What brings you up here tonight?"

"Just a business meeting," Rowdy said. "Me and Bridget, we're talking about a merger."

She snorted. "Merging my fist with your face," she muttered.

Ethan's heavy hand on her shoulder warned her to let him handle that. *As if.* Rowdy and his partner were her problems.

"It's late, gentlemen. I'm sure you can do business another time," he said.

No-Neck McGee turned to Rowdy and gave a quick nod of his head toward the truck. Rowdy nodded and grinned like a fool.

"Sure thing, Chief," he said. "We'll come by later. Don't want to interrupt official business."

Bridget gritted her teeth and ran her hand over the wooden pump on the shotgun. It was an antique, her grandfather's hunting gun, but it still worked. And oh, man, she wanted to fire off a warning blast just to see Rowdy hit the gravel. Possibly piss himself.

As if reading her mind, Ethan gripped her shoulder with a little more pressure. "Don't come back without an invitation,

Mr. Pritchard."

Rowdy smirked at her as No-Neck climbed into the passenger seat. "Gee, Bridget, hope you're not in trouble."

"Someone's been tampering with Ms. Donnelly's well. You two wouldn't know anything about that, would you?"

Rowdy shook his head with a more confident smile, now that he was on the other side of the Bronco from Bridget and her shotgun.

"Afraid not." He gave a wave as he climbed into the driver's seat. "See ya around, Bridget."

The Bronco left in a spray of gravel and she stared down the driveway for a long moment after the taillights disappeared around the bend. The sound slowly faded and she could hear the moment the car left the gravel driveway and hit smooth pavement.

The rage bubbled up inside her, warming her. Rowdy Pritchard had no idea what he was doing. He wasn't the sharpest tool in the shed, but his idiocy had been limited to petty shit—minor stuff that got him in trouble and fired on a regular basis, but nothing that had caused lasting damage. Something had changed. He'd upped his game. And this new guy, she'd never seen him before.

"Pack a bag," Ethan said, tossing the command over his shoulder as he stalked back to the house.

"What? Don't be ridiculous," Bridget said, following him.

"No. You're not staying here. Not alone, at least."

That thought took her breath away. Images of Ethan, in her bed, filled her mind and she blinked to clear her head. In the moment that it took her to recover and start to form a retort, Ethan had opened the door and ushered her into the house.

"Well?" he asked.

Her thoughts were still lingering on the idea of Ethan staying the night and she struggled to keep up with him. "Well, what?"

"Your family. You can stay with them tonight," he said with a firm nod. "Just until you get a proper security system. Have you considered getting a dog?"

He began checking the window latches, a methodical clockwise survey of the downstairs of the house.

"What the hell are you talking about?" Bridget said. "I am not staying with my family."

He ran a hand across his hair and stared at her. "You're not safe up here, all alone."

"I've been living up here all alone for six months without incident," she countered. "And Rowdy and his idiot friend aren't going to come back tonight. Especially after running into you here."

Ethan shook his head. His jaw was tense and she wanted to run a hand over that scruff and skin and kiss away that tension. But that was going to have to be another day. The two uninvited visitors had completely ruined the mood. Another reason to hate Rowdy.

"How sure are you that this is related to the neighbor?" he asked.

"You heard what Rowdy said about No-Neck being his business partner. He must think he's got an in with me because of—"

She bit her tongue before finishing that sentence and admitting that Rowdy was one of her regular customers.

Clearly, Ethan knew what she did, but she didn't have to sign the damn arrest warrant herself.

Ethan paused at the kitchen counter and rested his hands on the scarred and worn butcher block surface. He looked down, his hair falling over his forehead, and exhaled. He shook his head, then reached up and pinched the bridge of his nose. His gaze focused on something on the kitchen counter and he reached for it—the bullet that Rowdy had left in her mailbox. She'd brought it in with the rest of the mail and it was still sitting in the pile of junk mail.

With a curse, he looked at her. "That is a .223 round."

She nodded.

"Do you own a .223 rifle?"

She shook her head.

"Where did this come from?"

She sighed. "My mailbox."

"When?"

"After I disconnected the water the first time."

Ethan's eyes closed and a muscle in his jaw twitched. "Bridget, is there any other reason why Rowdy Pritchard would be threatening you?"

She bit her lip. "No."

He studied her and the intensity of his stare made her feel naked. But not in a fun way. Like he was seeing her flaws and all and wasn't at all sure what to do about her.

"Those many siblings you have, how about staying with one of them?"

She shook her head. "No."

Ethan tilted his head back, staring at the patched ceiling. "Why not?"

"Because I can take care of myself," she said, motioning to the shotgun, back in its place by the door. She might not have all the various belts that her brothers had earned, but she knew how to defend herself. And how to handle a firearm, should there be a need.

Ethan stalked across the room, took her hands and stared into her eyes for a long moment. Her stomach fluttered at the intensity of those warm amber eyes.

"Then you're stuck with me," he said.

The anger that had coiled in the pit of her stomach evaporated and was replaced by a warm glow at the thought of Ethan staying the night. She wasn't going to argue with that. Finally, things were looking up. She smiled.

"If you wanted to spend the night, Sheriff, all you had to do is ask."

"This isn't fun and games, Bridget. These people are trouble," Ethan said, his face grim. "I'll take the couch."

Bridget frowned. "Excuse me?"

He leaned in close and her head spun a little at the slight hint of his scent. The air between them crackled with chemistry. And he was turning her down?

"Bridget, this is…" Ethan blew out a long breath. He stroked her hair and kept her gaze. The longing, the heat, was all there. But something else, too. A very steely resolve. "But I am not taking advantage of a crime victim. No matter how beautiful she is."

Bridget blinked. "Did you just call me a *victim*?"

"Go get some sleep," he said.

"I am nobody's victim." She was so deeply insulted at the word that she could hardly think straight. Victims were people who suffered harm and she had suffered, at most, inconvenience. And now deep sexual frustration. But she was not a victim.

He kissed her cheek, sending a thousand tingles through her, and then he gently pushed her toward the stairs.

CHAPTER SEVEN

"And he slept on the couch. The couch!" Bridget paced around her desk to the bookcase, where a dozen framed family pictures mingled with binders and reference books, and then back to the wall, where her diplomas hung next to several vintage posters from historic wineries. It wasn't nearly enough room to burn off the anxious energy that threatened to consume her.

Grace turned in the upholstered chair and watched Bridget's progress back and forth across the office.

"Oh, and then he called me a crime victim. A *victim*! That's just fucked up."

Grace coughed and Bridget caught a glimpse of the smile behind the large cup of coffee.

"Sounds...frustrating," her friend said, biting her lip.

She clearly wasn't getting her point across to Grace. She'd been rejected by the incredibly sexy police chief. She was so far past frustration that it was barely in her rear view mirror.

"Things had started so well. But then as soon as Rowdy showed up, he went into cop mode." Bridget threw up her hands and continued her pacing. "Like I couldn't handle

Rowdy. He's a moron."

"Yes, but you don't know the other man. And you said you thought that guy was armed," Grace said, ever the practical one.

Her cautious approach made her an ideal in-house counsel for Donnelly Lumber and other assorted businesses that the family owned. But Bridget was in no mood for caution. She needed to go work out with Niall, hit something. Hard. And repeatedly.

"So the new police chief knows about your...business?" Grace frowned, a furrow forming between her eyebrows. "Did he say anything about that?"

Bridget shook her head and flopped into her chair. "No, not really. He dropped some hints, but he knows. I can tell. And Carl said the cops are on a short leash now when it comes to betting."

Grace tilted her head and pursed her lips. "You need to be careful around him. He's not Chief Grady. Chief Ford was hired to clean up that whole mess. And because the council put the vote off on his permanent contract, he may think he has something to prove."

She trusted Grace's judgment. But she didn't get the feeling from Ethan that he wanted to cuff her. Not like that, anyway. Their attraction had been real and intense. And how the hell could he have resisted it? Not that she had much practice resisting temptation, but had he made the slightest move toward her last night, she'd have jumped on it. On him.

But instead of acting on that, she'd ended up alone in her cold bedroom, knowing he was downstairs by the fire. It had taken every ounce of dignity she had to keep her from going downstairs, and then she'd ended up tossing and turning all night.

She turned to Grace with a deep sigh. "What's his story? Is the council going to approve his contract?"

Grace leaned back in the chair. "Yes, I think so. I mean, I'm still learning the ropes there, but once everyone gets what they want, they'll vote to keep him."

Bridget shook her head. "What a bunch of yahoos. What if he doesn't do what they want?"

Grace shrugged. "We didn't exactly have a deep pool of applicants to draw on. Chief Ford took a pay cut to accept this job. Moved out to Nowheresville, a town with a reputation for being a new frontier in public corruption. There's not a Plan B if we don't approve his contract. Valerie Childs made it abundantly clear that she did not want the job on a permanent basis. We need him."

"Why take less money to do a thankless job where you know no one?" Bridget mused out loud.

"I don't know, but I'm glad he did," Grace said. "He was far and away the most qualified candidate, even though he hadn't been in a supervisory position for very long in Bakersfield. And that was only supervising other detectives. But he had great references and a good record of commendations. He's what this town needs. Let's hope we don't screw it up."

She stood and gave Bridget a familiar look. *Don't screw this up.*

Bridget gave her friend a dismissive wave and Grace returned to her office across the hall to bury her nose in timber harvest plans and vendor contracts and other boring lawyer shit. And Bridget had her own boring accounting shit to do before an afternoon meeting with her father and several managers from various departments. She opened her computer and began her review of the financial reports and projections.

In the back of her mind, though, she was working at the puzzle that was Ethan Ford. Why leave a job in Bakersfield, where he had such a good record that he'd probably move up in the police department, to move to a corrupt little town? And for less money and more headaches.

She thought back to how skillfully he'd dodged a similar, if less direct, question from Mayor Strong last week. Where was he from? Who was he? Why was he here?

She'd add one more to that list: Was he a threat to her?

An hour later, she was immersed in numbers and making excellent progress toward completing her lengthy pre-meeting checklist, when her phone buzzed. Glancing at the screen, she saw Bree's number on the screen.

"Hey, Bree. What's up?" It could be an alert on the company's computer system. Some pervert in the lumberyard office trading soft-core porn with a friend, again. Or it could be the job she'd asked Bree to handle. That last thought made her nerves tingle.

"Everything's fine with the network," Bree said. "I thought you'd want what I found."

"So soon?"

"I'm good."

"Whatcha got?"

"Not much on Ethan Ford, but what I did find was interesting."

Bridget glanced toward the half-open door, but Grace's

office door was closed and no one else was nearby, so she didn't bother closing her office up. "Go on."

"I found an old court filing, but it's not criminal. It's a name change. Ethan Ford was known as Ethan Black until he was eighteen years old, when he legally changed his name."

That was interesting. Why would a teenager legally change his name? "Is that it?"

"No, not really," Bree said. "I wasn't sure how deep you wanted to go, but once I found this, it was easy to get more."

"Okay. What is it?"

"Ethan Black has a juvenile record."

Bridget sat up, then stood up, the adrenaline surging through her. She exhaled a long breath. She'd known he was hiding something.

"What is it for?"

"It's sealed. I can't get to it. And the records are old enough that I doubt they're online. But I did find an entry in family court," Bree said. "I think Ethan Black has a brother named Trevor. There are custody hearings that look like they relate to them when they were children, but I can't get into the sealed records."

Bridget nodded, recalling their conversation. "He mentioned having a brother."

"There are a lot of records for Trevor Black—arrests, warrants, criminal charges. No convictions, but most of my search was focused on California and the boy seemed to move around a lot," Bree said.

Bridget frowned. Now she felt really uncomfortable, prying into Ethan's background. She had no right to dredge that up.

"Anything else?" She almost dreaded Bree's response.

"I can send you a summary of Trevor Black's record. At various times, there were active warrants in South Carolina, New Mexico, and Wyoming. About six months ago, he was picked up in Kern County on an active out-of-state warrant, but was released without charges and the warrant was recalled."

Bridget bit her lip. "Okay."

"That help you?"

"Yeah, maybe."

"Ford's personnel file is clean. I didn't find any civil suits against him. He has good credit," Bree said. "If I see anything else worthwhile, I'll let you know."

"Thanks, Bree."

Bridget disconnected the call and remained standing by her desk, staring at the family photos arranged on the shelves in front of her. A dozen small frames displaying the Donnelly family at various milestones, including her favorite—a small snapshot of her father, holding a two-year-old with dark pigtails and wide blue eyes, both wearing hardhats and posing in front of the mill. Next to that, a photo of her with her two sisters at Elizabeth's recent college graduation ceremony, arms around each other, laughing at Niall, who had been behind the camera. Behind that, a picture of her parents on their thirtieth wedding anniversary, and past their smiling faces, a photo of her and Declan at the pub on Gavin's opening night.

The collection of photos was evidence of her place in the world, and she knew she was damned lucky to be a part of a close-knit family. And not for the first time, guilt flared inside her at her plans to leave Donnelly Lumber. It shouldn't be this hard to be her own person. Her siblings had all done it, but maybe they were smart enough to have never started down the path of working for the family company, at least nothing beyond a summer job at the mill.

That guilt mingled with her regret for digging into Ethan's past. It wasn't what she thought Bree would find. And it wasn't that helpful. She wanted professional background— like if he had been disciplined at work for anything that might turn the town council off when it came to their vote, sued for excessive force, fired from another job. But this was personal information and she wasn't comfortable knowing it. Now she had to carry it around like a live grenade.

It was nothing she could use, she thought, cleaning up her desk with quick movements, suddenly eager to get out of her office, even if it was to spend the rest of the day in a stuffy conference room.

She'd just have to hope that Ethan Ford didn't give a damn about some minor-league bookmaking operation in a small town. He'd been tasked with cleaning up his department and it looked like he was doing a good job of that—to her detriment. Thanks to him, she'd lost some of her best regulars.

Maybe he would leave it at that.

Chapter Eight

Ethan suppressed a yawn as he climbed into the department-issued SUV to make the short drive from his house to his office. His entire body ached from lying on the too-soft couch, wondering if he'd just made the biggest mistake of his life by turning down Bridget's obvious invitation. As a result, he was running on far too little sleep and way more unresolved sexual tension than he'd ever felt before.

His cell phone chirped as soon as he pulled away from the curb and he saw the police department's number flash on the screen.

"Chief, you have a visitor," the dispatcher said.

Ethan's stomach dropped. *Fuck.* It had to be Trevor. He should have taken his calls. Maybe he could have persuaded his brother to stay away from Lost Coast Harbor.

"Who is it?" he asked.

What he was really asking was which alias was his brother using these days. Which of the two names on the message slips in his desk drawer should he be using when he beat the shit out of him. Was he the Texas oilman's spoiled son? Or was he the Vegas high-roller who was branching into property development in the desert?

"It's Marlene Dewey, the councilwoman," the dispatcher said.

Ethan nearly sighed in relief at the unexpected name. He remembered Councilwoman Dewey from his interview, conducted via a sketchy video conference call. She was in her mid-60s, retired from her job, but he couldn't remember the details of what that was.

"I'll be there in a few minutes," he said. He thought about hitting the light bar, then almost laughed at the thought. He was a dozen blocks from the parking lot and walked into the back door of the police department within a few minutes.

Mrs. Dewey was waiting at the counter, chatting with Carl Spatz and comparing notes on their aches and pains. Ethan shed his coat and hung it in his office before making his way to the front of the building to greet the councilwoman, who he eyed warily. If each of the town council members planned to use his authority for their own gain, he couldn't imagine what she wanted. She wore a sweater vest over a long-sleeved red turtleneck and a long denim skirt. Her short hair was permed, with a tight coil that clung to her head.

"Mrs. Dewey, it's so nice to meet you in person," Ethan said, pushing down his suspicions. Librarian, he remembered as he saw her. She had been the town's librarian for thirty years.

"And you, Chief Ford. Hope you're settling in well in the new job," she said, shaking his hand with a surprisingly strong grip. "I was hoping to talk to you about something that's come up." She looked around the office and the few employees milling about. "In private, perhaps?"

"Let's talk in my office." Ethan waved her around the counter and led her back to his windowless room in the back, leaving the door open.

He held a chair for Marlene and then sat behind his desk. "What can I help you with, Mrs. Dewey?"

She smiled. "Call me Marlene, please."

He nodded with a smile and didn't say anything.

"It's my nephew, Dylan. He's gotten in a bit of trouble. My brother-in-law bought him a car that's way too fast for him and he keeps getting tickets. I'm just afraid that if he has to pay all of these fines, he's not going to be able to go to college," she said.

"How many tickets are we talking about?"

"Not many, really. Only a half-dozen or so," she said.

"That's quite a few, actually," Ethan said. "Does he work, go to school?"

Marlene frowned. "He's working for Hastings Enterprises, down on the dock. I think he's a supervisor there. He's saving up to go to college next year."

Ethan made a noncommittal sound. "And you're asking me to dismiss his speeding tickets?"

"He's a good boy, and this would help me out. I'd consider it a favor," the former librarian said with a smile. "Oh, and there are a few parking tickets, as well."

"Has your brother-in-law considered taking the car back and giving him a scooter?"

Marlene laughed. "Boys do love their cars, don't they?"

With great effort, Ethan didn't roll his eyes. He stood and escorted the councilwoman back to the front, promising to look into the kid's tickets and see if there was anything he could do to help out such an esteemed citizen.

Then he turned to Carl. "What's the deal with Marlene Dewey's nephew?"

"Kid's a shit."

Ethan sighed and nodded. "How much of one?"

Carl didn't bother hiding his disgust. "His speeding tickets and fines paid for the intern program last summer. You'd think he'd learn where the speed traps are by now, but despite the fact he got accepted into several colleges, that guy ain't too bright."

"Can you get me a list of his outstanding tickets?"

Carl's eyebrows raised. "You're not going to let him off, are you?"

Ethan shook his head and gave a short laugh. "I'll go talk to him about it. But no, I'm not."

He walked back to his office to grab his coat and keys. This new job was not shaping up to be the promotion that he thought it would be. It was supposed to be a chance for him to start over, leave the sketchier parts of his life behind him. Instead, he found himself dragged back into a way of handling problems that he thought he'd left behind years earlier.

It was a short drive to the commercial docks, and once he arrived, it was easy to find Dylan's car—a souped-up Camaro straddling two spaces, painted a brilliant shade of "why'd ya pull me over, officer?" red. Looking around at the dockhands milling about on the edge of the parking lot, Ethan made a show of leaning back against the car. He took out his cell phone, punched in a number, and requested a tow truck.

Then he waited, but not for long. A tall, skinny young man rushed across the parking lot within minutes of the first contact between Ethan's butt and the Camaro's paint job.

"Hey, fucker. Get the fuck off my car."

Ethan looked up, feigned an innocent expression, then as the kid got closer, opened his wallet and flashed the badge. Marlene Dewey's nephew skidded to a stop, his mouth open in outrage that his brain was able to rein in at the last minute.

"You're Dylan Jencks?"

"Yeah."

"Ethan Ford, chief of police," Ethan said, still leaning against the car. "You owe me and the good taxpayers of this county about two thousand dollars in fines for your unpaid speeding tickets."

"No, I don't," he stammered. "There's some mistake. My aunt will take care of it. But I don't owe two thousand dollars. There's no way."

Ethan watched the guy clench and unclench his fists, his throat convulsing in stress. "You're right. With the parking tickets, it's twenty-two hundred bucks."

A bead of sweat appeared on the young man's forehead. "Oh, come on. I'm gonna take care of it."

Ethan nodded toward the entrance of the parking lot, where the tow truck was pulling in.

"Yes, you are."

"Fuck, man."

Ethan pushed himself off the car and drew himself up to his full height, staring down at the skinny young man with the adolescent pout on his face.

"You sent your Aunt Marlene to clean up your mess?"

The guy looked back at the growing crowd on the edge of the parking lot, then at the slowly approaching tow truck, and then up at Ethan. His lips moved, but no sound came out.

"How old is your aunt? What, maybe sixty-six years old?"

Dylan nodded.

"You sent a sixty-six-year-old retired librarian to fight your battles?"

The kid swallowed again. "She's on the town council."

His voice was lower, less belligerent now and his eyes shifted toward the crowd again.

"That's pathetic," Ethan said.

"I didn't ask her to," Dylan said. "I need my car, man. I got to get to work."

He shifted and ran his hand through his hair. Dylan Jencks was tall, but thin, like he was still at least one growth spurt away from being a man. He might be twenty years old, but this was a kid. No experience. No responsibilities. And unless he made some changes, this was where he'd stay—loading freight at the docks, racking up speeding tickets, bored, and getting into trouble to pass the time.

With a sigh, Ethan's anger shifted. Marlene Dewey was the person trying to make him violate the law. Not this scrawny, aimless kid.

"Right, your job. How long have you been working here?"

"Three years."

"You like this job?"

He shrugged. "It's fine, I guess."

"Why does your aunt think you're saving to go to college?"

He turned red and shook his head. "I dunno."

"You applied and were accepted to several schools. But

you never went. You didn't tell your aunt that you turned down those opportunities."

Dylan looked up, his brows knitted in confusion. "Why do you care?"

"You want that car back?"

"Yeah."

"Then answer my question."

The kid shuffled his feet and expelled a breath. "I dunno. I never lived anywhere else."

Ethan nodded. "Yeah, I get it. This is comfortable. You don't have to grow up."

The kid nodded, but then looked away.

"Sorry, Dylan, but that's going to stop." Ethan waved the tow truck driver closer. "I'm impounding your car. You have a choice to make."

Dylan glared at him, his hands at his side still clenched.

"You can pay your fines in full and I'll give you back your car."

"What's the other option?"

Ethan gave him a long stare. He was probably going to regret this. It meant he'd be dealing with Marlene Dewey, as well as her deadbeat nephew. And yet, someone had done it for him. Looked past the immaturity, the paper-thin veneer of confidence, beyond the juvenile convictions, and the many, many scrapes with the law that didn't end with him behind bars. It was time to repay that man's favor. Hell, Ethan hadn't even been working, not at an honest job at least, when someone gave him a chance to start over.

"You can work off the fines at the police station. We need someone to wash the cars, keep the lawn mowed, move some boxes around."

"I already have a job."

"Guess you'll have two."

"But I work during the day." His eyes were darting around, as if looking for an escape.

"We're open 24/7."

Ethan stepped away from the car and watched as the tow truck driver hooked the car up to the winch, Dylan ran his hand across his head again as the car was lifted and the front end secured.

"My aunt might give me the money," he said, his voice weak.

"We both know that's a load of bullshit. If she'd still lend you money, she'd have done it by now. She's been reduced to using political capital to clean up your messes."

"Oh, come on, there's gotta be some other way," he moaned. "What if I know something about a crime? Would that help?"

Ethan looked sideways at Dylan. "You're willing to snitch out a friend to get that car back?"

"No, no, not like that. I mean, I saw someone knock the shit out of a car over at the VD a couple weeks back."

"What car?"

"Sweet little convertible Thunderbird. The newer model, you know. Red, totally sweet ride."

Bridget's car. Ethan's interest grew. Not enough to let the smart ass off the hook, though. Bridget hadn't mentioned that she thought her car's damage was related to the neighbor. But if her car was vandalized by the people threatening her, this might help him figure out how to protect her.

"What did you see?" he asked.

"I saw who did it."

"Who?"

"Some chick."

Great. Ethan tilted his head and gave Dylan a long stare. "Does the chick have a name?"

He shrugged. "Dunno. Never seen her there before. But she took a crowbar out of the trunk, smashed the hell out of the front end, then dropped it in the water. Cool as can be."

Son of a bitch. As soon as Dylan dropped that bomb, Ethan could picture her doing it. It wasn't even a stretch of his imagination. His jaw clenched so hard he thought he might break his teeth. He had no doubt that Dylan was telling the truth, though he had no idea why she did it.

"That help you? Maybe we can barter—"

"Nope."

Dylan hung his head.

"What hours do you work here?" Ethan asked, as Dylan watched his prized possession get hauled out of the lot, scraping along the pitted parking lot.

"Seven to four," he said. "Oh, man. My dad is going to kill me."

"Be at the police station by 4:30."

He stalked back to the SUV, his anger growing with each step. This time, though, it was directed at the Donnelly woman. She was trouble, pure and simple. He needed to stay the hell away from her. Nothing good could come of acting on his attraction for Bridget. Nothing.

Chapter Nine

B ridget walked down the back steps of Donnelly Lumber, her heels sinking into the carpeted steps and making almost no noise in the silent office. She was the last person in the corporate office and she turned off lights as she walked down the hall to the conference room.

Rolling her head, she could feel the tension in her neck and shoulders. She had started the day tense, and that was before a half-day meeting with her father, Grace, and a couple of managers at the mill, going over financial reports and timber harvest projections. In addition, she was distracted by the information that Bree provided and thoughts of Ethan's intriguing history kept pulling her focus away from her job.

Despite the compounding stress, she had turned down Grace's invitation to yoga. What she needed was a good workout at Niall's studio, pounding away at the heavy bag. A little physical activity to work out the anger and frustration and she'd sleep better tonight. Just as soon as she finished cleaning up her reports.

With a sigh, she took in the conference room table, cluttered with the remnants of a four-hour meeting, and began gathering the reports and her notes. She organized them as she went, sorting through the documents and returning binders and books to the shelves that lined the conference room walls.

The last records to put away went on the top shelf, and even though she was five-nine, Bridget had to drag a step stool to the shelves to reach it. As she extended herself and pushed the corporate record binder into place, she heard a faint creaking sound and the hair on the back of her neck stood on end.

Turning, she saw a tall and broad figure, leaning against the door frame. She jumped and her heart skittered at the shock, then again as she recognized him.

"Hello, Sheriff," she said, taking a deep breath to calm her nerves.

"Bridget Donnelly," he said, crossing his arms.

"You in the market for some lumber? I can direct you to the right person during business hours, but I'm afraid we're closed for the day," she said. Her heart still pounded too loudly, and she wasn't sure if it was the shock or the fact that he was staring at her with a dangerous expression.

"I found the right person," he said, stepping into the conference room.

It was the largest room in the Donnelly Lumber corporate offices—with a handcrafted conference table that could seat twenty people comfortably, wide enough to accommodate bookcases along three walls without feeling cramped. Two doors opened onto the hallway, and a long credenza stretched between them.

And even with all that space, as soon as Ethan crossed

the threshold, it felt intimate, much smaller than it had just moments earlier.

"What can I do for you?" she asked, and even to her own ears, her voice sounded heavy with desire.

He took a few more steps into the room, and she had the sense of being stalked, as if she were prey. When he was standing directly in front of her, he took her hand and helped her off the step stool. He let go of her, but didn't move back, so they were within inches of each other. Without her shoes on, she had to tilt her head back to meet his eyes.

"You're working late," he said.

His eyes never left hers and though they were no longer touching, her body nearly vibrated with the energy between them. "Yes, I was just finishing up for the day."

"You're the only one here?"

There was something in that question, something low and dark and primitive. Her heart thumped in her throat at the thought of being alone with Ethan again. At the fact that he even asked. At the sound of his voice as he asked it.

"I'm the last one here."

His eyes narrowed and his jaw tensed at her answer.

"We need to talk," he said, his voice growing husky as he stared down at her.

He reached up and traced a finger from her ear down her neck, the light touch sending a thrill through her that settled between her legs. Her hair was still up in a twist. Combined with the pencil skirt and crisp blouse, it was her attempt to look like a professional. But when Ethan looked at her, she knew he saw through that. Hell, the way he was looking at her made her wonder if he wasn't seeing through her clothing.

"What did you want to talk about, Sheriff?"

He swallowed, hard, and his gaze raked over her body. "Your car."

"Really?" Bridget ran a hand up to the drop pearl earrings that brushed against her neck, then let her fingers slide lower to the top button of the blouse. "You want to talk cars?"

Ethan's eyes followed her movement, his pupils dilated, and his pulse throbbed in his neck. It was delicious payback for his rejection last night.

"I know it was you," he said, lifting his gaze from her breasts to meet her eyes.

His words sunk in, through the thick layer of desire and need that had wrapped itself around her brain.

That was impossible. There hadn't been anyone around when she'd taken the lug nut wrench to her own car. Well, it was improbable, anyway. Someone could have been on the docks at Hastings, she supposed. But even then, it was dark and the parking lot at the VD was poorly lit. Any identification would never hold up in court.

She smirked. "Now, why would I do that?"

Ethan licked his lips and now she was the one growing uncomfortable. They were still mere inches apart, but not touching. All she'd have to do is reach out...

"I don't know why you'd do it," he said, his voice low and rough.

He reached up again, and brushed a stray lock of hair that had escaped her neat chignon, his fingers brushing her cheek with a spine-tingling touch. Her breath caught in her throat.

"I can't figure you out, Bridget, except that you're trou-

ble," he said, his finger tracing a path down her skin to the
top button that she'd been playing with. He hooked his finger in the fabric and tugged her closer, until she was against
him, pressed against his hard chest.

One arm wrapped around her, his hand resting on the
curve of her ass, pulling her tight against his hips. She made
no move to stop him, couldn't if she wanted to. Slowly, his
other hand found the pins in her hair and undid the careful
knot. Her hair tumbled down her back, and Ethan's fingers
raked through the strands. Then his hand cupped the back of
her neck, and when his fingers touched her skin, the contact
sent a jolt of electricity through her. Her mouth dropped
opened and she sucked in a breath.

"I know I should run, but damn, Irish," he said, then
brought his mouth down on hers. There was no soft kiss,
nothing to warm up—they were both too hot for that. It
was as if they were picking up where they'd left off last night,
before Rowdy's interruption, and Ethan's abrupt evolution
into a serious law enforcement professional.

Bridget heard herself moan and wondered vaguely what
would happen if another employee walked in, but then
Ethan's hands were running down her hips, gripping the fabric of her skirt and inching it up until his fingers found her
bare skin. At the first touch, her head spun. She groaned, but
the sound just spurred him to deepen their kiss.

Oh, God. This was dangerous. And it was better than her
frustrated dreams last night, better than any of the daydreams
she'd been having in this conference room hours earlier.

He moved forward, backing her up to the edge of the
massive table so she was trapped between it and the wall of

well-muscled chest. His arms bulged under the cotton shirt, and Bridget's hands gripped at his biceps to keep herself steady, since her knees seemed to be failing. He found the zipper at the side of her skirt and tugged at it with impatient fingers. His hand slipped under the fabric, along her lower back, tracing the lace edge of her underwear.

Bridget had a brief moment of panic at the thought of being discovered. Another office employee could return. A night manager at the mill could come investigate why the lights were still on in the main office.

Then Ethan pulled her away from the table, enough for the skirt to slide off her hips and pool around her feet. He lifted her easily, setting her on the conference table and moved between her legs. Strong hands gripped her thighs and pulled her forward until she was pressed up against his hard length.

He kissed her again, his tongue sweeping her mouth. Her body vibrated with need and she arched into the kiss. Ethan's hand behind her, in the small of her back, kept her pinned against him as his lips moved down her neck.

"Oh, God, Ethan," she moaned. "The door—"

"Locked it when I came in," he said, his breath brushing across her neck in a hot rush. "After all the trouble you chase, is that a risk you won't take?"

His voice, his words, made her body throb and she couldn't think of anything she wouldn't risk for a chance at more of his touch. Bridget ran her hand through his hair, the silky strands sliding through her fingers. His head lowered and he brushed his lips down her throat to the top button on her blouse. With slow and deliberate motions, he unfastened the first few buttons and leaned back, taking in the sight of her peach silk bra. Bending his head, he pressed his lips to the curve of her breast, just above the fabric.

Her head fell back and her eyes closed. Her entire universe had shrunk to the conference room table, and the center of that universe was the spot where his lips caressed her. Nothing outside mattered when he touched her.

And that made it even more risky. She couldn't forget that Ethan Ford could destroy all her plans, if she wasn't careful.

But then he pushed her shirt off her shoulders, unhooked her bra, and sank his teeth into the tender spot where her neck and shoulder met, sending her body into a spasm of pure lust that she'd never experienced before. And when he eased her back, so she was laying on the cool, hard surface, her mind nearly shut down all together.

"So beautiful," he murmured, his hands cupping her breasts, taking a hard peak into his hot mouth, tugging at it until she cried out as the pleasure crossed into pain and then back again.

She writhed under him, greedy for more of his touch. But he wouldn't be hurried. Instead, he alternated his mouth and fingers to tease and delight her. When she begged him for more, Ethan stopped, put his hands on her thighs and pushed her legs apart. She gasped and he gave her a predatory grin.

"I bet you taste good here, too," he said, his fingers inching up her inner thighs, slowly and softly and leaving a trail of tingles. When he brushed against the matching underwear, now wet with her desire, he groaned and the sound rumbled through her. His finger stroked her gently through the damp fabric and it wasn't nearly enough.

"More, damn it," she gasped.

With a low laugh, he pulled the last remaining barrier away and then pulled her to the edge of the table and dropped to his knees, kissing his way up her inner thigh.

"Thought of you all day," he murmured against her tender skin, while his fingers drove her into a frenzy. "Thought of doing this to you, and more. So much more."

"Oh my God," she gasped, as two fingers slid into her. Her mind had gone blank, unable to help her form words. All she could manage after that was a moan.

"I need to taste you, Bridget."

He spread her legs even more and kissed the inside of her thigh, making his way higher, until she was vibrating with need.

"More," she whispered. Her head fell back, resting against the wooden surface and she sank into the sensation of his hands, his mouth on her. And then one hot, wet lick across her core sent her careening to new heights. "Oh God, oh God."

Ethan's tongue teased and tortured her clit, his fingers slid inside of her. She writhed against him, relishing the rasp of his beard against her skin.

Last night, she'd imagined how Ethan would touch her, and she knew he would. Eventually. It was inevitable. Somehow it was better than her imagination could conjure. Ethan's mouth on her, sucking, kissing. It was overwhelming, it was too much.

And then the crest built to a peak, so intense and so fast it caught her off guard. Her body arched, clenched around his fingers, and she cried out, then bit back the sound with a moan. Her breath caught in her chest and her legs trembled.

She struggled to return her breathing to normal. God, the man's touch drove her crazy. Neither of them should be doing this, but they also couldn't seem to stop.

Ethan kissed her thighs as he pulled away, then rested his face against her leg.

"Why did you come here?" she gasped. She stared at the ceiling of the conference room, her body too spent to move.

She could feel him smile against her thigh. He kissed a trail up her body, then stood, leaning in over her again. A whiff of her own scent clung to his lips as he kissed her, soft at first, but then deeper.

"To keep you out of trouble," he said.

"You don't seem to be doing a very good job of that." She raised her face to look at him.

His eyes lowered to the shirt she barely wore, unbuttoned, that almost kept her from his view. Her bra was unhooked, draped across her chest. "Yeah, I know," he whispered. "This seemed like a better alternative to arresting you for filing a false insurance claim."

She sucked in a breath. He wouldn't. Couldn't. But the threat was enough to make her heart race in a whole new way.

"You'd do that?"

"That's sort of my job, Irish," he murmured, still stroking her trembling legs. Her body felt languid, far more relaxed than any workout would have left her. But with every touch, the need was growing again, a throbbing and aching that craved more of his touch, more of him. Even as he threatened to throw her in jail. Her body was such a traitor.

"Well, I guess it's a good thing I haven't filed an insurance claim," she whispered back.

He smiled and heat rushed to all the good places again. "Good, because I'd hate to have to cuff you."

She smiled. "Liar."

He kissed her again, pulled away and helped her off the table. "Get dressed. I'll take you home."

Her legs were weak, but she steadied herself and managed to fasten her bra and locate her panties and skirt.

"There's a game tonight. I'm going to the pub," Bridget said, stepping into her skirt. Ethan was behind her in an instant, his hands on her shoulders. His touch sent a shiver through her, reminding her that they had unfinished business. His beard grazed her skin and then the heat of his lips against her skin warmed her.

His hands roamed across her stomach, inching up her ribs, cupping her breasts and then teasing her nipples into hard peaks until they ached for more. Her eyes fluttered closed at the adoration of his hands on her soft skin. She reached for him, pulling him closer, rising up to kiss him. One hand playing with the buttons on his shirt, working it free so she could reach in, touch his skin.

His body jerked at the contact and his breath hissed out.

"Later," he groaned, and pressed his lips against hers. "Later, I'm going to take my time, make you scream for more. Make you mine."

Bridget's body hummed and was ready for that now, despite the fact that he'd just given her the best damn orgasm of her life. She unfastened another button on his shirt, her hands drifting toward his belt. He caught her hand as she brushed the bulge in his pants.

"We need to get out of here," he whispered. "I'm not doing this in a conference room."

"You started it," she said.

He nodded and swallowed hard. "I did. And now I need to get you home and finish this."

Her knees went weak at the words. *Yes.* She wanted that more than anything. But she had business to attend to. People she needed to talk with, and though Gavin would never know, money to collect.

He helped her into her clothes, an irony she found particularly amusing. She ran a hand over her hair, smoothing it enough that it wouldn't look like she'd just been ravished in her workplace.

"I need to be at the pub for a while," she said.

His face tensed, the whiskey-colored eyes darkened, and he shook his head slowly. His mouth was drawn into a tight line. "That's your regular schedule. It would be better, since someone is threatening you, to vary your routine."

She bristled at the command. It was her livelihood he was messing with. He hadn't come out and mentioned her side business, so she decided to dance around it, too. "It's not for long, just a couple hours."

He shook his head and all the tension that had dissolved after the lovely oral sex came roaring back and the muscles in her neck and shoulders knotted.

"It's my brother's pub. Nothing is going to happen to me there," she said. As much as she tried, she couldn't seem to stop herself from sounding like a petulant child. "You're welcome to join me."

Oh hell, why had she said that? She wasn't going to be able to do business right in front of him. Owen Nichols owed her at least a grand from the last few games and was cut off until he paid up. Since he'd texted her that he wanted in on tomorrow night's game, he'd be bringing her an envelope of cash.

Ethan crossed his arms and looked down at her, an incredulous expression on his handsome face. "Really, Bridget? You want me there?"

Okay, he knew. And they were done dancing around it.

"It's not a big deal," she said, and turned to gather the stack of reports that she needed to take to her office. She doubted he was going to let her brush this off.

He leaned back against the table next to her and rested his hands on the top. She frowned and grabbed a binder to take upstairs.

"You need to quit this," he said quietly.

"Why?"

"Because I don't want to arrest you."

It sounded sincere, as if he'd genuinely regret arresting her. But then he'd do it anyway.

"If I were doing something illegal, which I am not admitting, you'd arrest me? After that—" She waved her hands toward the spot on the table where she'd lost her freaking mind at his hands and under his tongue.

"It's my job," he said, his teeth gritted.

"And my job is at the pub," she shot back. The next few weeks were her Black Friday, her Christmas shopping season, the time when she'd earn a good percentage of her annual income. Things would quiet down after the championships, and then Ethan could go back to ignoring her little operation. And she could finish paying for having the land terraced, get irrigation pipes installed, and order vines.

Bridget stood up and reached for her computer bag. For a large man, Ethan moved fast—faster than she'd been expecting. He stepped into her path and she nearly ran fully into him. She raised her chin to meet his very determined gaze.

"You have a lot to lose if you get caught," he said.

This was too much. She wasn't going to be lectured like a child. And she wasn't going to suddenly change her long-term plans for someone who she had only known for two weeks. Even if she'd be trading that for mind-blowing sex. Because no matter how good the sex was, and she was positive that it would be excellent, she'd have to give up her future for it.

"I don't hurt anyone," she said. "I'm not forcing anyone to place bets."

He stepped forward, as if to intimidate her. "Bridget, you need to stop playing at being a criminal. It won't end well."

She took a step toward him, unafraid, reckless, and feeling the familiar rush of finding a good sparring partner. But the stakes here were higher. And this wasn't a game.

"Well, you'd know all about that, wouldn't you, Mr. Black?"

The words slipped out in a moment of temper and she instantly wanted to grab them back. Something flickered in his eyes, perhaps surprise, but it was gone in an instant. His eyes softened and he leaned back, just a little, but the distance felt far greater.

Fuck, when would she learn to control her mouth? That was supposed to be the leverage to keep Ethan from digging into her business, from shutting her down. And she'd just blown it.

But instead of begging her not to go to the town council with his secrets, Ethan took her hands in his.

"Yeah, I changed my name when I was a teenager," he said softly. "My mother abandoned my brother and me when we were very young and we grew up in the foster system. I took on the last name of my foster family when I was an adult and out of the system."

Oh, crap. That was not what she expected to hear and her insides twisted with guilt. Wow, she had really fucked this up good. Her mind scrambled to find a way to fix it, to take it back, but she knew it was too late.

"I'm sorry. I shouldn't have—"

"Hey, it's okay. You couldn't have known," Ethan said. He didn't even sound angry, which made it worse. "When I see the relationship you have with your family, Bridget—I'm not going to lie. It makes me a little jealous. I don't want to see you throw that away. You have no idea how lucky you are to have that."

Oh, God, it kept getting worse. Her stomach dropped and felt an unfamiliar emotion wash over her. She suspected it was shame. She knew she was lucky to have her family, her privilege. Was he right? Was she throwing all of that away? She'd welcome an earthquake about now, something to split the floor and let the earth swallow her. A tsunami. A kraken in the harbor. Anything to get out of this situation.

"Don't take that for granted," he said.

Unable to look him in the eye, she studied the way her hands looked in his—her pale hands dwarfed by his large tan ones. How gently he held them when she'd been a complete bitch to him.

"Where's your brother?" she asked.

He sighed. "Jail, probably. We don't keep in touch."

Not in California, she wanted to assure him, but that would reveal the depth of her background check on him.

"Why?"

"Trevor's been in trouble his whole life. We don't talk any more. It's too hard to see what he's become."

"What is that?"

"A con artist. A thief."

"When did you see him last?"

"It's been years."

She thought of her three brothers and how they drove her crazy, but also how much she adored them all. Niall, the big goof with the heart that was as big as the world. Gavin, who teased her mercilessly with great affection. Declan, the only honest one in the family, who always did the right thing, and would protect the family no matter what mischief they got into. And her sisters, Neve and Elizabeth, too. No matter what, she knew they each had each others' backs. Not having them would be horrible.

Having a brother, and losing him—that would be even worse.

"Am I proud of my brother and his life of crime? No, not at all. I didn't share that with the town council because it's irrelevant to my life here," Ethan said. "Trevor was never going to change. Changing my name put some distance between us. I knew what I wanted to do with my future, and I knew the path he was on."

"I understand," she said, forcing the words through the tightening in her throat.

He squeezed her hands lightly and she looked up at him. "I would very much appreciate it if you were to go straight home tonight. I'd worry less than if you went to the pub as you'd planned."

His warm brown eyes were searching her face, anxious and concerned, but not for himself—for her and her safety. She frowned and didn't say anything. Now that she had just become the world's worst person, she wasn't feeling nearly as social, so that wouldn't be a huge sacrifice.

"I asked Deputy McBride to keep an eye on your road, especially at night. Can you manage not to shoot any of the law enforcement officers?" A slight smile played around his lips and she nodded.

"Good," he said, then leaned down and kissed her. It was tender and gentle and made her feel even worse, a feat she wouldn't have thought possible.

"I'll go home," she said.

"Thank you." His relieved voice made her stomach tremble—but from guilt, not desire this time. "I'll call you tomorrow."

He brushed his lips across hers again, quickly, and then walked away, his footsteps fading on the carpeted hallway until she heard the soft click of the office door being closed behind him.

"Well, fuck." Bridget's voice echoed in the conference room.

She sat on an upholstered chair and put her head in her hands. Damn it all to hell, she had well and truly fucked this up. If Ethan spoke to her again, and she wouldn't blame him if he didn't, it would very likely be to arrest her for illegal wagering. And that meant the incredible sex she'd been promised was off the table.

And he turned out to be a really decent guy, so way to go, Bridget.

She picked up her laptop bag and the documents and took the back stairs up to her office, in case Ethan was still in the parking lot. She didn't want him to see that she was nearly in tears, that he'd had that effect on her.

No, Ethan didn't make her cry. She was making herself cry. Or at least miserable, since she wasn't actually crying. Yet.

Minutes later, she drove past the town boundary and started into the dark hills east of Lost Coast Harbor, her thoughts consumed with the two young brothers abandoned by their mother and left with just each other in a cruel social services system. And to come from that and become the police chief, that was really an accomplishment.

She turned off of the road and into her long driveway, but not before her headlights lit up a black and white cruiser on the side of the road. Ethan hadn't been bluffing about getting her more protection. She smiled at the thought of him watching out for her, but it was a thin and weak expression. She wasn't at all sure she deserved his care.

He was kind. And it really was a shame that his brother took a different path. Maybe if they'd been able to spend more time together, he could have influenced Trevor—

Bridget hit the brakes and the sedan skidded a few feet on the gravel. Her mouth opened and her brow furrowed as she replayed their conversation again in her head.

He'd said it had been years since he'd seen Trevor.

But Trevor had been arrested near Bakersfield just a few months ago. And then the charges were dismissed. She reached for her phone and brought up the email from Bree with the information.

Yes, it was all there—Trevor Black, arrested on outstanding warrants from South Carolina and Kern County, California. Taken into custody in a small town outside the Bakersfield city limits, but by Bakersfield police officers. Then released the following day with no charges and no extradition to South Carolina.

What were the odds that Ethan hadn't seen his brother or had a hand in his release?

In the darkened car, she quickly typed an email to Bree about getting more records from that event. Then she sat in the idling car, her hands gripping the steering wheel.

Trevor Black wasn't the only con artist in his family.

CHAPTER TEN

Early mornings in Lost Coast Harbor fell into two catego-
ries. When the sky was clear, the sun rising over the hills
east of town painted the scattered clouds pink and blue and
gently illuminated the neat rows of older houses below. And
when the sky was overcast, the sun didn't stand a chance. The
cloud cover gradually lightened in shades of gray. That also
usually meant that the gunmetal gray clouds were going to
stick around, with a flat and shadowless daylight.

Ethan drove to the office under a solid slate sky that indicated another dreary, gray day ahead. It was early, not yet sev-
en in the morning, as he parked in the employee lot behind
the police department.

He liked being the first one in the office. He could brew
a pot of coffee and take his time reviewing the fresh stack of
police reports from the night shift. The coffee would be especially necessary this morning, since he'd had another poor
night's sleep. This time it wasn't from trying to get comfortable on Bridget's couch. It seemed his conscience was making
a late arrival.

As much as he hated to admit it, he felt guilty about

manipulating Bridget. He hadn't lied to her. Well, not much, at least. It was for her own good. McBride had texted him that Bridget had arrived home and that it was quiet up on Townes Valley Road. So his strategy had worked.

Still, it didn't sit right. He liked her. A lot. She was fiery and smart and sexy as hell.

And had somehow found out about his name change. That was probably bad news.

Yesterday's encounter hadn't gone as he'd planned. But then he'd seen her in that conservative get-up, with the tight skirt that hugged her lean body, and with her hair pulled up, and his brain misfired. Or his judgment did, at least. All he could think of was tearing that blouse open and undoing that neat bun and unleashing the passion beneath the prim facade. And he'd been right, too. She'd responded to his touch just as he'd imagined, had fantasized about. His body still ached for more of her, even as his brain reminded him that she was pure trouble.

Ethan was still mulling over what that meant as he let himself in the backdoor of the police department and then walked down the short hall to his office. He inserted his key into the lock and the door gave, opening before he had a chance to unlock it. His body tensed. He locked his office door every night, without fail. He slowly pushed it open.

Bridget Donnelly sat in his chair, leaning back, her boots on his mahogany desk. Her bright blue eyes were wide and crystal clear, as if she'd never had a bad night's sleep in her life. Her long black hair flowed in waves over her shoulders, a sharp contrast to the crisp white button-down shirt that she wore tucked into dark jeans. Her full lips turned up in a smile that signaled trouble.

"Mornin', Sheriff," she said.

"How did you get in here?"

"I have many talents. Skills you'd appreciate."

His mouth went dry at the thought of Bridget's talents. "I do not doubt that."

Her eyes darted down to his desk, resting momentarily on a small black leather case, then back up to his. "Lock picking is one of them."

Ethan picked up the case and opened it, examined the thin tools, all neatly arranged. "Lock picks are illegal to possess."

Bridget's eyes sparkled at the challenge. She held up her hands, wrists together. "Guess you better cuff me."

"Don't tempt me," he said, walking around to the other side of the desk and leaning back against it, facing the sexiest felon he'd ever known. "What are you doing here, Bridget?"

"You lied to me."

It wasn't an accusation. If anything, she sounded impressed. He smiled.

"What gave me away?"

"You said you haven't seen Trevor Black in years, but he was arrested in Kern County a few months ago. And somehow, two outstanding warrants, including one from South Carolina, just evaporated."

There was no legal way she could have figured this out, not that fast. He'd picked up Trevor to keep him from getting hauled out of state to answer a warrant out of Hilton Head. He'd pulled some strings, flirted with a young deputy district attorney and gotten the Kern County warrant recalled.

A little more flirting and a few white lies, and omitting the fact that Detective Sergeant Ethan Ford was the defendant's long-suffering brother, and a sympathetic prosecutor in South Carolina had been persuaded to drop that matter, too.

And Trevor was a free man. For now.

It wouldn't last, and there was no way Ethan was going to stick around and risk his career for his reckless little brother. Not this time.

He raised an eyebrow. "Now, how would you know all that?"

She shrugged and gave him a modest smile. "Like I said, I have skills."

He grabbed her boots and pulled the chair closer, tilting it back and keeping her legs across his. He leaned in closer to her and detected a hint of her perfume, something a little spicy with a hint of sweetness behind it. "Why do you care?"

"If you're lying about that, what else are you lying about?"

"You'd be the expert on that."

"I didn't lie."

He gave her a hard stare. "You didn't tell me the truth."

"You didn't ask the right questions," she said. Her smile widened. "What did you do anyway? Your juvenile files were still sealed."

Shit. She really did do her homework. His two arrests when he was a teenager were in different counties. Finding both would take persistence. "Nothing you need to worry about."

Bridget squinted. "Why did you choose the name Ford? Was that really your foster family's name?"

Ethan laughed and briefly debating lying again. But a wise

man had once advised him to tell the truth whenever possible, because it was always easier to remember. That wise man was corrupt to the bone, but the advice was solid.

"No. I was driving this old Ford truck at the time. It was a good truck. Very reliable."

Bridget shook her head. "You nearly had me conned."

"Nearly?" He didn't have to remind her that she'd bought his story hook, line, and sinker.

She laughed. "You're good."

Of course he was good. He'd been trained by the best. And no matter how much he wanted to forget that part of his life, some skills couldn't be unlearned.

He pulled the chair in a few more inches, tightening his grip on her long legs and staring into those beautiful eyes.

"So what are you going to do now? Turn me in? Tell the council all about my misspent youth?" he asked, leaning in closer and inhaling her scent.

"Maybe I will. Our town council is understandably sensitive about the integrity of their police chief."

He raised an eyebrow. "Don't think you're going to blackmail me, Irish. It won't go well if you go to the council with a tale of my deception. Because I'll tell them the truth—a story of my redemption. And that story wins every time."

Her lush mouth opened, and her teeth bit into her full bottom lip as he leaned forward, close enough to kiss her, then backed up a couple inches.

"You've done this before," she whispered.

Her eyes were bright with excitement and he wondered if he'd revealed too much to the wrong person. Any sane woman would have run screaming by this point. Bridget Donnelly seemed turned on.

"You're not redeemed," she said. "You're a criminal."

"Takes one to know one, my dear."

She tilted her head back and laughed and Ethan closed the few inches between them, brushing his lips along her long expanse of pale neck. He was going to regret this, but damn, the woman drove him crazy.

Her hands gripped his arms, then moved up until her fingers were at the back of his neck, scorching him, and urging him on.

"You're trouble," she whispered, moving so he could kiss farther down her neck to the edge of the collar.

He laughed as she stole his line. "So are you."

Their lips met with a fury, a clash of tongues and teeth and hot breath and moans. The pent-up passions from the last two encounters released in a rush. He tilted Bridget back farther and consumed her mouth, and the antique wooden chair groaned, probably never having seen this much action. He lifted her to her feet, his hands at her waist. He kicked the chair away and pulled her between his legs.

"I'm not leaving this office until I've gotten what I came for," she said, wrapping her arms around his neck.

She licked her bottom lip and stared into his eyes. Trouble. Danger. Temptation that he should be able to resist.

"The door. Lock it." His voice was gravelly and low and he barely recognized it.

She walked to the door, turned the lock, and then stalked him across the office. He backed up to the sofa against the wall, suddenly grateful that the last chief had never gotten around to installing that window to the main office. Bridget followed, her eyes focused on him and her cheeks pink. She took long strides, but slow, and her slender hips moved like she was dancing to unheard music.

When she stepped close enough, he pulled her down, kissing her as she settled on top of him. His hands tangled in her hair as his tongue swept her mouth.

"What did you come here for, Bridget?"

She leaned into him, her hands on his chest and her long legs straddling his. "You, Sheriff," she said, in a voice low and sultry.

Her hips rocked against his cock, which was straining to be freed. Her sweet lips claimed him, tasted him, and then her hands began working at the knot of his tie.

"Why don't you wear a uniform?"

"Sometimes I do," he said, as her fingers brushed his neck, unfastening the collar. "Council meeting tonight after work. Gotta look respectable."

She gave him a wide smile. "Respectable? Like how you're rolling around in your office with the town's bookie?"

His hand landed on her ass with a light smack and she laughed again, a musical sound that made his cock strain against his pants. She sat up, her knees on either side of his hips, held up a finger and wagged it at him. "Don't start something you're not going to finish, Sheriff."

Before he could respond, her hands were moving down his chest, and then she shifted so she could unfasten his belt.

"Come here," he growled. He didn't care that his staff was going to start arriving any minute on the other side of the wall. He wanted her and waiting until they were in a more appropriate setting was no longer an option.

She shook her head and moved away, ever stubborn, pushing his legs apart so she could kneel between them on the couch. His right leg dropped off the sofa as her fingers worked at the button of his pants, then eased the zipper down, freeing his cock. His breath stuttered as her hand stroked him through the thin cotton of his boxers. He shifted his hips to help her remove the last barrier and then groaned as she leaned forward, her tongue flicking out and lapping the drop of moisture at the tip of his cock. It sent a shock through him, from his balls to the top of his head.

"You taste good, too," she murmured, and her breath across the sensitive skin was a whole new torture.

Then there was nothing but her warm, wet mouth taking him slowly, an inch, then one more. A wave of pleasure engulfed him. Her tongue swirled and hit every fucking nerve in his cock, setting them off like a string of firecrackers. His hands tangled in her hair, unsure if he was going to pull her up and fuck her or hold her there and let the exquisite torture continue. But he wasn't in control, Bridget was.

Her hand grasped his shaft as her mouth took more of him. Ethan couldn't look away from the sight of her dark hair draped across his lap. He smoothed it away and she looked up at him, the impact of those crystal blue eyes making his cock jerk again. The sight of her lips wrapped around him. Sliding, sucking. Her eyes met his, bright and clear and excited. She took him deeper, as far as she could.

"Come here." He needed her, he needed to be inside her. "I want to fuck you, Irish. I want to slide into you, feel you come around me."

Christ, this was such a bad idea. Maybe once they'd had

this…whatever it was. Once they'd acted on it, they could move on. Defuse the tension.

Her tongue deftly teased him and he let his head fall backward, falling into the sensation of being inside Bridget, letting her pleasure him. Falling into the delusion that this was something from which he'd be able to walk away unscathed.

"Goddamn it, Bridget," he said, his voice hoarse. "If you keep that up…"

In response, she slid his cock nearly out of her mouth, her hand on the shaft, squeezing him. Then she sucked him, her tongue swirling below the rim of his head, before sliding her mouth back down his cock, taking him deeper.

Then she cupped his balls and his body jerked, the fuse lit. Nothing stopping it now.

"Ah, fuck, Bridget," he groaned, the orgasm rocketing through him with a violent shake and he felt her tighten around him, swallowing him, and that thought made him come even harder.

In his thirty-seven years, he'd never met anyone who drove him this crazy. Drove him to risk his job, his reputation, his sanity, for another touch of her hands, her mouth. He could step back and see the mistakes he was making, and was powerless to stop himself. An addict. He needed her.

She hummed her satisfaction as she pulled back, licking him clean as she went. His breath was ragged, his legs weak, and he had no idea if he'd just shouted his pleasure to the entire Lost Coast Harbor police force. With a light sweep of her tongue over her bottom lip, his cock stirred again at the possibility of more. Greedy bastard.

"I'll see you tonight," she said.

"Tonight?"

She stood and adjusted her clothing, smoothing the crisp cotton shirt and tucking it into her jeans. "The town council meeting tonight," she said. She raised an eyebrow and smiled. "You might want to put on some pants before I open that door."

"Stay a minute," he said, and forced his body to move, to be roused out of the pleasure-drunk coma he'd fallen into the moment he'd come in Bridget's mouth.

"Can't. I have to go to work," she said.

"Just a minute," he said, as he got dressed. "I'll walk you out."

She helped him straightened his tie, close enough that he could watch the shadows cast from her eyelashes on her porcelain skin, and then be hit full force by those blue eyes when she glanced up at him. His stomach flipped and churned, a goddamn roller coaster he couldn't climb off.

Fuck. He was in trouble. She'd blown past all his defenses. Every pretense, all the facades lay flat on the ground when Hurricane Bridget hit him. He swallowed hard at the thought, of what that meant.

"I'll walk myself out," she said. "You have a good day, Sheriff."

Then she raised herself up on her toes and kissed him goodbye, leaving a hint of her perfume behind.

CHAPTER ELEVEN

S he should have brought a flask, Bridget thought, as she listened to the town council debate over whether to install parking meters in the town square. The crowd, if the two dozen scattered residents could be called that, looked around in boredom or concentrated on their phones. Even the five town council members seemed to struggle to pay attention to the staff member who was reading a report into the record.

An elbow hit Bridget's rib and she jumped at the sharp pain.

"Stop sighing," Gavin whispered.

"Stop hitting me," she whispered back, returning the elbow.

Molly Donnelly leaned across Gavin and gave them both a stern look that made the siblings sit up straight—an instinct honed over a lifetime of Sunday church services.

"So help me, God, I will ground both of you if you don't shut up," their mother hissed.

Bridget rolled her eyes, but tried to focus on the debate and not on the back of Ethan Ford's head, just six rows ahead of her. His wavy hair just barely touched the back of the suit jacket's collar and her fingers itched at the memory of running her hands through the strands.

"You're sighing again," her brother muttered.

"Shut up."

Gavin gave her a curious look, but she shook her head and then gave a quick nod toward their mother. Molly had insisted on coming to the meeting to support Grace, who was attending her first meeting as a member of the town council. But Bridget had no desire to alert her mother about whatever it was that was going on between her and Ethan. The woman was on a mission to get grandchildren and Bridget refused to put herself on Molly's radar.

"I move we table the vote on installing parking meters for another month, to better study the economic ramifications of this move," Councilman Kenneth Snell said.

Gavin expelled a long sigh and Bridget happily elbowed him in the ribs.

"Stop it," he whispered. "This means I have another month of comping Snell's tab."

"What's the big deal? Every town has parking meters," Bridget said.

"It could mean that my daytime crowd gets more tickets, which would drive them away. We like the tourists to stay and shop, and eat and drink, not have to leave in a hurry," Gavin said. "At this point, I just wish they'd make a decision. It's been four months."

Bridget wrinkled her nose. The council had a reputation for being slow to act on everything. So far tonight, they'd pushed off all the votes except for one on a study of whether to approve the permit for a St. Patrick's Day event in the town square the following year. It would take that long for them to make a decision, even though the party had been a huge success.

Grace sat on the far left of the dais, and Bridget tried to catch her eye as Councilwoman Fitzgerald droned on about replacing the town's streetlights with LED bulbs, which would be installed, no doubt, by Karen Merz' construction company. But her friend was studiously avoiding Bridget's gaze. The council tabled that item, of course, and moved to the last item on the agenda.

"And the last order of business is the introduction of our new police chief, Ethan Ford," Mayor Dale Strong said. "Chief Ford, thank you for coming tonight."

Ethan stood and walked to the podium in front of the mayor's seat in the center of the dais, and Bridget had to suppress another sigh at the sight of him—tall and broad-shouldered and so handsome in his suit. The thought of their morning encounter made her fidget in her chair and her brother gave her an incredulous look.

"God, you have got it bad for that guy," he whispered.

"Shh," Bridget hissed, but then saw her mother whispering with the woman on her other side, ignoring her children. God owed her no favors, but she thanked Him anyway.

Gavin gave a short laugh that he covered with a cough when Molly looked his way.

"As the other council members know, Chief Ford came to us from Bakersfield, where he had a distinguished career in law enforcement," Mayor Strong said. "We're very pleased that he agreed to come on as our new chief of police. Welcome aboard, Chief."

The council and the audience gave a polite round of applause.

"Now, we have moved the chief's contract approval to next month's meeting, so Ms. Ransom could be fully prepared to make an informed decision," Mayor Strong said. "But that's certainly not a reflection on your qualifications, Chief Ford. We're a very careful council and take our responsibilities very seriously."

"Of course, Mayor Strong," Ethan said.

"And it's so very unlikely that anything could come up between now and next month that would influence our vote, that it seemed like the best course of action," the mayor said.

Bridget nearly rolled her eyes. They were toying with him, letting him know that they had the power over his contract.

"Chief Ford, with the understanding that you've only been on the job for a very short time, do you have an update on the town's crime statistics for us?" Councilwoman Marlene Dewey asked.

Ethan dipped his head slightly and Bridget regretted that he was facing away, so she couldn't see his face. Though the view from behind was nice, too.

"Thank you for the warm welcome, Mr. Mayor, council members," he said in his rich baritone. "Thanks to the very capable work of Detective Sergeant Valerie Childs, who acted as interim chief, I do have the latest crime statistics for the council."

He went on to recite, seemingly without relying on his notes, the number of moving violations, petty thefts, and break-ins in the town in the prior month. Even as he got into the felonies, Bridget found her attention waning. As long as none of the Donnellys were in the police blotter, she didn't really care. The town's crime patterns didn't vary too much—petty thefts rose when tourism season arrived and people left their bags unattended, illegal grows were usually a problem left to the sheriff's department, and big crimes, like murders and assaults, just didn't happen here.

Well, not until recently, but then it was corruption, arson, and kidnapping. Some weapons trafficking. Attempted murder. But really, the recent crime wave was an outlier. Usually, the town was fairly quiet. Boring even.

"And are you doing anything about illegal wagering, Chief?" Mayor Strong asked.

An intense heat rose up Bridget's neck and face at the sudden turn toward her livelihood. She squinted at the mayor, who owed her two-hundred dollars from last night. What was he up to? Mayor Strong was a steady customer, who fancied himself somewhat of an expert on sports betting. He studied the stats and placed his bets after careful consideration of trades, past performances, and medical information on key players. He was cautious and generally won, and never bet that much, so he hadn't been on her radar to keep an eye on.

"I haven't had any complaints filed yet. If someone does come down to the police station to file a report, I would be happy to look into it," Ethan said.

"Well, I'm thinking that with the college basketball championships coming up, it seems like it's a peak season for illicit betting," the mayor said.

Bridget didn't like the way he pronounced the word "illicit," with extra emphasis so it sounded like a hiss.

"Uh, Bridget…" Gavin whispered in her ear. "Something

going on?"

She shook her head and waved him away, lest he attract any attention to her.

"Well, I haven't ordered my officers to bust up office betting pools," Ethan said. "If anyone has information on any illegal activity, they are always welcome to come in and talk with me."

The mayor caught Bridget's eye with a smug grin. "That is good to know," he said.

She seethed. Was Mayor Strong trying to get out of his debt? He had never failed to pay up before.

"Are there any further developments in the police department that you'd like to share with us, Chief Ford?" This question was posed by Kenneth Snell, member of the council and owner of The Rosewood Inn Bed and Breakfast.

"Only that we have a new intern program and our first intern," Ethan said. "Mr. Dylan Jencks will be working with the department through the summer."

Marlene Dewey gave a surprised gasp and then clapped a hand over her mouth when she realized that everyone had heard her. "My nephew, Dylan?"

Ethan nodded. "Yes. He's interested in learning more about a career in law enforcement."

Even from the back of the room, Bridget could see that Marlene Dewey's eyes were welling with tears. "He is?"

"Uh, Chief, I'm not one to tell you how to run your department, but is Mr. Jencks, ah—" Mayor Strong glanced over at Marlene, who flashed him an angry glare in return. "Ah—I just mean, that's an interesting choice."

"He seems eager to work with my officers. I'm confident

that he's going to do good work."

With a bang of the gavel, the mayor ended the meeting.

Bridget stood and gave her mother a hug good-bye, then got another elbow in the rib from her brother. "Looks like you've got competition," he said with a wink.

She followed his gaze and saw that Marlene Dewey had Ethan in a fierce hug.

"Guess I better up my game," Bridget said with a wink.

Gavin paled and shook his head. "Goddamn it, Bridget, do not say things like that to me. He's the chief of police, and if I have to kick his ass it's going to cause me all sorts of trouble."

She grinned. "What, you'd defend my honor? My maidenhood?"

Gavin muttered something under his breath and Bridget only caught a portion about smart-mouthed women before he walked away, shaking his head. Bridget found Grace near the dais, gathering her paperwork.

"Congratulations, Councilwoman Ransom," she said. "You survived your first meeting."

Grace smiled. "Not that I got to do much. We tabled everything."

"You got assigned to a lot of committees," Bridget said.

At this, Grace's smile slipped. "I'm not sure that's a good thing. What are you doing here, anyway?"

"I told you I'd come for moral support. That's what friends do," Bridget said.

"You're here to ogle the new police chief," Grace said, dropping her voice.

"Nope, that's just a bonus."

Grace shook her head, then straightened and her focus shifted to someone behind Bridget. She didn't need to turn her head to know it was Ethan.

"Councilwoman Ransom, it's a pleasure to meet you," he said, stepping forward and shaking Grace's hand.

"And you, Chief Ford," Grace said. "I apologize for the delay in voting on your contract. I tried to tell the other members that I would be comfortable voting this week, but it had already been moved."

"It's not a problem at all," he said, then gave Bridget a smile that lit her up from within. "Good evening, Ms. Donnelly."

"Chief Ford," Bridget said with a smile.

"Oh, you do remember my title?"

Her smile grew. "Sometimes."

Grace looked between them and then sighed and rolled her eyes. "I'm going home. See you at the office tomorrow, Bridget."

The crowd had thinned as Bridget and Ethan walked toward the doors leading to the lobby.

"And what are your plans for this evening, Ms. Donnelly?" Ethan asked, his voice dropping just enough to keep their conversation private.

His low voice triggered a deep throb within her. She was playing with fire, and damn if she didn't like it. Far too much.

"Chief Ford." The booming voice of Kenneth Snell interrupted their conversation and cooled her libido like a bucket of ice water.

"Councilman Snell," Ethan said, stopping shy of the door to the lobby.

"Hi Bridget," Snell said, giving her a brief nod.

"Mr. Snell, how are you?"

"Fine, fine. You don't mind if I steal the chief away for some city business, do you?" Snell gave her a look that implied it was vital law enforcement issues, but Bridget knew the bed-and-breakfast owner would most likely be asking for a favor—maybe a disabled parking placard for his Cadillac or something else he didn't deserve.

"Of course not," Bridget said, flashing a huge fake smile. "You gentlemen have a nice evening. And I'm sure you'll do a great job keeping our city safe and crime-free, Chief Ford."

Ethan bit back a smile at her facetious response. "Be careful out there, Ms. Donnelly."

She turned and walked out the front door of City Hall and into the cold mist, frustrated that the councilman had interrupted their conversation, which had been leading in a very promising direction. On the other hand, Ethan knew where to find her and she was certain he'd track her down. But if he didn't, she knew where to find him.

ETHAN FORCED A SMILE FOR THE INSIPID COUNCILMAN IN front of him. Kenneth Snell, mid-fifties, owner of The Rosewood Inn Bed and Breakfast. The Rosewood Inn was south of the town's center in a massive Victorian-style inn. Unlike most of the Victorians in Lost Coast Harbor, The Rosewood wasn't original. It had been built in the 1980s by a junk bond trader who had struck it rich.

He had then lost everything, as junk bond traders tended to do, and Snell had picked up the B&B at a bargain price. He added a fancy restaurant and gardens that he rented out for weddings and parties, and it was now the town's go-to place for special occasions. Ethan had yet to eat there. It looked a little on the fussy side for his taste.

"What can I do for you, Mr. Snell?" he asked. He hoped it was a fast bribery attempt because he had plans for tonight. Plans that included a very naked Bridget Donnelly, and no town council members in sight.

Snell clapped him on the back. "Well, it's an issue for the entire community, actually," he said. "You know that as chief of police, you have a lot of sway in the liquor license application process, right?"

Ethan nodded, though this was news to him.

"We're a small town, and every time a new business gets a liquor license, well, you know what happens," he said with a shake of his head.

Ethan tilted his head. "No, I'm not sure I do know what happens."

The councilman gave a dramatic sigh. "It's terrible. More alcohol in the community means more crime."

"I don't know that I have any statistics on that," Ethan said, waiting for Snell's ask. There would be one. It was just a matter of time.

"You see, there's a new business that is applying for a liquor license and I am very concerned about this, as a citizen. Not as a member of the town council. Although, since I've been elected to office now five times, I can tell you, this is a problem that has come before us time and time again."

"Uh huh."

"Now, I'm sure the young lady who is seeking the license is a fine, upstanding citizen, though we don't know a thing about her background, but I'm asking that you take a very close look at this. I, and many of this young woman's neighbors, are concerned that she's very young to be entrusted with this responsibility," Snell said.

"Who is the young woman applying for the liquor license?"

"Her name is Ivy Montgomery," Snell said. "She's new to town."

"And she wants to open a bar?"

Snell's mouth opened, then closed without making any noise, and then he tried again. "Not exactly. But if she were to get this license, that's essentially what she'd be doing. And right in the middle of a residential area, too. It'd be a real shame."

"What kind of establishment does she wish to open?"

He waved a hand. "She's opening it under the guise of a restaurant, but with this license, there's no limit on what she could do. I'm telling you, it's better to nip this in the bud."

Ethan would bet good money that Ivy Montgomery's restaurant was either within walking distance of The Rosewood Inn or had better food.

"I will look into it, Mr. Snell."

Snell smiled and shook his hand. "I appreciate that, Chief Ford. Hey, how about I buy you a beer down at Donnelly's?"

"I'm afraid I'll have to pass tonight, but let's do that soon," he said, moving toward the door before Snell could get another word in.

The cold, damp air hit him as he exited the building and he buttoned his jacket for the short walk to the police station. Bridget was nowhere in sight, and he guessed that she probably headed home. He debated, briefly, whether to call before going up there. Technically, she hadn't invited him. Also, she had a tendency to greet unannounced visitors with a twelve-gauge.

He was reaching for his phone when he heard someone calling him. With a groan, he turned, but it wasn't yet another council member trying to get some personal favor granted.

"Hey, Dylan."

"Hey, Chief," Dylan Jencks said, jogging up the block to him. "I just got a call from my Aunt Marlene. You told her?"

Ethan grinned at the young man's exasperated tone. "Yeah. She seemed happy."

Marlene Dewey's surprised tears of joy at the thought of her nephew suddenly gaining some career ambition guaranteed Ethan one vote on his contract. And he hadn't even had to compromise his principles to accomplish it.

"Yeah, she's happy. But I'm not really an intern," Dylan said. "And now she thinks I wanna be a cop."

"That is a problem."

"What am I gonna do now?"

Ethan shrugged and kept walking toward his office, Dylan falling into step next to him. "Guess you might have to finish the internship, enroll in the police academy, graduate, and get one of the best paying jobs available to someone with only a high school education, earn the respect of your peers and your community, and then retire with an above-average standard of living," he said.

Dylan's shoulders slumped. "Can't you tell her that I'm not good at being a cop? Maybe you could say I tried, but I'm just not cop material."

Ethan looked over at the kid. "You know that you don't get to be a cop just because you're working there. You're basically our janitor until you pay off your tickets."

"I could do more than take out trash and wash cars," Dylan said.

"Oh, no. No. You will be doing menial tasks. I am not giving you any responsibility for more than that. Anyway, you aren't even interested in being a cop," Ethan said.

"But I took out the trash and washed cars today and then ran out of things to do," he said. "Sergeant Spatz said if I couldn't find something to do tomorrow, I'd have to find the mouse in the break room."

That wasn't a bad plan, Ethan thought. "There has been a rodent problem in the break room for a while. You solve that and I'll get you a commendation."

"A what?"

"A medal."

"Oh. Okay," Dylan said. "I can do that."

Ethan was pretty sure that he had the power to get the kid a plaque, since he had the authority to reject liquor licenses.

"Hey, can I ask another question?" Dylan asked, matching Ethan's stride.

"Sure."

"Can I borrow my car? Just for the night?"

"No."

"Yeah, I thought you'd say that."

They reached the parking lot, and Dylan followed Ethan into the building through the station's back door. Ethan nearly tripped over a ten-speed bike leaning up against the wall in the short hallway.

"Is that your bike?"

"Yeah," Dylan said, his voice dejected. He pulled the bike away from the wall and headed for the back door. "See ya tomorrow."

"Good night," Ethan said, holding the door for the young man and his bike.

He closed the door and walked to his office, disappointed to not find Bridget sitting in his chair waiting for him. Closing the door behind him, he felt the stirring in his cock at the memory of her visit that morning and wondered if he was going to get a hard-on every time he walked into his office now. He pushed away those thoughts and focused on his task, filing the crime stats back in the designated drawer, locking his desk, checking his email, and then closing down the computer for the night.

It was busy work, and he was only doing it to distract himself from the thoughts of what he'd rather be doing. When the computer screen blinked to black, he pushed himself back from the desk. He had to make a decision—drive up to Bridget's house or go home.

If he went to her, it was over—he'd stay the night. They would pick up where they'd left things that morning. His cock stirred again, hardening at the memory, at the thought of what he'd do to her, of her tight, lean body and surprisingly full breasts above that narrow waist, her perfect alabaster skin turning to blush under his touch. His throat constricted as he recalled the sight of her lips around his cock, the feel of her hot and wet mouth surrounding him. How much he craved to be buried deep within her, making her cry out his name.

He'd never wanted something with this much intensity.

If he stayed home, he'd be the good cop, the upstanding chief of police. A man of principle. This choice had none of the attraction that Bridget held, but it was the right decision. He knew it.

He hated it.

Grinding his teeth, he reached for his keys, still undecided.

The faint beep in his coat pocket distracted him and he pulled out the phone and saw his brother's name on the screen. Another decision to make—be the big brother Trevor needed, or the one Trevor wanted.

He pressed the button on the screen.

"Hello, Trevor."

The fact that he'd answered the call must have surprised him, because his brother didn't respond for a long moment.

"Hello, Ethan."

His stomach clenched, anticipating the trouble on the other end of the line. "What do you need?"

Another pause and this time, he heard Trevor's breath hiss out.

"I've gotten into a bit of a mess."

CHAPTER TWELVE

Ethan paced the floor of his rental house, running a hand over his head. It was a nice house, three bedrooms, two baths, with hardwood floors, a big backyard, and a detached garage. Georgie, the police dispatcher and file clerk, had emailed him a selection of three available rentals and Ethan had picked this one. Any of them would have been fine, but the one he chose had a front porch and fit his image of what a small town should look like.

It came furnished, all the pieces in a simple, modern style, and that had made his move incredibly easy. He'd sold or given away most of his belongings, and the things he cared to keep fit in the back of his truck with room to spare. It wasn't the first time he'd left town in a hurry, but this time he wasn't outrunning the angry victim of a scam or a determined investigator.

Those days were long behind him. But his brother was still there.

"Fuck." Ethan groaned, diverting his pacing to the kitchen to grab a beer.

He should be at Bridget's house, undressing that gorgeous

woman, teasing her until she made those sweet sounds he loved, and sinking into her until they were both spent and satisfied. Placing the cold bottle against his temple, he closed his eyes. Between his brother's intrusion into his new life, and the mayor's cryptic remarks about illegal gambling, he was in no position to go to her. He would be terrible company, and it was very likely a poor career move to start dating the woman who everyone in town knew was a bookie.

In the front of the house, he heard his cell phone chirp and he walked toward the sound. The phone was buried in the pile of overcoat and suit jacket that he'd dumped in a chair as soon as he'd walked in the door and by the time he'd found it, he had missed the call. He checked the caller ID and saw that it was Trevor again.

Ethan twisted the cap off the beer and took a long drink. He'd been too abrupt with Trevor earlier, practically hanging up on him when Trevor had caught him at the office. He hadn't wanted to talk to him there, at the police station, about what was probably Trevor's latest criminal activities. But now, here in his own house, with a beer in hand, he was ready to confront it. He hit the redial button.

When his brother answered, Ethan could barely hear him over the background noise. His greeting was filtered through music, voices, and the chaos of a rowdy bar.

"Hey, Ethan. Hold on."

The noise grew quieter and it sounded like Trevor walked outside to take the call.

"Thanks for calling me back."

"Sure. What's up?"

"I'm fine, thanks. And how are you?"

Ethan closed his eyes and the muscles in his neck tightened. "Are you under the impression we were raised with any sort of manners? Just tell me what you did this time and what you need me to fix."

There was a long pause and Ethan wondered if he'd been too hard on Trevor. The tough-love approach still felt new to him. He'd always ended up bailing his brother out, sometimes literally, but five years ago he'd drawn the line—no more. Of course, he'd crossed that line last fall when Trevor got picked up near Bakersfield. But Ethan had told himself then that next time, he'd hold to it.

"It's not like that this time," Trevor said. "This time it's different."

Ethan rolled his eyes, not buying Trevor's bullshit for a second. It was always the same. Trevor Black was handsome and charming and free of any conscience. He was the perfect con artist, so there was no reason for him to change.

"What happened?"

"I met someone. A girl. A woman," Trevor said. "She's different, Ethan. Not like the rest."

"Oh fuck me," Ethan said, his voice coming out on a breath. "So, what's the story? Her father's demanding you marry her? She's pregnant? What is it?"

He heard Trevor's quick inhale and when his brother spoke again, he heard something new in his voice.

"No, nothing like that. You know what? I'm fine. Everything's fine."

"Bullshit, Trevor. You don't call me when everything's fine. You call me when you're neck-deep in trouble," Ethan bit out the words.

He had long since resigned himself to the fact that he had missed out on that average American childhood almost everyone else he knew had experienced. He and Trevor had floated through so many foster families that he had lost count. When he'd told Bridget that her family's closeness made him jealous, he wasn't lying. He'd give anything to have a relationship with Trevor that didn't involve deceit and suspicion.

"You're right, Ethan. I should have been better at staying in touch, but I never thought you wanted me around, so it was easier to stay away," Trevor said.

"Stop it. We don't con each other. You know that."

"I meant it."

Ethan drained the last of the beer. Trevor was right, Ethan had tried to separate himself from the criminal, the con artist. But not his brother. He would have loved to spend time with Trevor. Just not his baggage.

"I'm a cop. I can't be hanging around scammers and criminals," he said.

"Well, you'll be happy to hear that I'm going straight."

Ethan couldn't stop the snort of disbelief.

"I am."

"Let me guess—you're going straight, as soon as you hit one last score."

"It's just—ah, you know what? Just forget I called."

He was seized with an immediate fear that if his brother hung up, it might be the last time they would speak. It was irrational, because Trevor was thirty-four years old and more than capable of taking care of himself.

"Trevor, wait."

"What?"

He took a deep breath. "Are you in trouble? Do you need help?"

He'd never forgive himself if something happened to his younger brother, the only family he had, if he could have done something to help him.

"No. I can handle it myself," Trevor said.

He paused, exhaling slowly to calm himself. "Okay. Keep in touch."

"Yeah, I will."

The call disconnected and Ethan was left holding the phone in one hand and the empty beer bottle in the other, unsure which one he wanted to throw. He gritted his teeth and started toward the kitchen for a refill, when a knock on the front door sounded behind him.

He flipped on the porch light and saw the unmistakable outline of a tall, slim woman on the other side of the frosted glass door. He opened it and as soon as his eyes met hers, his tension ebbed a bit.

"Bridget," he said, holding the door for her. "I wasn't expecting you."

"I know. I like surprising you." She stepped into the small foyer and looked around, an eyebrow cocked. "This doesn't look at all like what I was expecting."

He closed the door behind her and leaned against it. "What were you expecting?"

Her full lips pursed and she looked at him, then around the modern furnishings. "Something more old-fashioned, maybe rustic."

"Can I get you something to drink?"

She smiled and slipped out of her coat and handed it to

him. "Yes, I'll have what you're having."

He held up the empty beer bottle and she nodded. "Come with me," he said, laying her coat across the pile of outerwear in the chair and then leading her to the kitchen.

He grabbed two more beers from the nearly empty fridge and opened hers before handing it to her.

"Would you like a glass?"

"No, thank you," she said, then tilted her head and studied him. "Are you okay?"

Ethan reached up and brushed a lock of hair from her face. It was cool to the touch from the outdoor air, but her soft skin was warm. "I'm fine."

Her eyes narrowed. "You're lying."

He took her hand and led her back to the living room. "Yes, I am."

"Why?"

"Because I don't want to talk about it."

"Then just tell me that you don't want to talk about it."

He flipped a switch and the gas fireplace came to life. He settled on the couch next to Bridget and let his arm fall behind her. She scooted closer to him, leaning against him and he wrapped his arm tighter around her shoulders. She fit him perfectly, like the other half of a matched set.

"I'm not good company tonight, Bridget," he said, and kissed her head, breathing in her warm scent. It soothed him, eased the knot of muscles in his neck and shoulders.

"You don't have to be," she said. "I just wanted to see you before I went home."

He smiled and stared into the fireplace, the flames dancing around the fake logs. He rested his head on the top of

Bridget's. It was nice. Romantic, even. He could get used to the feel of her in his arms, snuggled up against his side.

"What's put you in such a bad mood?" Bridget asked, her voice soft.

He took another drink and considered what he should share with Bridget. He was used to keeping his family life, such as it was, closed off from even his closest friends. But then she took his hand in hers and the warmth seeped into his skin, disarming him.

"My brother called," he said.

Bridget stiffened under his arm. "Your brother?"

"Yeah, Trevor," he said, remembering that she seemed to have learned a lot about Trevor already. "He only calls when he's in trouble."

She turned, looking up at him. "Is he all right?"

"I'm not sure," Ethan said. "He says he'll take care of it, but won't tell me what it is."

"Is he in danger? What are you going to do?" She shifted, setting her beer on the coffee table and pulling her knee up so she was facing him, her eyes wide and concerned.

He stroked her hair, brushing the soft strands from her face. "I can't do anything. I'm not even sure where he was calling from."

"But can you find out?" She seemed alarmed that he wasn't running out the door to help his brother. Which was probably what she would be doing if one of her brothers were in trouble.

He kissed her forehead. "Trevor can take care of himself."

"Then why did he call you?"

A fine question. Ethan wished he could answer it. "Who

knows? He's called me for bail. For money. For…well, lots of reasons."

He wasn't about to share the details of some of Trevor's earlier escapades—not the time Ethan had to extract him from a Juarez jail. Or when Trevor had been caught in the middle of a scheme in Atlantic City and Ethan had to come in and layer another con on top to get him out. Bridget certainly didn't need to know about that.

She frowned at him, her brows drawn together, and he touched the side of her face. "We don't have the kind of relationship that you and your siblings have."

The sadness in her eyes surprised him, and for the first time since he'd met her, she seemed to be at a loss for words.

"Bridget, sweetheart, don't worry about Trevor. He's going to be fine," Ethan said.

"I'm not worried about him. I'm concerned for you."

Her direct gaze knocked the air from his lungs. She *was* worried about him. He tried to recall the last person who had that concern for him and came up empty. He smiled and traced his thumb along her bottom lip. "Thank you."

She smiled back. "For what?"

He leaned closer, until his lips were hovering over hers. "For coming over tonight."

Bridget raised her chin, bringing her lips even closer. "You're welcome," she whispered, her breath feathering across his skin.

When their lips met, the spark shot through him. His heart slammed against his ribs as he deepened the kiss, tongues gliding against each other. Bridget's sweet sigh urged him on and he threaded his fingers into her hair and kept his hand at the back of her neck.

There was a small voice in his head, warning him about the dangers of playing with fire. He was doing exactly what he'd done in the past—taking the path of pleasure, ignoring the signs that this wasn't the right thing to do. Acting impulsively, heedless of the consequences.

He ran a hand down her back, drawing her closer, taking in the heat radiating from beneath her crisp cotton blouse. The slight tremor under his palm made his entire body react with a need that startled him in its intensity. His desire for Bridget was a steadily moving inferno that swept through him and swallowed up every good intention in its path. With every stroke of her tongue and brush of her lips, the need grew until it was greater than anything he'd experienced before.

Greater even than his need for self-preservation.

IF SHE WERE A BETTING WOMAN—AND DESPITE HER PROfession, Bridget wasn't—she would lay odds that Ethan Ford was going to break her heart.

He already had a little, with the sad way he spoke about his brother, with a longing that made her chest ache. But there was no way she was slowing down to think about the risks. Not now. Not when the man had one large hand gripping her hip like it was a life raft in a stormy sea. Not when his lips burned down her neck, marking her, and her body begged for more.

She swung a knee across his lap and straddled him, closing her eyes as his beard tickled her neck and sent shivers throughout her body. Ethan groaned as she pressed her body against his, then leaned his head against the back of the couch and watched her through hooded eyes. She reached up and caressed his face, running a hand over the short, trimmed beard on his jaw.

"Too rough?" he asked, his voice low.

Her body answered the question with a deep throb at her core. She shook her head. "No, I like it."

"You sure? I can shave."

"No, I don't want you to."

"Cause I like going into soft places and—"

She gripped his face with both hands and stopped him from talking. "Talk is cheap, Sheriff."

A slow smile spread across his face, his warm brown eyes lit up, and his grip on her tightened. With a quick move, he set her aside, stood and pulled her close to him, his hands on her hips. Bridget tipped her head back to look at him and wrapped her arms around his neck.

"Take me to bed, Ethan."

He blew out a long breath when she said his name, his eyes dilating with passion. When he leaned toward her, she stood on her toes and met him halfway in a kiss that made her head spin and her body shake. When they broke apart, panting, he grabbed her hand and tugged her toward the front door, where he flipped the lock and turned off the porch light. He hit another switch and the gas fireplace went dark. Then he pulled her down the short hallway, past the stairs, and into a darkened room. Without turning on a light, he lifted her easily, took a few long steps across the room and dropped her into the middle of the bed, where she landed with a bounce.

Ethan followed her down, his body covering hers and

enveloping her in his scent, an intoxicating mix of soap and leather and something unique to him. Bridget took a deep breath, inhaling it in. She ran a hand up his chest, working the buttons on his shirt free. Her fingers fumbled with the buttons, anxious to feel his hot skin. Then his shirt was wide open, and he shrugged it off and she splayed her hands on his chest, trying to feel as much of him as possible—the hard muscles under the warm skin bunching at her touch.

He lay on his side, one hand tangled in her hair, tilting her head back to look her in the eye.

"What are we doing, Bridget?" Ethan asked, his voice a low groan.

His heart beat under her fingers, keeping time with her own. "You carried me in here, Sheriff."

He was right, of course. The idea of getting close—especially this close—to law enforcement was scary. Thrilling, but risky. Her brain cautioned against it, but her body urged her forward.

"You want me to stop?" she asked, keeping her eyes on his but running her fingers down his chest, across the ridges of muscles, the trail of hair that tapered down his stomach. "I'll stop."

His eyes darkened and his breath became ragged. "I want you."

She leaned in to taste him, her tongue flicking against his nipple. He groaned, but let her explore his body. Her eyes fixed on a scar, a slash of six inches of jagged tissue that started at his shoulder and extended into his chest. She bent closer and kissed the long-healed wound and his body twitched. She looked up at him, but he held himself still and she resumed her exploration of this new territory.

Her territory. She wanted this. Wanted to claim it for herself.

Pressing her lips to his skin again, she moved down his body, unfastening his belt and then the button of his pants. His cock strained against the fabric and she bit her lip in anticipation and with the memory of that morning. A searing heat pooled between her thighs, and her body begged for more of him. Right now. But she denied herself that immediate gratification. This time, she wanted him slowly, and he seemed to be on the same page.

"God, Bridget," he breathed.

He lifted his hips and let her slide off the wool pants, then the boxers, and kicked them aside and lay back on the bed. She licked her lips at the sight. *Jesus, Mary, and Joseph.* He was just the finest specimen of a man she had ever seen. His thick-muscled thighs clenched when she ran her hand along the long length of skin from his knee to his hip. His cock, thick and hard, rested on his flat stomach and she trailed her fingers along the length of him there, too.

His breath skipped. "You're wearing entirely too many clothes, Irish."

She tore her eyes from his body and met his gaze, hot and intense.

"Shh, patience," she whispered and moved lower on the bed, dragging her lips along the ridge of his abs. Slowly, she lowered her head to kiss the tip of his cock, lapping up the drop of moisture there, and then ran her tongue along the sensitive rim below the head. Ethan's body contracted and his moan rumbled through him.

"Bridget, God," he hissed.

She slipped him into her mouth, grasping his shaft with one hand and swirling her tongue. One of his hands gripped the bedspread, the other tangled in her hair as she took him deeper.

"You're killing me, Irish," he whispered and his body tensed. With a rough breath, he pulled her away, guiding her up his body and then kissing her with a fevered urgency. "I can't take too much of that, beautiful."

He sat up and began undressing her by pulling off her boots, her socks, and then he ran his hands up her legs to the waistband of her jeans, which he unfastened and eased over her hips. As he pulled them off, he kissed her bared skin. His hands reached up, under the hem of her shirt and his fingers hooked the waistband of her panties and slid the lace away from her throbbing sex.

"So beautiful," he murmured, rubbing his beard along her thigh as he crawled up her body. Bridget tensed as his fingers brushed her sensitive folds and stroked her. She closed her eyes and arched into his slow, almost feathery touch. Her pulse beat in her throat as Ethan's hands pulled away, gliding up under the shirt, across her stomach.

He made quick work of the buttons on her shirt, pushing it open, and bent his head to kiss her stomach. His hands stroked her breasts, tracing the lace edge of her bra with a finger and cupping the weight in his hands. Running a hand behind her back, he expertly unclasped the bra and pulled it away, discarding her shirt at the same time. Then he returned to her, his lips more urgent on her breasts, teasing and sucking until she cried out his name.

"I like the sound of my name on your lips, Bridget," he murmured. He cupped a breast and ran a tongue around the tip, which made her throb everywhere. "I want to hear you say it again."

He began kissing a trail down her body, centering himself between her thighs, until his beard scratched at the soft skin of her inner thighs. Her legs quivered at his touch, and then his fingers stroked her and she nearly came off the bed.

"Ethan," she cried out.

"Yes, baby?"

His fingers went deeper, parting the slick folds and circling her entrance and her mind went blank with want, with need, a desire so intense it shut down every other instinct she possessed.

"Oh, God."

His tongue followed his fingers and the first long stroke hit her clit and made her cry out again. His fingers probed deeper, filling her, and she arched into his touch. A swirling kiss with his tongue across the tight bundle of nerves sent her reeling as his fingers slid in and out. With a crook of his knuckle, she teetered on an edge, and went over. Her vision went black but for the dancing lights, her body contracted, and she shouted his name.

He kept her there, his tongue darting against the nerves until she was panting and begging—but for what she had no idea. More? She couldn't take more of this. But oh God, she wanted more.

He pushed her legs apart, opening her wide and then slipped his tongue inside her.

"Oh, fuck, Ethan," she gasped, as another wave of pleasure hit her. She was helpless under his hands and his mouth.

"That's it, Irish," he whispered, stroking her with one hand while kissing his way up her body. Her entire body trembled and her breath was ragged. "Now let's do that again when I'm inside you. I want to feel you tight around me. Hot, wet, slick."

The words enflamed her. That was what she'd been begging for. She reached for him, her hands encircling his girth.

"I need you," she gasped. "Inside me. Now."

Ethan crawled to the side of the bed and fumbled with the bedside drawer, returning with a condom. She took it from him and pushed him back onto the bed, then opened the packet and rolled the condom onto him, her hands lingering and stroking him while she did it.

"Come here," he groaned, pulling her on top of him.

Bridget straddled him, using her hand to guide him to her entrance, slick and ready for him. When he eased inside, she gasped and slowed to let her body accommodate him. Slowly, she lowered her body down onto him, every inch bringing a fresh flood of sensations.

"Oh, Jesus." Ethan groaned, gripping her hips. In the dim moonlight streaming through the bedroom window, she saw a sheen of sweat on his chest, his forehead, and the tight clenching of his jaw. "You feel amazing, Bridget."

She rolled her hips and his breath hissed out. And then he thrust upward, and a wave of pleasure rolled through her. She dropped her head back and moaned. Ethan's hands slid up her body, cupping her breasts, pinching the nipples just hard enough that the nerves fired more sensations to her core.

"Ethan, oh, yes," she said, rocking against him.

He grunted, his hands gripping her hips, harder now, keeping her tight against him. He pulled her down to him, then rolled her underneath him and drove into her, deeper. She wrapped her legs around him, raised her hips to meet his thrusts, and threw her head back as the orgasm built.

"Goddamn. I can't hold back," he groaned, his breath on her neck.

"Yes, Ethan, God, please." She was no longer capable of forming sentences, or thoughts. She could only hang on to him, gripping his back, as she fell apart again. But this time, Ethan was there with her. With a shout, her body tensed and another tsunami of pleasure rippled through her as his cock jerked inside her.

He rested his forehead against hers, his heart pounding against her chest and both struggling to catch their breaths. Bridget's body was limp and her brain was flooded with endorphins and oh, Lord. The man knew how to please a woman. Not that she'd thought a man who looked like that would be an amateur, but damn.

Ethan kissed her, his cock stirring inside her and her hormones were off and racing again.

"Stay the night," he whispered, kissing her neck.

"Mmm," she moaned, the delicious sensation of his beard against her skin distracting her. She hadn't planned on spending the night. Hell, she'd only come over on a whim. She should go home, but then he pressed another kiss where her neck met her shoulder and she shivered.

"I want to sleep next to you." His lips skimmed her collarbone. "And wake up and do this again."

Of course she'd stay. Her body was never going to let her

turn that offer down.

Then he kissed her hard, his tongue sweeping through her mouth as if they hadn't just made love and collapsed, sated and exhausted. Her body tingled and started to come back to life as soon as he'd touched her.

Dear Lord. She was willing to admit that she might be in over her head.

Chapter Thirteen

"I have Councilwoman Fitzgerald on line two for you," Georgie said, poking her head into Ethan's open office door.

Ethan rubbed his face and felt the last of the just-fucked glow from the last night slip away. It was only eleven in the morning. He'd arrived at the office in such a good mood, he'd practically been whistling. Though he tried to hide it, he knew he was doing a poor job of it, so he'd just closed his office door and did paperwork. He didn't want to have to explain why he was smiling.

Having to deal with the pushy councilwoman was going to put a dent his good mood, he just knew it.

"You want me to make your excuses? I can say you're busy," Georgie said.

"No, but thanks for the offer," he said, reaching for the phone. "Good morning, Ms. Fitzgerald. How are you?"

"I won't beat around the bush, Chief Ford. We really need to nail down that contract for the renovations. The council approved those funds with the intention of having the work done as soon as possible, and it's been months."

Now that he was alone in his office, Ethan didn't bother to hide his annoyance with the councilwoman. At least on his face. In his voice, he conveyed a professional and reasonable response. "I understand completely. But keep in mind that I've been chief of police for less than a month and the prior chief didn't put the request for proposals out, so I'm starting at square one."

"We don't need to put this out for a bid, Chief. Karen is more than happy to do it for a modest increase over the cost of the materials."

"You know we can't do that," Ethan said. "But I do hope that she puts a bid in. I've heard very good things about her craftsmanship."

He'd heard no such thing, but it seemed to go a long way toward mollifying the council member.

"You know there are several smaller projects that could be broken out, and that work would be under the threshold for a bid," she said.

The woman was beyond pushy. "I'll look into it, and if that is allowed, I will see if there's some work for Ms. Merz' company."

The councilwoman exclaimed her effusive thanks and Ethan hung up as quickly as he could. He shot an email to Valerie about the status of the renovations and if there were smaller projects not subject to the mandatory bidding process. He hit send as a knock sounded on his open door.

"Uh, Chief?" Dylan Jencks stood in the doorway.

"Hey, Dylan. You're about five hours early for your shift," he said.

"Yeah, well, it's sunny out, so I thought I'd wash the squad cars now. Last time I washed them at night, my fingers just about fell off," he said, a frown on his face. Then he stood a little straighter. "I was wondering if there was anything else I could do? I mean, besides the rodent problem? Does anything need repaired? I'm good with repairs."

"Can't think of anything, but if something breaks, I'll let you know."

Dylan frowned again, but gave him a nod. "Okay. Carl said since I'm here, I should help myself to the lunch in the break room. I hope that's okay. It smells really good."

It was Ethan's turn to frown. "What lunch?"

Dylan waved toward the front of the police station's break room. "It's a big fancy lunch. Is someone retiring?"

Ethan stood and walked out of his door to find the main office empty. There was a mouth-watering scent of roasted chicken in the air which grew stronger as he approached the break room.

The small room was packed with uniformed officers, detectives, and clerical staff gathered around a table full of chafing dishes.

"Chief, you've got to try this chicken," Carl said, waving at the table. "It's stuffed with something that will change your life. What is it again, Ken?"

Councilman Kenneth Snell beamed at the praise. "A sage stuffing with mushrooms and leeks. My chef's speciality," he said. "I hope you don't mind, Chief Ford. I wanted to show a little appreciation for the police department's hard work."

Ethan gritted his teeth and gave Snell as much a smile as he could without baring his teeth.

"Jump in there, Dylan," he said, patting the kid on the

back. "Mr. Snell, do you have a minute?"

He led the councilman back to his office and closed the door behind him.

"Your gift is very generous," he said.

Snell smiled. "Just my way of saying thank you."

Ethan lowered his eyes and took a long breath. "In the future, please check with me. We have a strict policy against gifts of any sort. I will be enforcing it."

"Well, not today, I hope," Snell said with a laugh.

It wasn't like he'd snatch that chicken breast away from Carl, if the sergeant would even let him. "Please don't take offense. I do appreciate the gesture. But this is the last time."

"Of course," the councilman said. "I completely understand. We're hired you because of your reputation for integrity. I admire a man of principle."

Ethan did not roll his eyes at Snell's words, but it took everything he had.

"And since I'm here, how's that little matter of the liquor license going?"

Ah, yes, there it was. The real reason Snell was hand-delivering a gourmet lunch for the police department.

"I have not had time to investigate Ms. Montgomery's application, but I do plan on looking into the matter shortly," he said.

Snell stood. "Excellent. I'm sure you'll do the right thing."

Ethan quickly ushered the councilman out of his office, promising to have someone return the dishes later. The food did smell incredible, but he couldn't bring himself to join the rest of the crew for lunch. He had only been chief of police for a few weeks, and he couldn't even get the basic rules enforced. Sure, he probably at least cut down on the number of officers who were placing bets with Bridget, but his job was to lead this office.

It probably wouldn't help his leadership when it got around that he was sleeping with Bridget, either.

Georgie knocked on the door and leaned into the office. "I brought you a piece of pie before Carl could clean up the dessert tray. Between him and Dylan, there's not going to be a crumb left."

He took the plate with a piece of lemon meringue pie. "Thank you, Georgie."

"And Curt McBride faxed over some papers for you to look at." She put a small stack of documents on his desk. "Said he'd try and come by this week and introduce himself in person, but in the meantime, he thought you'd want this."

Ethan flipped through the papers as Georgie left the office. At the top of the stack were property records from a nineteen-acre parcel off Townes Valley Road, purchased seven years earlier by a couple, Phillip and Doreen Anderson, who had a mailing address in Palm Desert, California. The taxes were current and no building permits had been pulled.

At the bottom of the stack was a handwritten note from Curt McBride. He'd left a message for the Andersons and would call when he had more information.

He debated calling Bridget to find out if she knew the Andersons, but that would have just been an excuse to hear her voice. Even the thought of her made his stomach flip. An image of her stretched out on his bed flashed through his mind and his cock hardened. Damn, he wanted her. No. It went far beyond that. It was a need, a deep and desperate need.

Forcing himself to focus on work, he pulled the liquor license application for Ivy Montgomery's restaurant and reviewed it. It was a routine form and there didn't seem to be any reason to reject it. He picked up the office phone and dialed the restaurant's number.

"The Vine, how can I help you?" a friendly voice answered.

"Hello, are you open for lunch?" Ethan asked. Since he'd boycotted Snell's lunch delivery, his stomach was growling. Maybe he could check out the restaurant and get a bite to eat at the same time.

"Not for lunch today, but we open at five for dinner."

"Is Ms. Montgomery available?"

"This is Ivy."

"Hello, this is Chief Ethan Ford—"

"Is this about my liquor license? Is there a problem with it?"

"Oh, no, not at all. I was hoping to come by and talk with you about your plans. I understand that the neighbors may have some concerns about it," he said.

"Only the one neighbor," Ivy Montgomery said, and he heard the frustration over the phone.

"Are you free now to meet? I won't take up much of your time. I'm sure you're busy preparing for this evening," he said.

"I have to pick up my daughter, but I could be back here in about thirty minutes."

Ethan agreed to meet her at the restaurant and hung up, slipping the liquor license application into an envelope and stared at the clock on the wall. He had thirty minutes to kill and wondered if he should see if there was anything he could do for Trevor. They'd never have the kind of bond that Bridget had with her siblings, but he and Trevor had been through a lot together. It wasn't like he had to break the law for his little brother. He could just check in and see if he was safe.

He hit the button on the phone before he could change his mind, but still almost hung up before a woman answered the phone on the second ring.

"Hi, Judi," he said. "It's Ethan."

His greeting was returned with a high-pitched squeal. "Oh, my God! Ethan! It's so good to hear from you! How are you?"

His foster mother's enthusiasm made him smile. "I'm fine. How are you and Bob?"

"We're fine, but we sure miss you. Where are you now? Trevor said you left Bakersfield?"

His stomach clenched at the question. He loved Bob and Judi Keogh, and was grateful for the years he had lived with them and the care they'd provided, but that didn't mean he trusted them. Regardless of their parenting skills, they were con artists. He hadn't told them of his new job and he didn't intend to. "You spoke to Trevor? He called me, but wouldn't tell me where he was. I need to reach him."

"Oh, honey, I don't know. I thought he was down in Delano for a while, then working in the oil fields. But you know Trevor. He doesn't stay in one place too long. You got his cell phone?"

He and Trevor had always stayed in touch with Judi, even when they weren't speaking to each other, but Trevor was closer to their foster parents. His brother would never admit it, but Ethan suspected that Trevor still worked the occasional scam with Bob. And Judi was always available by phone, since it was her work's lifeblood.

"No, why don't you give it to me?" He had the number Trevor used yesterday, but his brother often kept more than one cell phone, and it wouldn't hurt to gather any other ways to contact him.

Sure enough, she had a different phone number for Trevor, so Ethan made a note of it. "Thanks, Judi. How's business?"

"Busy as ever. People always need advice," she said.

"From dead people?"

"From the spirit world, dear," she replied.

He snorted. "I can't believe people still fall for that."

"You can't prove I'm not communicating with the dead," Judi said. It was a debate they'd never resolved.

"Guess it's true what they say about a sucker born every minute."

"And thank God for that," she said.

"Is Bob on the road?"

"He's back tomorrow, been off in Florida on business."

Ethan closed his eyes. God only knew what that meant.

"You guys ever going to retire?" He knew the answer to that was no, not unless they got arrested and the state forced them into retirement. Still, he hoped. Not just for their sake, but all the potential victims of their cons who were out there, unaware that the sweet couple from a California suburb was plotting to separate them from their savings.

"When you love what you do, it doesn't feel like work," Judi said with a laugh. "Oh, I've got a client calling. You keep in touch, Chief."

His stomach dropped a little with her deliberate use of his title. "Stay out of trouble, Judi. Give Bob my best."

He hung up, studied the phone number he'd written down, and wondered if Judi really didn't know where Trevor was. It wouldn't be the first time she'd covered for him.

The Keoghs had been very good to him and Trevor, doted on them, made sure they were healthy and went to school. Tried to impose some discipline on two basically feral children. Ethan was fourteen and Trevor was eleven when they went to live with them, the last in a long line of foster children who they'd taken in over the years. Knowing that they weren't going to continue fostering children, they treated Trevor like the baby of the family.

And they still did. It didn't hurt that Trevor was the one who followed in their footsteps, going into the family business.

Ethan found a bottle of aspirin in his desk and popped a couple of pills in his mouth as he dialed the phone. It went to voicemail and he listened to his brother's voice on the outgoing message.

"You've reached the voicemail of Alex Ferguson at Prairie Property Development. Please leave a message and we'll return your call as soon as we can."

Ethan hung up without leaving a message, his stomach churning. He knew this scam, knew it well. His brother swept into town looking to buy up undeveloped property for his fledgling company that was going to build a subdivision. He'd let a few trusted locals in on a secret—a major development project, maybe a casino or a big box store, was going to triple the land's value overnight once it was announced. But he was always up front with one piece of information—the project was highly confidential. Trevor came by the information through illegal means, and it was therefore illegal to act on it.

Soon, he'd have plenty of unscrupulous opportunists throwing money his way. And damn if Trevor wasn't the best at immediately picking out the characters who were most willing to break the law to make some money.

If anyone got suspicious, that's when Trevor's partner might come into town. Dressed in an expensive but understated suit, he'd hang out at the county assessor's office, buying up expensive copies of parcel maps. He'd refuse to say whom he worked for, but his business card was from a law firm that specialized in bringing casinos to small counties. He'd be seen in the middle of the day, snapping photographs of empty fields and back roads that led to nowhere. Making notations on a map that he hid from view if he thought anyone was watching him.

Investors who might be suffering cold feet suddenly felt warm again. And after the money was raised and transferred to an escrow account, then Trevor would start spending it—telling the investors that he'd hired surveyors, planners, architects and construction firms, and paving companies that would lay the roads.

And then there'd be a dire announcement about the project. A bankruptcy in another state. A setback with financing for the new development. That would tank Trevor's entire project. It was a risk that Trevor had warned the investors of all along. Since he'd make a show of putting up his own money in the project, they'd all believe him when he stood in front of them, his eyes welling up with tears, and explained that they'd lost their investments.

They didn't blame him. Hell, more than once a victim had even slipped Trevor a few hundred dollars to help him get back on his feet so he could try another subdivision in the future.

The best cons are the ones when the victim either doesn't know he was conned, or can't go to the police because of his own illegal activity. And Trevor was the best at what he did.

Which should have made Ethan feel better about falling for Trevor's lies, but it didn't. Of anyone, Ethan should know better. He'd worn that expensive but understated suit a few times.

Well, that settled it. His brother was on his own now.

It was time for Ethan to make that new start he'd promised himself. Cut himself off from the old life, and his old way of doing things. Do the right thing, even when it was hard.

He rubbed his forehead, where an ache was forming that wasn't going to be beat back by a couple of aspirin.

He wasn't sure what that meant for any future with Bridget, unless he could convince her to give up her illegal side gig. How much money could she be making from it, anyway?

By five o'clock, most of the Donnelly Lumber office staff were gone, with only Bridget and Grace still working in their offices. Through the open door that faced her friend's office, Bridget heard Grace typing away, probably drafting a memo to let the pervs know about the new surveillance on the email server.

Bridget finished her accounting tasks and shut down her work computer, then pulled her personal laptop from her bag and turned it on. She didn't hide what she did on the side, but she also didn't broadcast it. Once her coworkers left, she felt more comfortable catching up on the work she'd been neglecting.

That was Ethan's fault. He may not be actively trying to shut her down, but he had distracted her enough that she hadn't been paying attention to her clients. She still took their texts and calls and entered their bets into her ledger, but she hadn't been doing the detail work that ensured her profits—moving lines to compete with online wagering, sending texts to clients who hadn't been in touch. It wouldn't hurt her in the short term, but she had a three-year plan and a vineyard to build, and she needed to keep on top of things.

There was a pause in the clacking, Bridget looked up from her own computer screen. She heard the squeak of Grace's chair and then the sound of her coworker closing the blinds in her office. A moment later, Grace stood in Bridget's doorway holding a gym bag.

"You coming to yoga with me?"

Bridget wrinkled her nose. "I always fall asleep."

"That's because it's relaxing." Grace always had a peaceful Zen air, no matter what crisis was exploding around her. It was a trait that Bridget envied, but she doubted that yoga was to credit. It was just the way Grace was built and no amount of downward-facing dogs were going to give Bridget that tranquility.

"I'm going to pass. I have work to do tonight."

"Suit yourself," Grace said. "You going to be long? Want

me to lock the door on my way out?"

Bridget recalled the last time the front door had been left unlocked after hours and Ethan Ford had found his way to the conference room. Her body flushed warm at the memory. But tonight she had work to do.

"Yes, you better lock up. I won't be too late. Enjoy your stretching and chanting."

Grace waved as she headed down the hall to the stairs, and Bridget turned back to her laptop. She opened a spreadsheet and started entering figures from her ledger, keeping an eye for any unusual trends or deviations from her customers' betting habits. Everything seemed normal, though traffic wasn't as high this year. Last year during the run up to the college championships, she'd been making about twenty percent more. She frowned and checked the stats again.

Nope. Definitely down. And some regulars who she'd expect to see were absent.

And the trend didn't start when the new police chief arrived on the scene, either, so it couldn't entirely be blamed on Ethan and how distractingly sexy he was. Some of the downturn was due to his crackdown on his officers gambling, but even that didn't explain the trend.

She dug through her computer bag and found her other cell phone, the one she reserved for business—a burner phone taken out with a fake name and prepaid data plan. While running an illegal gambling operation had certain risks, Bridget really hadn't worried too much about the law coming after her. But why take chances?

Checking her text messages, she saw that she had entered every order into the spreadsheet. She hadn't missed anyone's bet.

Over time, she expected to lose a certain number of clients. There was too much competition now. Gamblers could go online, get their gaming fix by joining a fantasy league. And frankly, the demographics of people using bookies tended to skew old. Every year since she took over Oscar's business, she'd had to send flowers to someone's funeral.

She didn't expect such a sudden drop in business. She sighed and ran a hand through her hair. Well, drastic times called for drastic measures.

She quickly calculated the line on tonight's games and made some adjustments. Then she texted out a message to her contacts, moving the lines to make them more favorable. She wouldn't make as much, but it would lure in a few more wagers. And her business strategy was to make money with her commission, no matter who won. But to keep her books balanced, she needed a certain number of clients. That hadn't been a problem, but if this trend continued, it would be.

Within minutes, she got several return texts. That was better, but the fact that she'd had to reach out to them troubled her. She added the bets to her spreadsheet and reviewed the list again, noting one client in particular who hadn't yet placed a bet on the game tonight. Owen Nichols was a very reliable client, so she reached for the phone again.

"Hey, Bridget," he said.

"Hey, Owen. Did I miss your text about tonight?"

"Oh, uh, no. I mean, I still owe you a little and I don't want to get in over my head."

He was totally lying. Owen was constantly in over his head. He wouldn't know how to be any other way. "You've been making payments on that, so you're not cut off."

"Thanks, but I'm gonna take a pass on this game," he said.

She paused, letting the silence settle between them. Some people can handle the absence of conversation, but Owen wasn't one of them. He bet with his heart, not his head, and he was a huge Arizona fan. If he was holding back on tonight's game, something was wrong.

"I just don't like owing you money and then running up more debt, and my plan to win big and square up hasn't panned out yet," he said, and Bridget rolled her eyes at his "plan." Still, she remained quiet.

"Okay, see I did put a little bit of cash down, but with someone else. Just 'til I get you paid off."

Bridget sat up in her chair, her eyes narrowing.

"Oh sure, that's cool," she lied. "Who else has a line on the game?"

"I'm not comfortable talking about it, you know," he stammered.

"How about this. You owe me, what six hundred? Let's call it three hundred and you tell me everything you know," she said.

Owen blew out a breath and she knew she had him. "Well, I don't know who he is. But he moved the line on tonight's game and I literally can't lose."

And *that* was why Owen was one of her favorite customers. She'd really hate to lose him to someone else. Especially since up to now, she'd been the only game in town.

"Owen, it can't be that good a line," she said. "Plus, how do you know this guy will pay?"

"I hear he's got a good bankroll behind him."

"Says who?"

"Rowdy Pritchard," Owen said.

Her blood boiled at the sound of his name. That fucker. Everything in her life was going along swimmingly, but now every time Rowdy entered her life, things fell to hell.

She remembered back to Rowdy and his buddy showing up at her house. What if they weren't talking about water? What if that guy was trying to move in on her territory? Lost Coast Harbor barely supported one bookie. Having competition wasn't going to help her get her vines planted.

"Good luck tonight, Owen," she said.

"Hey, you're not going to tell anyone I told you, right?"

"Of course not," she said, and hung up the phone.

Bridget frowned and rubbed her forehead. If she knew who was taking action, she'd find a way to fight back. Maybe she should have talked with Rowdy. Had this been what he'd been harassing her about?

She snapped her laptop shut and slipped it into her bag, then reached for her phone. She stared at it frowning.

Why hadn't she heard from Ethan? Wasn't it customary to at least send a text after a night of mind-blowing sex? Bridget frowned. Maybe he was having second thoughts. There were…complications involved with dating a law enforcement officer. And for him, getting involved with someone who he knew was acting a little outside the law.

No, they could make this work. Her situation was only temporary. The first grapes would be harvested in three years, and a year after that, she'd bottle the first wine from her own land. The bookmaking business was a good cushion against the vagaries of vineyard production, at least in the first few years. With her job at Donnelly Lumber, and the extra cash from bookmaking, she'd be sitting pretty, hedging against the risk of starting a winery.

Ethan just needed to understand that the gambling wasn't a long-term career for her.

Bridget rolled her shoulders and felt the tension that had built there. It had crept in over the course of a day filled with tedious obligations and work stress on two fronts. Maybe she should have gone with Grace to yoga.

Then she remembered how loose and relaxed she had felt that morning, waking up next to Ethan, snuggling up against his hard and hot body in the dark. How he'd wrapped himself around her, still half asleep, slowly stroking her body in the warm cocoon of blankets until they were both awake and desperate for each other again.

That beat the hell out of yoga.

She studied the phone as if it had answers to her dilemma. Call Ethan, or wait? Tell him about the development with Rowdy, or not? Explain that she was only planning on breaking the law for a short period of time, or leave things alone there?

Maybe she was rushing into things. This wasn't the best time to get involved with someone, particularly with someone who could arrest her. And who had promised that he would.

But oh, hell, she wanted him. Wanted to drive over to his house right now for an encore performance. Wanted him so badly her body ached for it.

The phone in her hand buzzed and startled her so much she nearly dropped it. Her heart, already racing from the shock, jumped again at the name on the phone. With a slight tremble in her hand, she hit the button to connect.

"Evening, Sheriff."

CHAPTER FOURTEEN

The Vine was a small, cozy bistro in a converted bungalow-style house that was separated from the sidewalk by a garden of wildflowers and herbs. Inside, the dining area was softly lit by candles on white-draped tables. It could have seemed fussy or formal, but warm and casual touches made it feel welcoming.

Ethan watched Bridget take the last bite of his dessert and close her eyes in pleasure.

"The creme brûlée is amazing." She sighed, her eyes fluttering open.

Good Lord, he was getting hard just watching her eat.

"Thank you for bringing me here," she said with a smile.

"Thank you for eating that dessert in the most pornographic way possible," he said, leaning forward and taking her hand.

She gave a modest head tilt and smiled. Then licked her lips slowly, the smile turning wicked. Ethan's heart rate sped up. Inviting Bridget to dinner had been a whim, and it was quickly turning into the best part of his day. He'd had his doubts about being seen with her in public, now that he knew about her other profession, but Trevor wasn't the only one adept at convincing a person to give up something. The chemistry between him and Bridget was off the charts, and something that he'd not experienced before. He wasn't willing to give that up without a fight.

"I'd heard we were getting a new restaurant, but I didn't know it was open already," Bridget said, looking around. Then she frowned a little. "It is open, right?"

It was open, but they were the only diners that evening so far. They were alone in the small dining area, except for the waiter who largely left them alone, and Ivy Montgomery, who poked her head out of the kitchen occasionally, her nervous energy spilling out every time the door swung open.

When Ethan had stopped in to meet Ivy, she'd explained that she was waiting on her liquor license to have her grand opening, but the approval kept getting delayed. She had walked him around the gardens with her adorable two-year-old daughter on her hip, and then showed him the wine list and beer menu that she planned to use. She couldn't understand why it was so controversial, except that Kenneth Snell had tried to drum up opposition to her plans among the neighbors.

Ethan had already planned to sign off on the license—there was no reason not to. But when he learned that Ivy was a single mom, he'd pulled out the paperwork and signed it on the hostess stand. Kenneth Snell could go to hell. Ethan wasn't keeping a working mother from supporting her daughter so the council member didn't have to face competition. Now Ethan just had to figure out a way to spin it to Snell that would make it sound like having a new and well-received restaurant in town was to Snell's benefit.

"We're getting in before the grand opening," Ethan said. Another reason he'd wanted to bring Bridget to the tiny bistro was that he'd seen Ivy's reservation book—and it was nearly completely empty. He had expected a few more customers would have found their way in to sample the exquisite food and comfortable ambiance, though.

"She is going to do really well. That food was so wonderful," Bridget said. "And I love it here, so romantic. But not fussy, like at The Rosewood."

"Is that where everyone goes for a nice meal here?"

"Not after they hear about this place," Bridget said.

Her skin glowed in the soft warm candlelight and Ethan's chest tightened at the thought of touching her again, dragging his lips down her neck. Her soft black sweater clung to her curves, dipping to a deep V. A silver charm on a thin chain drew his eye to the swell of her breasts.

When he raised his gaze to her face, Bridget was watching him with an amused smile on her face. She reached up and fingered the necklace, playing with the small seashell cast in silver, running it along the chain.

"Do you have plans for later?" she asked, her blue eyes nearly smoldering in the low light.

God, did he have plans. Hot and filthy plans. His pulse picked up at the mere thought of it.

"Maybe," he said, dropping his voice. "Do you?"

Her lips turned up and she nodded.

"Don't tell me it involves checking scores at Donnelly's later," he said. He stroked the back of her hand lightly, brushing a finger across her skin with the lightest touch. Her eyes fixed on the movement and her lips parted.

"No, I'll get a text with the final scores," she said.

"You don't watch the games?"

Her eyes met his and she tilted her head before answering. "Sometimes, but it's easier not to watch."

"I thought you'd be a sports fan," he said. "Isn't that how someone goes into your line of work?"

"I do like sports, but it's different now. A lot of people who wager on games like having something at stake. It makes the game more exciting," Bridget said, her voice low, even though there was no one around to overhear their discussion. "But it puts more stress on me, while the game is underway. When I watched the games, I would constantly be calculating the outcomes, in terms of my payouts. So I stopped watching, and it got easier. Now it's just numbers and odds and statistical calculations."

He had never been into gambling, having learned early in life that the house always wins. Unless you have some inside information, some sort of angle, putting money down on a bet was for suckers. That was Bob's best advice, and though his foster father had imparted some questionable values and virtues, Ethan was grateful for that lesson.

"Do you take bets on all sports?" he asked.

Bridget's back straightened and she started to pull her hand away, but he held it in his.

"Why are you asking?" Her voice sounded disappointed, and a little suspicious.

"I'm curious," he said. "I'm not gathering evidence."

She studied him for a moment, serious and still, but then relaxed by a small measure.

"Major games, Super Bowl, World Series, other championships. End of the season tournaments. I couldn't keep up with a full roster of college championship games, so I pick and choose which games I know my clients are interested in. If someone wants to put money on a game and it's not something I'm following, I take the bet as a broker for a friend who works in Vegas, and then I get a small cut," she said. "And I'll handle some boxing, but it has to be high-profile. No MMA fights, ever."

"Why not MMA?"

"Niall trains a number of fighters, some of whom are ranked. I didn't want the conflict," she said.

That was interesting—he'd found himself an honest bookie. Not that it made a huge difference—it was still illegal. But he understood this code. It was like how Trevor targeted other scammers, who he could argue didn't deserve to hang on to their money because they'd stolen it.

He started to respond, but saw Ivy poke her head out of the kitchen again. Bridget pulled her hand away and sat straighter as the chef approached the table with a carafe of coffee. Ivy was petite with short dark hair and huge brown eyes. She barely looked old enough to drink, let alone open a restaurant and sell beer and wine, but according to her paperwork, she was in her late twenties.

"I hope you enjoyed your meal. I really appreciate that you signed the liquor license approval for me after so many delays," she said, topping off Ethan's coffee. "I'd like to get your dinner tonight."

He returned the smile. "Thank you, that's a very nice gesture, but I can't accept a gift. Department policy."

She gave him a sweet smile, and Bridget jumped in.

"Ivy, tell me more about your wine list," she said. "Will you be featuring local wines?"

Ivy's face lit up. "Of course, and if you have any recommendations, I'd love to hear them."

"I have several," Bridget said. "Of course, the Napa Valley makes some of the best wines in the world, but there are so many undiscovered wineries in Mendocino County. I can send you some names, if you'd like, and my favorite varietals and vintages."

"I would appreciate that," Ivy said, slipping a card out of her pocket. "I'm doing my best to use local produce and meats. The seafood is easy, of course, but I've also found an organic ranch not far from here that will be supplying me beef and lamb."

"My parents are going to love this place," Bridget gushed. "You have no idea how much Lost Coast Harbor needed a nice restaurant to compete with The Rosewood. That place is a museum. We had to go there for every wedding, funeral, prom—and it still looks exactly the same. It's a little creepy."

Snell was going to have to watch his back. Ivy Montgomery had just won over an enthusiastic supporter and Ethan had no doubt the bistro would be a roaring success.

When they walked out of the restaurant, a fine mist was starting to settle over the darkened town. He walked Bridget to her car and then stood with her.

She looked up at him and all traces of her usual sass were gone.

"It's just temporary, you know," she said. "I'm not doing this forever."

His heart jumped. That was exactly what he wanted to hear. No need to manipulate, beg, or connive her into going legit. Ethan smiled and squeezed her hands.

"Three years, maybe five at the outside, and I won't need to do this any longer," Bridget said.

"Five years?" Ethan felt like someone had just thrown a bucket of ice water over him. "Five more years?"

She nodded. "Maybe three. I have plans, and I need to stick to them. I've worked it all out. Even though this year's profit is falling short of my projections, it should be enough. I'm still on track to meet my goals."

He blinked and stared at her. She could have been talking about timber harvests, or residential housing construction, or any other legal industry. But she wasn't.

"Bridget, you're telling me that you plan on running an illegal gaming operation for the next half-decade," he said, still holding her hands and trying his damnedest to not raise his voice. He glanced around the quiet street, but they were alone.

"Well, I thought I'd try being honest with you. Maybe that was a bad idea."

He closed his eyes and took a deep breath. When he opened his eyes, Bridget was frowning, a furrow in between her brows, and he hated that she was now on her guard.

"I'm glad you were honest with me," he said. "This puts me in a difficult situation. And I don't understand why you want to do this, even for three or five years."

She bit her lip and then looked up at him through thick lashes. "You know, Chief Grady never gave me this much grief."

"Chief Grady was a corrupt son of a bitch," Ethan bit out. "And being like Chief Grady is not my career goal."

"I'm not asking you to be corrupt," she said. "Just reasonable."

Ethan blinked and started to respond, then shut his mouth. The warm glow from the good food and his engaging companion had faded. Now he stood in the cold mist, his stomach tight at the direction their conversation had turned.

"Maybe we should talk about this later," he said, wondering if he could salvage the rest of the evening.

Bridget's lips pursed and she took her hands from him. "Yes, another time."

She reached for the door handle and he stopped her. "Wait a minute."

"I don't want to talk about this anymore," she said, raising her face.

The stubborn tilt of her jaw reminded him that his goal had been to convince her to give up the gaming business, and he'd been too distracted or delusional to even try. The night couldn't end like this.

He shook his head, then reached up and slipped a hand behind her neck. "No, I was wrong. We need to talk about this."

"Not tonight," she said, her eyes troubled. "I should go."

She stood on her toes and kissed him, a light brush against his lips that sent a jolt through him, before she pulled away too soon. That wasn't nearly enough Bridget for him—and he pulled her close and kissed her properly, backing her up against the car and slowly exploring her mouth with his tongue, tasting her, claiming her. Her pulse fluttered under his fingers where he had her wrist in his grip.

When he leaned back, his heart was pounding. He hadn't bargained for this, his wild girl, so hot and sweet and sexy. His playbook said walk away now, leave her wanting him, but he wasn't sure he could do that.

Neither of them moved for a long moment, staring at each other, each daring the other to make the next move. To cede their ground.

The buzz of a cell phone made his heart skip, and he and Bridget reached for their phones at the same time. He saw a text from Curt McBride from earlier that he had missed, but the alert had come from Bridget's phone. She studied it with a curious expression, then shoved it into the pocket of her coat.

"I'm going to go home," Bridget said, her voice husky and low.

"Will you let me know you got home safely?" he asked, leaning in and stroking her cheek until she met his gaze.

She nodded and kept her eyes on his for another long moment until she reached for the door handle, climbed in the car and left without saying another word.

He watched her drive off then walked off toward his truck. He had no idea how to break the impasse, but it wasn't going to end like this—with them on opposite sides of the law. Either she had to end her career as a bookie, or he had to look the other way and follow in the footsteps of his predecessor, the deposed and indicted chief of police.

Or he had to walk away and not see her anymore.

Chapter Fifteen

Bridget sat in her car, shivering, but not from the cold. Her stomach was still sour from the discussion the previous night with Ethan. Thinking that they could resolve their differences was probably delusional. She'd misjudged his character—she'd thought he wouldn't care about a small-time bookie, but damn if he wasn't honest.

She had no idea what to do with an honest man.

She'd gone to a yoga class with Grace after work, and worried the problem over in her mind the entire time. There was nothing relaxing about stretching and posing while her brain was whirling with thoughts of Ethan Ford the whole time. She hadn't even fallen asleep when they were doing shavasana at the end of the class, which was saying something, because she felt like she'd gotten no sleep the night before.

That must be the reason she was now sitting outside the VD by the Sea, waiting on Rowdy Pritchard, still wearing her yoga gear. In her sleep-deprived state, it had seemed like a good idea to agree to meet him. She needed to know what he was up to.

"I really think you're overestimating my value in this situation," Grace said from the passenger seat. She bit her lip and stared out the window into the dark parking lot.

"I didn't bring you as muscle," Bridget said. "And you volunteered to come with me."

"Because I didn't want you going alone. I thought you'd turn me down and ask Niall to come with you."

"Niall has something going on."

Grace motioned toward the shadows near the docks. "Is that them?"

The two bulky figures walked across the parking lot toward her car and Bridget slid the button on her stun gun to the on position and slipped it into a pocket of her hoodie. Then she reached into the other pocket to check for her pepper spray canister. Niall would be crazy mad at her for coming without him, but she was taking precautions—meeting in a public place, with defensive weapons. There were several people milling about outside the bar, smoking, and though they couldn't be relied on to help her, it did make her feel a little less vulnerable. And she had Grace with her, though she wasn't sure what good a five-foot-four-inch attorney would do if things went ugly.

Not that she expected Rowdy to suddenly turn violent. She'd known him since fourth grade, when his family moved to Lost Coast Harbor, and while they weren't friends, there was a level of trust that came from that shared history. His companion, however, was a different story. She didn't like the look of the silent man who was a half-step behind Rowdy as they crossed the parking lot.

Bridget climbed out of the car and Grace joined her.

"Hello, Bridget," he said, flashing her a cocky grin full of crooked teeth. "Hey, Grace. Nice seeing you."

Grace gave a forced smiled to Rowdy and shoved her hands into the pockets of her jacket.

Bridget was in no mood for small talk. She nodded toward Rowdy's friend. "Don't think we've been introduced."

"Call me Fury," the dark-haired man said.

The sound of the man's surprisingly high-pitched voice took her off guard and she saw Grace do a slight double-take, also.

"No. That's stupid. I'm not calling you Fury," Bridget said.

The man's beady eyes widened a little and he turned his block head toward Rowdy, who just shrugged. "No big deal. This is Martin. He and I have a business partner who is interested in coming to an arrangement with you."

Bridget stood still and waited for more information, her hands in her pockets, resting lightly on the pepper spray and the stun gun. When she didn't ask Rowdy to give her more details, he shifted uncomfortably and threw a glance at Martin.

"So, yeah. Our partner wants to carve up the market, you know. Share the available resources when it comes to recreational sports betting."

At least Owen's information was correct, so the three-hundred dollars it cost her wasn't wasted.

"Who's your partner?" Bridget asked.

Martin shook his square head. "You don't need to know that."

"He's for-real, though, trust me," Rowdy said.

She wouldn't trust Rowdy farther than she could throw the six-foot-tall dockhand, and she was getting impatient to hear what deal the stupid duo in front of her was proposing.

"Get to the point, Rowdy," she said.

"My boss is taking money for certain games now. But he wants to expand," he said. "He'll stay away from basketball, if you back off other sports."

Interesting. Not something she wanted to be part of, but the fact that he was proposing it was intriguing. She wasn't interested in handling only NBA and college basketball games. She'd found a nice balance of high-profile games that her clients wanted to put money on. It took a long time to find that sweet spot, and a lot of research and number-crunching—something she doubted that Rowdy Pritchard and No-Neck McGee were going to do.

"What's wrong with the free market?"

The two men looked at each other, then back to Bridget. "You're not a full-service bookie, Bridget. He's willing to pick up the slack."

"Nothing stopping him."

"Your brother might," Rowdy said, and his hand crept up to his neck. It had been Ethan's hand at his neck, not Niall's, but Bridget knew what he meant.

"Niall isn't going to bully someone into giving up his business," she said. "Unlike you and No-Neck here."

"What do you mean?" Rowdy seemed puzzled again. "That thing at the St. Patrick's Day party? That was just a misunderstanding. No big deal. I just wanted to talk with you, that's all."

"Wait a minute. Are you saying that you didn't put the bullet in my mailbox?" she asked, watching Rowdy closely. He was a moron, a bit of a bully, and not too bright. But she'd never known him to be violent or threatening.

His surprise looked genuine. "What? No! I wouldn't do that," he said. "Jeez, Bridget, we've known each other for years. I would never do that."

She glanced between Rowdy and Martin, probably looking as confused as they did. If Rowdy, No-Neck, and their likely fictional partner weren't involved with the property next door, then she had two problems to deal with.

"Well, if you won't tell me who your boss is, I'm going to leave. I'm not interested in your proposal," she said.

She started to turn, but Rowdy grabbed her arm, his fingers tight around her bicep. She yanked her arm away at the same time she heard a loud and rapid snapping sound that sent her heart racing. Rowdy flopped to the ground with a yelp.

Grace stood over him, her handheld stun gun poised for another jolt. Martin started toward his comrade, but when Grace raised the device, he backed up with his hands raised.

"We're leaving now," Grace said, looking between the two men.

"Jesus, Grace! I wasn't going to hurt her," Rowdy gasped, rolling to a sitting position on the wet asphalt. He rubbed his thigh, where Grace zapped him. "Fuck, that hurts."

"You need to stop being so fucking grabby," Bridget said, her heart still racing from the sudden burst from the stun gun. "Tell your 'boss' that I'm not interested."

Rowdy struggled to get off the ground, favoring his left leg. "Christ, this is a business meeting. You don't just shock the shit out of someone at a business meeting."

"Business meetings don't take place in the parking lot of a

dive bar," Bridget said.

Rowdy ran a hand through his hair. "Just listen. My boss, he's gonna do what he wants, because he's got the money to do this. He'd like to have an arrangement, so it's easier for everyone."

She still only half-believed that there was a boss or a partner. Rowdy had been a fairly regular client of hers over the last few years, and he might think what she did was easy. He'd be wrong. And the block-headed friend might be a savant, for all she knew, but she wouldn't put money on that. His eyes had an angry and vacant stare that didn't imply a great love of statistics and probability.

"Okay, well, just fair warning," Rowdy said, holding his hands up. "If you're not interested in sharing, he'll drive you out."

She nearly laughed at that. No one was running her out of Lost Coast Harbor. She was a Donnelly Devil, for fuck's sake. No one was going to mess with her. Not unless they had no clue the hell they were about to bring down.

She turned to No-Neck and took a step forward. He was a scant inch taller than her, and she looked him right in the eye.

"I don't know what the hell you think you're doing, but I don't scare easily. You guys want to play at being bookies, knock yourself out. But don't threaten me."

No-Neck blinked, but otherwise his ruddy face remained impassive.

"Fine, we'll tell our partner that you're not interested," Rowdy said. "But you're making a big mistake. A word from him and you're out of business, Bridget."

Bridget shook her head. "You can tell your partner, if there is such a person, that I'm not afraid of a little competition."

The two men walked away, Rowdy limping and practically dragging his left leg, and Bridget watched them until they disappeared into the shadows near the docks.

"See, that's why I brought you," she said to Grace, who was sliding her stun gun back into its case. "Nice work."

"It was my pleasure," her friend said. "I've hated Rowdy Pritchard since our eighth grade dance when I wouldn't make out with him and so he told everyone I kissed like a mannequin."

Bridget climbed into her car, giving Grace a wary look. "That's a long time to hold a grudge."

She shrugged. "And now I can let it go."

"I guess we both got something out of this," Bridget said, starting the car. "Now I know what Rowdy is up to."

"But that doesn't solve the problem with the water," Grace said. "Are you going to tell Chief Ford that it wasn't Rowdy tapping the well?"

Bridget frowned and bit her lip. "If I tell him Rowdy isn't the person stealing water, then he's going to want to know how I know that, and then I'd have to either lie to him or tell him that it's because Rowdy is trying to horn in on my illegal side-business. I hate those options."

Grace gave a thoughtful nod. "You could tell Curt McBride that it's not Rowdy, so he knows not to waste his time investigating him."

That was a slightly better option. She still wasn't crazy about going to the cops, because it just invited trouble. And she had a feeling that if Rowdy and No-Neck did start taking bets, they would screw their clients over and that could invite more law enforcement scrutiny. So she had enough trouble on its way.

She dropped Grace off at her house on the outskirts of Lost Coast Harbor, then drove home, her mind churning over how best to solve the problems—and in a way that would let her still be with Ethan. She wasn't ready to give up on that.

By the time she rounded the last curve before her driveway, she had made a decision—she'd call McBride and tell him that Rowdy wasn't the person tapping her well, so he didn't start investigating the wrong guy. That might also head off any law enforcement probe into Rowdy's new venture, which could have blowback on her. And then she could tell Ethan that she'd agreed to work with the sheriff's department, as he wanted, on the water issue.

Since she'd installed the fence, she hadn't had any problems with the well, so that was probably going to go away, also. And she would just keep quiet on any more talk with Ethan about illegal activity. She didn't want to put him in a bad situation. Mostly because she wasn't entirely sure that if pressed, he wouldn't arrest her.

Satisfied that she'd come to a good compromise, she parked the car at the end of her driveway and got out and walked around to get her mail. The box was empty, but her hand brushed up against a cold, lumpy, metal object. With a start, she jerked her hand back and then peered in, squinting into the dark hole.

A faint illumination came from the interior light from her

car, and it was just enough to see the unmistakable outline of a hand grenade.

CHAPTER SIXTEEN

The Lost Coast Harbor police station was eerily quiet on the weekends, at least during the day. The phones were picked up by the dispatcher, so Ethan ignored the occasional ring as he worked through the pile of reports on his desk. With all the interruptions during the week, he hadn't had time to finish everything he needed to do. Police work involved paperwork, something he'd known since his days in the police academy. But somehow all of it made its way across the chief's desk at some point, and he wasn't doing a good job at keeping up with it. Between Bridget, Trevor, and the town council's demands for favors, he was being pulled in too many directions to focus on his job.

He initialed the last police report in his stack, and then turned to the next folder—the information Valerie left him about the construction funds. He looked for a small project that he could throw to Councilwoman Fitzgerald's girlfriend. As he went down the list of improvements the station needed, his frown deepened.

It had been easy to see what Marlene Dewey wanted. She had said she wanted to get her nephew out of trouble. But what she really wanted was for Dylan to grow up. Her mentions of the car. Inflating his job at the docks. The talk of his college aspirations. Those were all tells. She wanted to be proud of him. That was an ask he could work with.

But Lynn Fitzgerald wasn't as easy to figure out. It could be greed motivating her, but he'd be damned if he was going to hand over a quarter-million-dollar remodeling job to the contractor with the coziest relationship with the town council. Maybe Lynn wanted power, being able to impress her girlfriend with her ability to steer big contracts to her.

Ethan flipped back to the beginning of the renovation list to see if there wasn't something that would appease her.

"Hey, uh, Chief?"

Dylan Jencks stood in the open door of his office, holding a large, empty glass jar.

"Hi, Dylan. What are you doing here today?"

"Carl and I are going to take care of that rodent problem today," he said. "We thought it would be easier when there weren't as many people here. Hope you don't mind. It might get a little loud."

Ethan motioned toward the jar in Dylan's hands. "That have something to do with your mouse plans?"

Dylan grinned. "Oh, no. It's the new swear jar. Carl says we can't take gifts anymore, so this way the department can buy its own donuts."

He spun the jar around to show off the hand-lettered label.

"That's a great idea," Ethan said. "Thanks, Dylan."

Dylan smiled and turned away, calling out a greeting to Georgie in the dispatch room. Dylan had been spending more time at the police department, and volunteering for more assignments. That had been Ethan's plan, but he was starting to run out of tasks for the "intern" to do.

Ethan turned back to the papers on the desk and rubbed his face. He'd worked all morning and it was now mid-afternoon. While his desk was cleaner, that wasn't how he wanted to spend his weekend.

The cell phone on his desk vibrated and he glanced at it, anxious to see his brother's phone number or Bridget's. Instead, it was a text from Curt McBride.

All clear on Townes Valley Road.

He stared at the phone for a moment trying to decipher the message. Then he hit the button to call Curt. The call connected, but the deputy sheriff's voice was cut off almost immediately, and then the line went dead.

Ethan walked through the empty office, past the open door to the break room where Carl and Dylan were in a deep and animated discussion about their eradication project. He opened the door to the dispatch office and leaned in. "Hey, Georgie, did the sheriff's office have a call on Townes Valley Road?"

Georgie set her knitting aside to check the log on the computer. "Sure did. They responded to a call last night about a hand-grenade in a mailbox. Want the address?"

Ethan's posture stiffened at the news and his gut filled with fear and anger.

"No, I got it," he said, barely managing to get the words out. He dialed Curt again as he stalked back to his office and grabbed his keys and coat. This time, he got through to Curt on a staticky connection.

"Hi, Chief. I'm up in the hills, sorry about the connection," Curt said. "Wanted to give you an update. That dud grenade was a replica. There was no actual risk of explosion."

"When did this happen?"

"Bridget didn't call you?"

Ethan squeezed his eyes shut and expelled a long breath. "No. What happened? When?"

"Ah, jeez, I'm sorry, Chief. I would have called you myself, but she said she'd take care of it," Curt said.

"Tell me what happened. Now." The command came out harsher than he'd intended, but it worked.

"Ms. Donnelly found the grenade in her mailbox last night. Called me straightaway. The bomb squad dispatched and immediately saw that it wasn't a live explosive, so we opened up the driveway and let her go home," Curt said. "We kept a car in the area all night, though. Just to be safe."

A sharp bolt of pain shot through his head and Ethan rubbed his forehead in a vain attempt to relieve it. "If you could do me a favor, Curt. No matter what Ms. Donnelly says, call me if there are any developments."

"Of course, no problem."

"Did you get anything off the device?"

"Won't know for a few days. The bomb squad took it back with them and they'll let me know the details. But it wasn't a risk to her. It was a hoax."

"It was a message," Ethan said. "Did you reach the Andersons?"

"No, but I spoke with their nephew who lives in Mendocino. They're a retired couple who bought the property as an investment during the recession. Got it at a foreclosure auction for a song, but then Mr. Anderson had a stroke, so they don't travel now and they're thinking of putting it back on the market."

"So they're not growing pot on it?"

"Not that they know of," Curt said. "We're close to having enough for a warrant. I'd rather get permission from the Andersons. Less paperwork. I'll let you know when we're going in. Maybe you could keep Ms. Donnelly away?"

"Yes, I can do that. Call me if you hear anything," he said. He grabbed his coat from the chair by the door, locked his office, and stalked to the dispatch office to check out. Minutes later, he was driving east, his jaw set. His stomach clenched at the thought of someone threatening Bridget, and at the thought of her staying alone at her remote farmhouse.

That was about to stop.

In the daylight, it was a nice drive up to the farmhouse and far easier to navigate than at night. As soon as the road started climbing in elevation and the farther from the coast he drove, the more the weather improved. By the time he reached the turnoff to Bridget's house, it was sunny and warm.

He pulled into her driveway and saw the little red convertible parked in front of the house, freshly repaired.

Climbing out of the truck, he looked around for any signs of trouble, but it was a peaceful scene—a soft breeze rustled the trees around the house. Getting no answer on the front door, he walked around to the back of the house to the deck.

When he'd been to the house before, it had been too dark to see anything. Now, as he stepped up to the railing, he took in the view. And it took his breath away.

The house sat on the edge of a shallow valley, terraced land stretched out below, following the gentle curve of the hill. The soil was dark and damp from the recent rains, but it also looked like it had been freshly tilled. A path from the house led past the terraces, and he started in that direction. As he stepped onto the path, Bridget came into view. She was wearing a long-sleeved T-shirt and faded jeans, with rubber boots that reached halfway to her knees. She was holding a bucket and stretched as she stood up from the ground where she'd been kneeling.

Mid-stretch she noticed him on the path above her and she froze.

He walked toward her, down the slight grade, and she met him halfway. He reached down to take the bucket. His hand brushed against hers and sent a warm tingle through him.

"Hello, Ethan. I wasn't expecting you."

The sound of his name on her lips sent a thrill through him, even as he missed her teasing nickname for him. She wore no makeup, and looked as lovely as ever, if a little younger. A smudge of dirt marred one cheek and he reached up to rub it away, his hand lingering over her soft skin.

All the anger and frustration and fear he'd carried with him on the twenty-minute drive melted away as he stared into her eyes. She was too reckless and stubborn when it came to the threats, but for now she was safe and unharmed, so he let himself relax.

"I don't know what to do with you, Irish."

She looked down and bit her lip, then smiled, and his heart skipped a beat. "Then let's figure that out."

～

ETHAN FORD FILLED THE FARMHOUSE KITCHEN, EVEN though it was a large kitchen by any standard, and open to the dining and living areas. Or maybe it was that Bridget was just so aware of him here, wearing jeans and a gray and black checked shirt with the sleeves rolled up. He smelled incredible, and when she had looked up to see him standing on the sunny path, her heart had nearly burst out of her chest.

And now she couldn't stop staring at him, drinking him in. She really needed to get a grip. It had only been two days since she'd seen him. It wasn't like he was returning from war or something.

He still hadn't told her why he was there, and that made her nervous. It had to be about the grenade, but she didn't want to bring that up. While it had been a shock to find a possible explosive device in her mailbox, the sheriff's deputies had quickly figured out that it wasn't real, and she was left with just an uneasy feeling of dread and a fair share of paranoia. It had been enough to make her call Grace and tell her to ready the spare room. But this morning, she'd returned home, determined not to be intimidated by the ham-handed tactics. So far, whoever was sending these messages hadn't done anything that could actually hurt her—the bullet, the fake grenade.

She'd run this theory by Deputy McBride, who disagreed and pointed out that the threats were escalating. But he'd also said that they were investigating the threats and the water thefts. That gave her some comfort. Deputy McBride made her promise to tell Ethan about it, and she intended to. But just not right now. Not when they were carefully avoiding the land mines.

Bridget took a deep breath to compose herself, and then handed him a globe wine glass one-third filled with a pinot noir.

"Would you like a tour?" she asked, picking up her glass of wine.

Ethan's curious expression deepened and he nodded. "Of course."

She led him out to the deck and then down the stairs to the path that led from the detached garage. It was narrow, but widened after a few yards, enough that they could walk side-by-side. Ethan shifted his wine glass and took her hand in his, the touch sending shivers through her. She couldn't even blame the weather for the reaction—the late afternoon sun warmed the small valley.

"It's beautiful up here," he said, taking in the slightly sloping green hills. To the west, a gray bank of fog settled over the ocean and the coastline, but the property was at an elevation high enough to avoid that most of the time.

They came to the bottom of the first terrace and she stopped at the landing. Below were several more terraced plots, leveled to no more than a five-percent grade. Wide enough for multiple rows of vines, which would follow the curve of the hillside. The south-facing exposure ensured plenty of sun, and the sheltered valley meant there'd be enough heat to ripen the grapes.

Ethan studied the landscape, then turned to her. His smile caused his eyes to crinkle. "You're building a winery."

A slight tremor ran through her stomach as she raised the glass of wine and smiled over the rim.

"Yes, well, a vineyard to start. It takes three years to get the first harvest, so I have time to figure out if I want to bottle my own wine or just sell the grapes to other wineries. But I'd like to try my hand at winemaking. I think I'd be good at it," she said, suddenly feeling shy talking about it. The vineyard was her baby, her secret project, and very few people knew her plans.

Ethan stared at her, his mouth still turned up. "You're amazing."

She laughed and shook her head, looking away. But he pulled her closer and put a finger under her chin so she had to look at him. A slight breeze ruffled his hair as he stroked a finger along her cheek.

"How long have you been working on this?"

"Since before I purchased the property, really. It's perfect for growing grapes—good soil, good water, exposure, temperature," she said. "And it was difficult, but I got the ground prepared fast, so I can get the vines planted in a month or so."

He looked up at the farmhouse, which overlooked the terraced property and then down the slope, then he turned back to her. "This is what you're spending your money on?"

And at a rate that scared her. Between buying the property and having the soil prepared and terraced, she would have been tapped out, except for her extra income. Her loan applications had all been rejected unless she could pledge more collateral, which she didn't have. A fresh round of rejections were sitting on her desk in the upstairs spare room she used as an office.

She looked out over the land and could see it in a year's time—the trellises filling with vines full of new green leaves.

Her heart thrilled at the thought of it. This was hers. Not the Donnelly family's. She hadn't even put her own name on the mailbox yet, wanting to keep this apart from the family still.

"Yes, the work on the terraces, the irrigation system, and the vines, which I'll order in a few weeks."

Ethan was quiet for a long moment and her stomach grew more nervous.

"What kind of grapes?"

His question made her smile with relief. "Pinot noir, to start. Fifteen acres. Next year, I'd like to put in some petit verdot vines. I think they'll do well here, especially on the rockier terrain."

He smiled again and pulled her close, kissing her forehead. "Is this going to be a full-time venture?"

Her skin tingled where his lips touched. She finished her glass of wine and they started back up the slope to the house. "Not right away. Eventually, I hope it will be."

She left Ethan outside on the deck, watching the sun dropping toward the horizon and went inside to get the bottle of wine. She stirred the simmering pot of Irish stew on the stove and then caught a glimpse of Ethan from behind, the low winter sun behind him.

God, he was beautiful. The warm, golden rays cast a halo about his hair, and the near-silhouette effect highlighted his broad shoulders and long legs. His hands were resting on the rail and he was leaning forward, as if studying the landscape that stretched out in front of him.

Bringing the bottle with her, she returned to the deck and refilled their glasses.

"Your family must be proud of you," Ethan said.

Bridget bit her lip and hesitated before answering. "They don't know. I mean, my sister Elizabeth knows, but she's not going to tell my parents because I know all her secrets."

Ethan turned and leaned back against the railing, a confused expression crossing his handsome face. "Why not tell them?"

This wasn't that easy a question for her to answer. "It's complicated. But basically, I don't want my dad to think I'm quitting the family business."

"But you want to do this full time?"

"Yes, someday," she said. "There're six kids in the family and I'm the only one who works for Donnelly Lumber. No one else is even interested—Declan has his bookstore, Gavin has his pub, Niall has his studio. Neve is off in New York."

"And Elizabeth?"

"She's in college."

"Business major?"

"She's had so many majors in the last ten years. And while she's earned a ridiculous number of degrees, none are in business. I don't see her bringing her archeological skills back to Lost Coast Harbor to run a timber business or build houses," Bridget said.

Ethan nodded, and sipped his wine. "You don't want to let your father down."

"I know I need to tell them. Eventually, they're going to come up to visit and see the vines. It's not like I can hide it forever. I just haven't wanted to deal with it yet," she said. "I want to do something on my own, without the help of my family's name, or connections, or money. I know people think the only reason I got my job at Donnelly Lumber is because it's my father's company, and that's fine. To a certain extent, it's true. But I want this for me."

That was why it was so hard to talk about. If she failed, that was on her and her alone. Right now, if she failed the only people who would know were Elizabeth, Grace, and now Ethan.

The sun hit the horizon and they watched in silence as it disappeared behind the clouds, lighting up the sky with a faint pink tinge that grew into a vibrant tapestry of blues and purples. Ethan placed a hand over hers on the railing, keeping her hand warm as the evening air cooled.

She still didn't know how to reach a compromise with him that would let her stick with her plan, but not make him compromise his values and the thought made her sad. He was like no one she'd ever known before and when she was with him, she'd never been happier. But she wasn't good for him. Being with her could cost him dearly—if not his job, then at least his authority with the officers who worked for him.

That was a high price.

She glanced up at his face, lit by the waning sunlight. The sight of his profile unleashed butterflies in her stomach, and when he turned and met her gaze, that grew into a tremor.

"What are you thinking?" he asked, squeezing her hand.

"How much I'd love for you to stay for dinner," she said.

"Anything else?"

"Dessert, too."

He smiled, leaned in and kissed her, lightly. "I'd like that, too."

And then, later, she'd tell him about the grenade.

CHAPTER SEVENTEEN

Ethan paced the living room, the glass of wine in his hand, and studied the space for clues about Bridget. A pot of stew on the stove simmered and bubbled and made his stomach growl. A tall bookcase against one wall was filled with a varied selection of books, some of which looked like they were fifty years old, nestled against newer books on grape vines and wine production.

On the mantle, he picked up a framed black and white portrait of a beautiful young woman with dark hair, light eyes, and a familiar jawline. There was no doubt this was a relative of Bridget's, and he'd guess her grandmother, since it had been her house. He moved on to other photographs on the shelves, scattered along a long table, and among the books. He recognized Gavin, from the pub, and Niall, the martial artist.

A family portrait of the six Donnelly children and their parents against a studio background showcased the family traits—Bridget and Gavin with their black Irish coloring, took after their mother. The youngest girl, who looked to be about four years old in the photo, and a lean boy with a serious expression in the middle clearly had gotten their father's genes, with thick, dark blond hair and blue eyes. Then a girl and boy with copper hair, which must have been the twins, Niall and Neve.

A soft laugh escaped him when he saw a smaller photo behind the formal portrait—it was a photographer's proof from the same sitting, but captured a moment of chaos. The twins slapping at each other, Bridget kicking one brother, the youngest child with her mouth open wide in a cry of protest while another brother pulled at her hair. Both parents reaching out toward different sides of the group to corral their offspring. He could practically hear the chaos of six lively children.

Setting the photo back in place, Ethan moved to the living area, and his gaze fell on a stack of sports magazines on the end table. It reminded him that there was unfinished business to take care of before they could move forward.

From upstairs, he could hear the shower running and he swallowed hard, trying not to think about Bridget, naked and wet. It wasn't working, and it wasn't making it any easier to keep his distance from her. As if he had a chance of doing that.

The water stopped, and a few minutes later, Bridget came down the stairs, freshly scrubbed and wearing jeans and a soft sweater in a shade of blue that matched her eyes.

"I feel better now that I'm not covered in sweat and sunscreen and dirt." She smiled and his nerves buzzed with sexual energy. He really needed to get a grip because his body was making too many decisions for him at this point.

"Whatever you have on the stove smells delicious," Ethan

said, rising from the couch.

"Irish stew," she said.

He set his glass down on the counter between the living room and kitchen and watched her stir the bubbling pot. She topped off their wine glasses and he laughed. "I'm pretty sure you're trying to take advantage of me."

With a flourish, she emptied the rest of the bottle into his glass. "You're damn right, I am."

"Is that so I can't drive home?"

Her coy smile made his heart race. She walked around the counter and picked up their glasses, handing one to him. "You think I'm letting you go that easy, Sheriff?"

Ah, fuck, he was in so much trouble.

He set the glass down, took hers and placed it on the counter, then pulled her close. He ran a hand up her back and with his other hand, brushed her hair away from her beautiful face.

"I've missed you, Irish," he said.

When he kissed her, everything in his world fell into place. What didn't fit, fell away. He savored her lips, the soft moan that escaped her, the feel of her body pressed up against his. His heart hammered in his chest when her tongue touched his. It had only been two days, but he kissed her like he'd been starved for her.

This was all he needed, this troublesome woman. And God, she was trouble. But he didn't care. This was like nothing else he'd experienced, and damn if he was going to throw it away. He would convince her to see things his way.

When he pulled away, Bridget was flushed, her eyes wide. "Why did you come up here?"

He traced his finger along her swollen lower lip, his entire body at her disposal. "Because I was mad at you," he said, his voice low. "You didn't call me about the threat. You put yourself at risk by staying here last night."

She turned her head and captured his finger in her mouth, sucking gently, and raising her eyes to his. His entire body tensed, but especially his cock. Her lips turned up into a sexy smile.

"You came up here to yell at me and tell me I'm stubborn and I need to quit being a bookie," she said, her voice husky with passion.

"Yeah, something like that," he said, fastening his arms around her, keeping her close.

"Why haven't you?"

He stared into her piercing blue eyes. She had learned him fast, faster than he would have thought. It was a con artist's survival skill to be able to read someone fast, learn them, what makes them tick, what they want. Really want, not just what they'll admit to wanting.

She'd just done that to him and that realization was like a kick to the stomach.

"Night's not over," he said with a grin.

She raised her arms around his neck. "I'm glad you came."

"Why didn't you call me last night?"

"You would have come storming up here, dragged me back to town, and lectured me about being alone in my own home," she said, raising her chin. "And there wasn't a real risk of danger."

He shook his head, reaching for the anger he'd nursed on the drive to her house, but it was strangely missing. "There was a real threat, Bridget. I don't want you to get hurt."

With a small smile, she stood on her toes and leaned in, kissing his neck. She pulled him down to get closer and her breath stirred across his skin. "I stayed with Grace last night," she whispered.

He smiled and pulled her tight against him and inhaled her scent. "Thank you."

"I'm not totally reckless," she said, pulling him into the kitchen.

Ethan followed reluctantly. The meal was the last thing on his mind now. But Bridget was good company, and an excellent cook, and he found himself relaxed for the first time in what felt like forever. That wasn't the right word. Content. He was content to sit with her at the rustic wooden table, watching the flames in the fireplace, talking about different varietals of grapes and the climate they needed, the maintenance of vines, and the pros and cons of establishing a winery versus just selling grapes to other vintners. It was comfortable and it felt like home.

And yet, in the back of his mind, that voice nagged at him. This wasn't home. And she wasn't just a beautiful woman, who loved wine and gardening and books. Bridget was far more complicated than that. Her phone chirped and she reached for it. A smile flitted across her face before she turned off the phone.

"Was that the scores?" he asked.

She nodded, and then stood and took their dishes to the sink. Ethan followed and waited for her to elaborate, but instead she ran water into the sink and started washing dishes.

"Did you have a good night?" He wasn't sure why he asked the question because he didn't want to know. Didn't want to talk about it.

She threw him a curious glance, then returned to the dishes. "It was fine."

Picking up a dishtowel from a hook, he dried the dishes after she rinsed them. "That's it? Fine?"

"Do you really want to know?" she asked, shooting him a cautious look.

"Yes, I do. I'm curious about how you do it," he said. "And how you got into it."

"I'm good with math. I like sports. It was a good fit." She kept her eyes on the dishes.

"Maybe someday you can give me the unabridged version."

Her frustrated sigh said more than enough. "I think it might be better if we don't talk about that."

But if they didn't talk about her being a bookie, how was he going to convince her to quit?

"And it's been such a nice evening. I don't want to ruin that," Bridget said, splashing him with the dishwater. "I'm sure you can't tell me things about your job. So we can just talk about anything else."

She seemed to have come up with a map to avoid the land mines. But that wasn't going to solve some core problems.

Bridget turned and leaned back against the kitchen counter and watched him wipe the last dish. When he hung up the towel, she flipped off the overhead light. Then she stepped forward and closed the distance between them, her gaze on his chest, and then slowly moving up until she was staring into his eyes.

"Or we could just not talk. We do really good with not talking," she said.

He wasn't going to argue with her about that. Whatever their differences, they were on the same page there.

He reached out and touched her face, leaning in and hovering over her lips. "We can't not talk forever."

"But why not try?"

She raised herself up on her toes and closed the distance between them, her hands on his face, her lips against his. He was suddenly aware of his own heartbeat, pounding in his chest, and then all he could feel was Bridget, her hands sliding under his shirt, against his skin.

"How about this? You answer my questions, I'll make it worth your while," he said.

Her smile grew. "Oh really?"

He took her hands in his. "How did you get started as a bookie?"

She tilted her head, and then paused a moment before answering. "My dad's friend Oscar was a bookie. He taught me everything I know."

"How old were you?"

"That's a separate question," she said.

"Oh, now you know how to follow the rules?" He leaned forward and kissed her, slowly, deliberately, until she was rubbing against him and panting when he pulled back.

"How old were you?" His fingers slipped through the long strands of silky hair, brushing it away from her face, baring her neck.

"Teenager, maybe fifteen or so. But I didn't start taking

bets until I was in college."

He bent his head, pressing his lips against her neck. Her pulse quickened under his touch, her head fell back. Her reaction to his touch sent a thrill through him. His impulse was to drive her crazy, keep stroking, kissing, until she was trembling and begging for more. But he held back. There was a purpose to this seduction.

"How many clients do you have?"

Bridget groaned as his lips left her skin, and looked at him with eyes clouded with passion. "About sixty. It varies, though. Sixty reliable regulars."

Ethan's fingers played with the hem of her sweater, then slowly lifted it over her head, leaving her standing in front of him in a sleek satin bra that showcased supple curves. He sat down on one of the kitchen chairs and positioned her so she was straddling him, sitting on his lap and facing him, giving him exactly what he needed.

His hands cupped her breasts, and then he leaned forward, running his tongue along the top of the cups. He slid one strap down, exposing her to his view and to his mouth. He bent his head, pressing his lips to the curve of bare flesh, then licked and sucked until she was moaning and grinding against him.

When he pulled away, Bridget's full lips were parted, her breathing heavy. "Are we done with this interrogation yet?"

With a low laugh, he shook his head. "Let me have my fun, gorgeous," he whispered into her neck, then scraped his teeth across the skin, relishing her soft cry. "Have you ever had a client threaten you or felt that you were in any sort of danger?"

Bridget squirmed in his lap. "No, I'm the only bookie around. I don't have to take clients who I don't trust or who don't pay. Once in a while some lowlife will try and get in on some action, but they usually lack the math skills to compete. I'm honest and I pay out properly. I don't have problems."

He ran a hand up her back, skimming soft warm skin, and wondered if she was telling him the truth. "You've never had a client go sideways on you?"

Bridget's eyes met his and she tilted her head to the side. "No."

"Never had a client not pay?"

"A few got in over their limits. I've cut people off who owed me money," she said, leaning in and resting her hands on his chest. "They pay up eventually."

He really didn't like the thought of Bridget dealing with problem clients—even though he knew that having a massive MMA fighter standing behind her made her slightly safer. Ethan knew from his work on both sides of the law that gamblers were going to find a game, a table, or a deck of cards, if they wanted to play—and being cut off wasn't going to stop someone from playing if they had money to spend.

"Your brother help you there?"

"All he does is glare," she said, then rocked her hips against him and gave him a smile that made his heart race again. "I'd rather not talk about my brother right now."

He pulled back and cupped her face with one hand, keeping her lips just inches from his. "You risked a lot to build this vineyard."

Her blue eyes dilated at his words. "I'm not afraid to take risks."

Damn if that wasn't true.

"Are you?" Her voice was low and husky and shot straight to his gut.

He wrapped an arm around her waist and stood, lifting her and setting her in front of him. His fingers found the button on her jeans and he slid the pants over her hips, taking his time exploring her stomach, her sleek curves. He should fear getting in over his head with her. God knows he was. It was only going to lead to trouble, and yet...

"Not nearly enough," Ethan managed to gasp as she stepped out of the clothes, and stood before him in only a pair of black lace panties.

He reached for her.

"Damn it, Bridget." He hissed as he pressed his lips against her skin. "I can't get enough of you."

They moved toward the stairs, trying not to break contact, then stumbled over the couch. Ethan caught her before she would have flipped backward onto the cushions, and she laughed as he kissed her. The sound enveloped him, warmed him.

"We'll never make it upstairs," she gasped, pulling at his shirt.

They tumbled onto the couch, clothes flung to the side until Bridget was naked and he was wearing only his jeans. She was underneath him, writhing against him while their tongues tangled. Her hands were in his hair, pulling him closer.

"You're wearing too many clothes, Sheriff," she whispered in his ear.

Her playful nickname for him was a reminder that this

was exactly what he shouldn't be doing. He closed his eyes, trying to summon the strength to walk away. Knowing he would never do it.

Bridget's hands fumbled with his belt, and then pushed his jeans down over his hips. Her hands on him made him lightheaded, and when she gripped his cock in both hands, he groaned.

"Fuck, Bridget," he gasped. "We should slow down. We have all night."

"Next time, slow. But oh my God, I need you."

That was all he needed to hear. The last of his clothing was shoved away and he grabbed Bridget's hands and stretched them above her head, pressing her into the soft couch. Her eyes widened at the restraint and her mouth opened slightly. Her legs wrapped around his waist and she arched against him.

He bent his head to kiss her skin, glowing in the firelight. He dragged his lips down her neck, slowly making his way to the swell of her breasts, flicking his tongue against her nipple.

"Oh, God, Ethan," she gasped when he took it in his mouth, sucking gently.

He released her hands and pushed himself up to look at her, her hair spilling around her face. Eyes bright with passion. Those lips. Her tongue ran along her bottom lip and he groaned.

He moved away to find his pants and the condom in the pocket. He returned to her, pulling her legs off the couch so she was bent over the cushion and he was behind her. Sweet lord, that ass was going to be his undoing. He bent and kissed the small of her back, the smooth round curves.

He cupped her sex with his hand, stroking the heat, the wetness, and Bridget threw her head back with a moan.

"Oh, God, you're so wet, so hot," he whispered.

"Please, Ethan," she gasped. "Oh, God, please."

He eased a finger inside her, brushed a thumb across her clit until she clenched around him, the orgasm threatening. He withdrew, then slid two fingers inside and her cry nearly undid him.

"Yes, oh, yes," she groaned, her legs trembling.

He rolled the condom on and rubbed the head of his cock against her wetness, then eased into her tight heat. Bridget's hips bucked and he sank deeper, his heart pounding.

"You feel so good, baby," he groaned, gripping her hips and thrusting into her again.

Her hair spilled over her back and he leaned forward, gathering the silky strands and pulling her head back. He reached around, wrapping an arm around her waist to keep her as close as he could. He couldn't get enough of her. He wondered if he ever would.

Bridget's cries grew louder as he reached between her legs, stroking her as he thrust into her. The tension grew around him as she arched and shuddered with the force of the orgasm. She tightened around him, sending him over the edge with her.

"Oh, Jesus," he gasped.

He fell against her, collapsing against her body. His breath was ragged, and his legs were shaking.

After a minute, he pulled out and went to discard the condom, coming back to find Bridget stretched out on the couch, an arm thrown above her head, the low light from the fireplace caressing her skin. He knelt down next to her, kissed his way up her body, and then smoothed her hair away from her face.

"Fuck, Bridget, what are we doing?"

She purred under his touch and smiled, then sat up and wrapped herself in a throw from the back of the couch. "Come on, Sheriff," she said, standing up and taking his hand. "We have all night, and I don't want to waste a minute."

Chapter Eighteen

Bridget snuggled up against Ethan's chest, her fingers stroking his hot skin, trailing through the trail of hair that led down a set of rippled abs. His heart beat under her touch, and his heavy breathing stirred her hair.

"Goddamn, Irish," he gasped. "You're trying to kill me."

She laughed and pressed a kiss to his chest. It hadn't been the slow and sweet sex that she'd promised him. Well, it had started off that way, but quickly grew out of control. The antique bed was still standing, but at this rate, she wasn't sure it would last the weekend.

Her body was limp and sated and she still couldn't get enough of him. Her hand touched the scar on his shoulder that extended into his chest. The only light in the room was from a nearly full moon outside, but the disruption to his otherwise perfect skin was clear in the low light. "What happened here?" she murmured.

Ethan blew out a long breath. "A bar fight."

She lifted her head. "Really?"

He grinned and nodded. "My first year on the force was one long blur of medical reports, but this one did stand out."

"What happened?"

"My partner and I tried to break up a fight between two guys in a bar, and some other guy jumped us," Ethan said. "The two guys were just fighting, but the third guy had a broken bottle."

Bridget's stomach dropped in an empathetic reaction to his injury. She ran her hand along the ragged tissue, as if her touch could erase the wound. "That sounds scary."

He laughed, a low soft chuckle. "It hurt like hell, but it wasn't life-threatening."

His hand stroked her hair and she sank into the sensations. This was right and perfect, lying there in bed with him. She could lie there next to him all night, just listening to him talk, wrapping herself in his deep, warm voice.

"Tell me another story," she sighed. "Tell me about your brother."

His body tensed and she instantly regretted the words. But with a sigh, Ethan relaxed and continued running his fingers through her hair absently.

"What do you want to know?"

"Everything. When were you in foster care?"

He tightened his grip on her and for a minute, she thought he wasn't going to answer her question.

"From when I was about six, and Trevor was three."

She closed her eyes. So young. "Were you with the same family the whole time?"

"No, not at all. Sometimes we weren't even kept together. I have no idea how many homes we bounced through. A dozen, at least," he said, his voice lower. "When I was thirteen, Trevor and I went to live with the Keoghs and we stayed there until we aged out of the system."

She wasn't sure where to go from there. "What were they like?"

He laughed again, a low rumble she felt under her fingers. "Well, Bob and Judi are, uh, interesting. Hard to describe. But they were good to Trevor and me. They'd raised a dozen foster kids, and they knew we were their last ones before they retired from that. They treated Trevor as their baby. Doted on him."

"They sound like good people," Bridget said.

"Not exactly," he said, and Bridget looked up at his face. "I mean, they were good parents. Made sure we went to school, ate well, learned some manners. And we had been in some bad situations, so it really was a blessing that we were placed with them. And they love us, in their way. But they're different."

"Different how?"

"They're con artists, sweetheart," he said, kissing the top of her head.

"Really?"

"Judi is a psychic advisor, which means she separates the gullible from their money," Ethan said. "And Bob has a number of skills that are in demand around the country. He travels around, works with other con artists to scam people."

Bridget raised up on an elbow and stared at him. He didn't seem to be joking, but he'd flat-out lied to her before. Ethan must have seen the skepticism on her face, and he gave her a small smile.

"I'm telling the truth," he said.

"Huh."

"Yeah, well, they try to justify it by saying that they don't scam civilians, just other con artists," Ethan said, looking weary. "And Judi says what she does gives people comfort, even if it's all lies. But it's all fraud."

"Civilians?"

"Straights. People who obey the law. Normal folks."

"Ah, got it," Bridget said, the words sinking in, but not quite fitting into what she thought she knew of the man in her bed. "And Trevor?"

This would explain his brother's criminal record.

"Yeah, Trevor followed in Bob's footsteps and was a real natural at it."

Bridget was quiet for a long moment, her hand still over his heart.

"I'm sorry," she said. It was hard to know what to say. The Donnelly Devils had nothing on Ethan's family. "I can see why you changed your name."

"Oh, right," Ethan said and paused for a moment. Bridget's stomach tightened in anticipation. "About that. I wasn't exactly truthful about why I changed my name."

She raised an eyebrow and he continued.

"When I was a teenager, I got in a few scrapes and I was on law enforcement's radar as Ethan Black," he said. "So I changed my name and moved to a town about an hour away. That way, I could keep working with Bob and not draw attention."

Her eyes widened. "You worked with your foster father?"

Ethan nodded. "I was good, too. Not as good as Trevor, but we did all right."

"How did you end up a cop?" Bridget couldn't keep the

incredulity out of her voice.

He blew out a long breath. "I was enrolled in community college, just to kill some time. Bob thought it would make me look respectable. And I got some extra work as a research assistant to a professor who was a retired cop. Merle saw right through me. He knew what I was doing. He knew I was probably up to no good. But instead of kicking me out of school, or even firing me, he took me under his wing."

Ethan's voice was steady and he didn't seem upset about talking about his past, but Bridget worried that she was prying or making him uncomfortable.

"He gave me some direction for the first time in my life, or at least some direction that wouldn't lead straight to jail," he said. "I transferred to a four-year university, majored in criminal justice, and then went to the police academy."

"How did your family feel about that?"

"They were not happy. Well, at first they were, but then they realized that I wasn't interested in being on the take for them," he said. "Trevor thought I was going to be his get-out-of-jail-free card."

"Did you help him?"

"I have, but not as a cop. Except last year, when he got picked up outside of Bakersfield. I made a few calls, got him released. I thought that he would grow up, mature. But that's not happening." He blew out a long breath, stirring her hair. "I knew if I didn't leave, I'd be in that situation again and again, having to decide between my career and my brother."

"Have you talked to him, since he called?"

He shook his head. "No, I called a number Judi gave me for him. Got some voicemail message for some property development company, which is a con he's pulled before. He's not going to change."

Bridget rested her head on his chest and listened to his heart beat. "Do you think he's in danger?"

Ethan sighed and tightened his grip around her. "No, I don't think so. Trevor prides himself on never getting caught. The best con is one that the victim doesn't even know happened. And he's good at that. Like Bob, he goes after people who aren't in a position to go to the police for help, if they do figure out that they got taken."

She absently stroked the skin on his stomach until he put his hand over hers. "If you keep that up, Irish, we'll never get any sleep," he said, his voice low and groggy.

She smiled and kissed his chest and sank into the protective embrace of his arm. Ethan Ford was not the man she thought he was when she first met him. He was far more interesting, and despite his confession of his former days as a con artist, he was a far better man than she could have guessed. Lost Coast Harbor needed someone like him.

And boy, was the Donnelly family ever going to love him.

Her eyes flew open as that thought jolted her out of her drowsy state. Where the hell had that come from? She didn't take men home to meet the family. Too complicated, too messy to introduce people to her rambunctious siblings and expose them to Molly's not-so-subtle questions about future plans.

Ethan murmured something soothing and patted her arm, and she relaxed again. She'd worry about her subconscious later, once she'd had a good night's sleep and was thinking more clearly.

She had just about drifted off when she heard the faint beep of her work phone from downstairs. She'd forgotten to plug the phone in to charge overnight, and her mind started worrying over who could be trying to reach her this late. Ethan's breathing was slow and steady, and when she was certain he was sound asleep, she eased away from him and out of bed. Throwing on a robe, she crept downstairs to check the message.

It was Rowdy, and it was brief.

My partner wants to talk with you. Can you come now?

Bridget's stomach dropped and she glanced at the clock. It was almost two in the morning. She didn't know who she'd be meeting. She didn't know why the meeting was happening in the middle of the night, or even why he wanted to meet her.

And if she tried to leave the house, Ethan was certainly going to stop her.

But if she went to the meeting, just to see who the partner was—that wouldn't be too unsafe. She could drive to town, see who showed up, and learn who was trying to destroy her business. She wouldn't even have to get out of the car.

And if she didn't go, it meant that the ground outside would stay fallow, barren, and she'd be another year enmeshed in Donnelly Lumber. If her father decided to retire, she'd be stuck there, probably forever. That was the suffocating fear that kept her awake at night, and it was what shook her out of her paralysis.

Bridget bit her lip and stared at the phone, then at the stairs. In between lay the small piles of clothing that they'd left behind in their haste, and her gaze fell on Ethan's pants, his utility belt still threaded through the belt loops. And the handcuffs in the small pouch attached to the back.

She looked back up the stairs at the darkened bedroom.

No, she should not do that. She could take his truck keys and that would keep him from following her. His keys weren't in his pants pockets, and she didn't see them laying around. Her stomach fluttered with nerves as she examined the cuffs. That would slow him down. She just needed a head start, so he couldn't follow her to the meeting.

She found her clothes and dressed in the dark, then made her way back upstairs as quietly as possible. She put the handcuff key on top of the low dresser about eight feet from the bed, where he couldn't miss it. Her hands trembled slightly as she walked toward the bed, where Ethan lay with one arm cast out to the side. His face was relaxed in the blue-white wash of moonlight.

This was a terrible idea. Tonight had been amazing, and not just the naked parts, either. He'd trusted her with the story of his childhood and his foster family. Guilt gnawed at her insides and she hadn't even worked up the courage to do it yet. She should forget it, get undressed, climb back in bed next to him.

And then abandon all the plans she'd made for her future.

That thought made her sick to her stomach. This was her land, her future, at stake here. And it wasn't like she hadn't tried to find another way to raise the money. If she couldn't get the vines in this spring, it would be another year's delay, and even worse, much of the work she'd done to prepare the land would be lost.

Memories of how the warm soil slipped through her fingers and the scent of the freshly turned dirt filled her nose flooded through her, overtaking the guilt. With slightly unsteady hands, she silently threaded one cuff through the headboard and fastened it around a wooden slat, wincing as the metal clicked. If he woke up, she could always say she was planning on handcuffing him and having her way with him again. Though that wouldn't explain why she was completely dressed.

Ethan's breathing was slow and heavy and his arm was cast out to the side. Gingerly, she lifted his hand and fastened the metal bracelet around his wrist, keeping it as loose as possible. He barely stirred and she studied his face in the moonlight—his features relaxed and peaceful.

With some luck, she'd be back in an hour and he'd never know.

And maybe she'd keep him handcuffed to the bed and have her way with him again, just to assuage her guilt. A warm thrill ran through her at the thought. That would ensure her trip was as fast as possible.

And then she slipped back down the stairs, put on her shoes, and snuck out of the house.

ETHAN STIRRED IN THE WARM COCOON OF BLANKETS, a slight disturbance registering deep in the recesses of his mind. The bed was too soft, and it took a moment for him to wake enough to remember that he was in Bridget's bed. His eyes still closed, he reached for her, but his arm stopped with a jerk.

His eyes opened wide, but in the dark room he was disoriented. His right hand was secured to the bed. With his own damn handcuffs. He reached over to the other side of the bed and felt the cool sheets.

"Bridget?"

The house was silent.

"Bridget!"

He sat up, the cuffs sliding along the vertical wooden slat of the headboard. "Oh, for fuck's sake."

He tugged on the handcuff and the metal bit into his wrist. With a growl, he gave another yank and the old headboard groaned in protest.

"Goddamn it, Bridget."

His clothes, his cell phone, his keys—everything was downstairs. Even if he dragged the bed to the door, which he could easily do across the hardwood floor, he'd be no closer to unlocking himself.

"Son of a bitch." His muttered curses echoed in the silent house.

What the fuck was she thinking? And where the fuck was she?

Grabbing the metal cuff with both hands, he yanked, twice, and the slat snapped, freeing him from the bed, if not the cuffs.

He stomped downstairs to find his clothes and his keys, and only halfway succeeded there. But he found his phone, and dialed McBride as he dressed in the dark living room.

"Chief," McBride answered, his voice groggy. "Everything okay?"

"Can you put out an APB on Bridget Donnelly's car?" he asked. "I think she just left her house, probably heading to Lost Coast Harbor. She's driving a red Thunderbird convertible, 2005."

"Yeah, let me call it in. Need help?"

Ethan glanced at the cuffs dangling from his right wrist. "No, just pull her over and hold her, and I'll meet your deputy there."

He found his shirt across the room from the couch, his shoes where they'd been hastily kicked under a chair, and he finished dressing while still looking for his keys. He could have sworn that he'd left them in his pants, but they were gone, and he suspected that Bridget took them.

She really didn't want him to follow her.

Too bad, Irish.

He had left his truck unlocked, and it took him less than a minute to hot-wire the vehicle and head toward Lost Coast Harbor. His phone rang as soon as he pulled out of the driveway.

"My deputy is pulling her over about a mile from the city limits. You're lucky there's no one on road this time of night," McBride said. "How soon can you get there?"

"I'm maybe fifteen minutes away." Relief flooded through him that she was safe, but the anger was still at a full boil. He hung up, his jaw clenched painfully. He had no idea what he was going to do once he got there. He supposed he could arrest her, but he knew that he wouldn't.

Rounding the last curve before the Lost Coast Harbor city limits, he saw the flashing lights on the side of the road and pulled over, parking behind the squad car. He left his truck running and stalked up to the young deputy who was arguing with Bridget as they stood between the two vehicles.

Bridget's eyes widened at the sight of him and she had the

decency to look guilty.

"Chief Ford, I'm so glad you're here," the deputy said. "Need me for anything else?"

"Yeah, I want this car impounded."

"That's my car," Bridget said. "I need my car."

He raised a hand and pointed at her and the squad car's headlights glinted off the silver handcuff dangling from his wrist. The deputy's eyes widened, and he looked away with a sheepish expression. This was the sort of gossip that blazed through a police department and he expected that by Monday morning, it would be common knowledge in the Lost Coast Harbor station.

"You'll get your car back. But not tonight."

He grabbed his phone and found a number in his contacts. "Dylan, hey, it's Chief Ford. You awake? You sober?"

"Uh, yeah." Dylan's voice sounded like he'd been sleeping, which was what sane people did at half-past two in the morning.

"How far are you from—" He turned to the deputy. "Where are we?"

"I can give him directions," he said, and Ethan handed him the phone.

While the deputy gave brief instructions to Dylan, Ethan stared at Bridget. She stared back, that stubborn chin raised. He didn't trust himself to speak yet.

The deputy handed him the phone. "Dylan? Take the car to the police station. Leave the keys with dispatch. Thanks for doing this."

"No problem, Chief. I'm about a mile from there," Dylan said, his voice more animated, probably from the thought of being able to drive again.

He nodded at the deputy. "Do you mind staying a few more minutes until he gets here?"

The young deputy shook his head. "That's fine."

"I'll take Ms. Donnelly home," he said.

Bridget glared, but climbed into the passenger seat of his truck. It was a long and chilly ride back to the farmhouse. Ethan fumed and Bridget stared out the window, facing away from him. Her body was tense and he had no idea what she was thinking. Or where she'd been going.

When the truck rolled up and came to a stop in front of the house, Ethan turned to her. "Do you have my keys?"

She was still for a moment then shook her head.

Leaving his truck running, he got out and walked toward the front steps, leaving her in the cab. She climbed out and followed him to the door and they both reached for the handle at the same time. When his fingers brushed hers, his body reacted, despite his rage and disappointment.

"Why?"

She shook her head. "Something came up. You couldn't go with me."

He closed his eyes for a long moment and composed himself. "Where were you going? And what sort of emergencies do bookies have?"

Bridget turned, her eyes sparking and her jaw set. "You know we can't talk about this."

"Goddamn it," he said, pushing the door open. The cuffs still hung from his wrist. "Where the hell is the key to the cuffs?"

She walked briskly through the dark and quiet house to

the stairs and he followed her. In the bedroom, she turned on the light and stared in dismay at the broken slats in pieces on the unmade bed.

"That's what you get for handcuffing someone to the bed without their consent," Ethan snapped.

"The key's right there," she said, pointing at the dresser. "You could have dragged the bed a few feet and reached it."

Ethan gritted his teeth, and for the first time saw the silver key on the edge of the dresser. He picked it up and released the cuff from his hand. "Glad to know you had this all planned out."

She whirled around. "I told you, something came up. It wasn't a plan."

"No, this was definitely no kind of plan," he said. "You need to tell me what's going on."

"No, I don't."

"Not as a cop, Bridget," he said. "But what if whoever is leaving you these messages is willing to go further? What if it's not related to the property next door? Have you thought of that?"

His gut churned, because it was something he thought about all the damn time. He hated that she was living in the remote house, alone, and there was someone out there who was bothering her.

She blinked and looked away, her brow furrowed. She was hiding something.

"What do you know?" he asked, lowering his voice.

Her large blue eyes met his and he saw the sheen of tears there.

Shit, he was an asshole. She was being bullied by her

neighbors, and he was doing the same thing.

"Come here," he said, reaching her for, but she backed up.

"I'm sorry," she said.

"Bridget," he said, shaking his head. "This doesn't work without a little bit of trust."

"How can I trust you when you keep promising to arrest me?"

Ethan crossed the bedroom in two long strides. His instinct was to hold her, to ease that tension from her face. But he didn't know how to resolve their positions.

"I came here to make a new start," he said. "To be a good chief of police for this town."

She put a hand on his chest, but not to push him away. "I'm sorry," she whispered.

"I don't know how we get around this. I can't just enforce the law when it's convenient, and ignore it when it affects someone I love," he said.

"You're asking me to give up something important to me," she said. "My future, my dream."

"Yes. I guess I am," he said with a nod. "And you're asking me to give up something, too. I was brought in to clean up after a police chief who was on the take. My dream is not to be the next corrupt chief of police. I'm trying to do the right thing here, Bridget. And you're on the wrong side of that."

The silence between them spoke volumes. Neither one willing to budge.

After a long minute, Ethan nodded, his lips pressed tight.

"I'll have McBride add a patrol around the house," he said, and put his handcuffs in his pocket. He gave her one last look, waiting for her to give in, trying his damnedest to keep hold of his resolve.

Then he turned and stalked out of the room, and out of the house, before he changed his mind.

CHAPTER NINETEEN

Seven in the morning was way too early to be up and dressed and trying to project a professional appearance. Especially when one was trying to act like there was a perfectly reasonable explanation for her car to be parked at the Lost Coast Harbor police station for most of the weekend.

Grace dropped her off in front of the police department and Bridget used the front door this time, since she was sure Ethan would have left her keys with the person on duty. And by coming in this early, she'd hopefully be able to avoid seeing him.

Not that she didn't want to see him. She wanted to see him so bad it made her ache. But thirty hours after their fight, she still didn't know how to fix anything. She'd spent Sunday moping and even avoided her family's mandatory Sunday dinner, claiming a headache. Her father had doubted her excuse but didn't pry and she knew she had sounded ill, but that was from the stress of not sleeping and trying to keep from crying.

She hadn't felt this horrible since that night in the conference room when she'd slipped up and let Ethan know that she'd dug into his background. Then, he'd made her feel guilty by telling her about his tragic childhood and strained relationship with his brother. Sure, he'd included a little white lie to twist that knife a little more, but this time he didn't have to. He was right—she was not good for him. It was going to hurt his contract approval, compromise his authority at the police department. She couldn't do that to him.

The public counter was unstaffed and she stood for a few minutes, waiting for someone to notice that she was there. When that didn't happen, she leaned across the counter and tried to see into the open door that looked like it was a break room. The phones rang and were answered, so someone was working.

She made her way behind the counter and saw an older woman sitting behind a glass door in front of several computer monitors. Bridget knocked softly and the woman turned and smiled, waving her in.

"Hi, can I help you?"

"Yes, I need to get my keys. Chief Ford said they'd be here."

"For your little sports car?"

Bridget nodded.

"The keys are in his office."

Her stomach flipped at the thought of having to see him. This guilt was really for the birds. She couldn't remember ever feeling so horrible.

"Is he in?"

"No, not yet," the woman said. "Want me to call and find out what time he'll be here?"

Bridget shook her head. "No, I'll stop back by later. Thank

you."

The phones lit up and the woman turned back to the switchboard in front of her.

Bridget let herself out of the room and glanced back toward Ethan's office. His keys weighed in her coat pocket. She'd found them buried deep in a corner, where they'd probably slid out of his pants pocket. Even if she didn't have them, the lock on his office door was no barrier to her. Maybe she could leave him a note. Explain that she was terribly sorry that she'd handcuffed him to her bed and not in a fun way.

The police department was still empty, so she walked quickly to the back and tried the knob. It was locked, and she found the correct key on his ring and opened the door. Turning on the light, her eyes went to the couch against the wall and her body tensed at the memories. She moved quickly to the desk to find her keys, return his, and get out before he found her there. The desk was also locked and she huffed an impatient sigh. He was so paranoid.

She found the desk key, left the keyring in the center of his desk blotter where he couldn't miss it, and within a few seconds she was rummaging through the drawers. There were plenty of neatly organized files and office supplies, but her keys were nowhere to be found.

She could at least let him know she had come by. She took a pen from the cup on his desk, and looked for a piece of paper. A mesh basket full of reports sat on the corner of his desk, so she flipped through the stack looking for a blank page she could use. Then her gaze fell on the top page in the stack, and her hand froze.

Scrawled across the form in blocky handwriting was her name. She snatched up the page and read it, trying to absorb the information on the form. Then she slowed down and read it again.

It was a complaint, an anonymous caller reporting that Bridget Donnelly was running an illegal gambling operation. There was very little information provided, except that she often took bets at Donnelly's Pub, which wasn't even true. Well, sometimes it was true, but only on rare occasions.

The paper shook as she stared at it, and she realized that her hands were trembling. The report was dated Saturday, but that didn't mean that Ethan had read it. He'd come to her house in the late afternoon, and unless he worked yesterday, he might not have seen it yet.

Her instincts were to take the report with her, but that wasn't a solution. There could be another copy in the office, and it only delayed the inevitable. She set the document on his desk and straightened up as the door knob rattled, sending her heart racing.

Ethan walked in and her body reacted with a throb, an ache that she hadn't expected. If he was surprised to find her in his locked office, he hid it well. He dropped his coat on the chair, then closed the door behind him.

"I was looking for my keys," she said.

"I figured as much," he said, coming around the desk.

She stayed still and he leaned close to her, and then reached past her to the bookcase behind the desk, pulling the keys from behind a small plaque. He held them up and she reached for them, her eyes on his.

"Change your mind?" he asked, as their hands met around

the key fob. Heat and desire rushed through her and made her insides tremble. But instead of replying, she looked down at the police report on his desk, then back up at him.

"Don't worry, sweetheart," he said, his voice cooler. "There's no corroborating evidence. An anonymous report is merely a tip. Not enough to swear out an arrest warrant."

Somehow, that did not make her feel better. She swallowed and tugged the keys from his hand, tightening her fist around them. They were inches apart, not touching, and it was killing her.

"I need to get to work," she said, her voice barely audible.

"You're free to go," he said, so close she could feel the heat coming off him.

If she raised her eyes and looked at him, she'd lose her resolve. But she did it anyway. And he was staring at her with a longing that took her breath away. She could have that, if she'd just give up everything else.

The keys bit into the palm of her hand and she realized she'd tightened her grip. She stuffed the keys into her purse and turned to leave, and Ethan made no move to stop her.

When she turned back, any hurt or desire or anger was masked with a stone-cold expression.

"See you around, Bridget," he said.

She nodded, and left, managing to keep it together until she was in her car and driving away.

HER CHILDHOOD HOME WAS A WELCOMING REFUGE IN HER unhappy state. Bridget turned into the driveway and parked, wiping under her eyes in what was a vain attempt to hide how raw and exhausted she felt. Not that it would do any good. If her mother was home, she'd know in an instant.

She let herself in through the kitchen and then walked down the hall to her father's home office, where he ran all of the Donnelly companies. He looked up and smiled when she knocked on the open door.

"Good morning, sweetheart," he said, getting up to give her a hug.

Her father, tall and broad and imposing, had raised his six children to be self-sufficient and tough. She hadn't been handed her job at Donnelly Lumber. She had had to earn it, and continually prove herself to keep it. Sometimes she wondered if she was the only Donnelly child tough enough to work with Richard, or just the most stubborn. Or maybe the other five were simply smarter than her. They were all off living their own lives, while she was stuck building a family empire that she resented a little more with every passing year.

"Did we have a meeting this morning?"

She shook her head. "No, I just wanted to talk to you about something. If you have time."

"I always have time for my controller. Want some coffee? Your mom's around here somewhere."

"No, no thanks." Maybe she could get out before Molly Donnelly saw her and started grilling her about why she looked so sad.

"Is everything okay?"

"Sure."

"Come with me. I need some coffee," Richard said, leading her to the kitchen.

He took two cups out and poured the coffees, then added cream to hers. "You look like you could use this."

She must look pretty bad if her father picked up on it. "Yeah, probably."

He sat at the kitchen table and motioned for her to join him. "What's going on?"

She took a sip of the coffee, then pushed it away, her stomach too sour to handle it. "I'm starting my own business venture. I won't leave the company right away, but I'm not going to take it over when you retire."

The words tumbled out in a rush before she could change her mind. All the months of planning exactly how she'd tell her parents that she was abandoning their lifetime of hard work, and then she just blurted it out. Smooth.

"Oh." Her father sat up a little straighter and his lips turned down. "Why don't I make you Chief Financial Officer?"

Bridget closed her eyes and shook her head. "It's not about a title."

"It would come with a raise," he said.

This was a mistake. Panic rose in her chest and crowded out the air in her lungs. It was as close to drowning as she'd ever felt, the thought that she'd be trapped in her family's business for the rest of her life.

"No."

He set the coffee down on the table with a thump and the liquid splashed over his hand. "I don't understand. What brought this on?"

"What are you two fighting about?" Molly walked in, grabbing a dishtowel and wiping up the spilled coffee in front of her husband without missing a beat. "Bridget, why do you look so tired?"

"Bridget is quitting," her father said.

"I'm not quitting. Not for a few years," she said, glaring across the table. His annoyance for pursuing her own business instead of his was turning her guilt into anger.

"Bridget, what's going on?" Molly sat next to her, one hand on her arm.

"I'm putting a vineyard in this spring," she said. "Within a few years, I'll be able to produce about eighteen hundred cases of pinot noir. If it goes well, I'll add other varietals."

Molly beamed at her. "That's wonderful news!"

Richard scowled. "It's terrible news, Mol," he said. "This is a family business. If Bridget quits, what am I supposed to do? Hire Niall to keep the books?"

He threw his hands up in frustration and leaned back in the chair.

"You'll find someone else," Bridget said. "I'm not leaving right away. You'll have three years to find someone and train them."

"You're a Donnelly," he said.

Like she could forget that. Her entire life was built around that reality. And her father was always going to equate that privilege with responsibility—like the obligation to run the family business.

"She's also a Flynn," Molly said, before Bridget could answer. "And if she wants to use the Flynn family land for a vineyard and winery, I think it's a great idea."

"The CFO title will come with a substantial raise," Richard said, his jaw set.

"I'll take the raise and the promotion," Bridget said, and the lines around her father's mouth eased slightly. "But I'm still leaving once the vines are producing grapes for production."

"Damn it," he said, slapping his hand on the table.

"I've earned that promotion," Bridget said.

Her father grumbled, then gave a begrudging nod. "I thought you wanted the company. You'd certainly be good at managing it."

"I thought I wanted that, too, but it turns out there's something I want more."

Molly smiled and patted her hand. "It's very exciting, Bridget. We're very happy for you."

She doubted that Richard shared his wife's sentiments, since he was still frowning.

"If this is good news, why do you look so miserable?" her father asked.

She gave a weak laugh. "Because I didn't want to disappoint you. You've spent your life building the business and none of your children want it."

Richard ran a hand over his thick hair, so much like Declan's, and then he reached across the table and squeezed her hand. "I spent my life building up the family business because I enjoy it. I like building things. I like being a good steward to our timberland. It makes me happy. But if that doesn't make you happy, then I don't want you to be obligated."

She smiled and the weight on her shoulders lifted slightly. As tough as he was, she'd never doubted that he wanted her to be happy, just like all his children. "I'll do whatever I can to help with the transition."

"Is there anything else I should know?" he asked with a

sigh.

Bridget figured he'd keep trying to convince her to stay, at least for another few months.

"I need to come up with the money for the vines and I can't get a loan because I haven't paid off the mortgage on the property yet, and I used my savings for the down payment and the terracing."

"And what about, you know, the extra income?"

They never talked about the fact that she'd taken over Oscar's operation, but he knew about it, of course.

"Business is a little down," she said. "I've got some new competition, I guess, and there may be a legal problem."

Might as well lay it all out for him so he wouldn't be surprised if things went to hell.

"Legal problems?" he asked. "What sort?"

"Someone filed a complaint with the police," she said.

Her father let out a long exhale and his brow furrowed. She could almost see him calculating the cost of getting her out of a legal mess. It wouldn't be the first time he'd had to use his wallet to save one of his kids. But this time, she'd turn down his help. She was no longer a teenager, and this wasn't a house party that got out of control.

"Well, good thing you've got some pull with the new chief, right?" Molly said with a smile.

Her eyes widened. "Mom, I can't ask Ethan to do that. And how the hell did you know about him, anyway?"

Richard laughed. "If you think Molly Donnelly doesn't know what's going on with her children, you haven't been paying attention all these years."

"Does this mean you'll be quitting the bookie business?"

Molly asked.

She bit her lip, uncomfortable with hearing her mother talk about her side business so openly. "Well, it wasn't ever my long-term plan to be a bookie."

"Who's the new competition?" Richard asked.

"Not sure yet," she said. "But it could set my plans back a few years."

Richard leaned in, his face serious. "Do you need a loan?"

That was the last thing she wanted. "No. And what ever happened to 'Donnellys earn their own money.' Is that no longer the family motto?"

"But you would be doing it on your own. I'll charge you interest. It's just another business venture."

She shook her head. "No, Dad, I don't want that. And as your Chief Financial Officer, I have to tell you it would be a terrible investment for the company. It's a start-up, in an industry with a high rate of failure, and there's nothing to secure the loan with."

Her father frowned. "I don't care about that. I have faith in the company's founder. The offer stands."

"I'll figure something out," Bridget said. "I need to get back to the office."

"Missed you at dinner Sunday," Molly said, standing up as Bridget rose.

"Hmm-mmm," Bridget said, eyeing the door.

"Sunday dinners are the only time I get to spend with my children, now that you're all grown up."

Molly wielded guilt like a sharp sword, and Bridget did her best to deflect it.

"Sorry, I just wasn't feeling well," she said, moving toward the exit.

"Maybe next week you can bring Chief Ford with you."

Ethan wasn't exactly eager to spend time with her, even if Bridget were inclined to subject him to her family's weekly dinner. She made a noncommittal sound, then quickly hugged her parents and fled.

Not keeping that secret from her parents made her feel lighter, even if it hadn't solved her problems. And though she hated doing it, she had to consider her father's offer of a loan. She'd never truly feel like she built the winery on her own, though. No matter how successful it became, she'd just be another child of a wealthy man who got her start due to her family's status and money.

Bridget gripped the steering wheel and pulled out of the driveway. Was she willing to give that up, trade that satisfaction for the ability to go to Ethan and tell him that she was out of the bookmaking business?

Before she could answer her own rhetorical question, a blue Bronco blew through a stop sign and she had to slam on the brakes to avoid a collision. It was a familiar car, but she'd never seen it in this neighborhood, where the Donnelly family home was side-by-side with other prominent and successful Lost Coast Harbor residents. She watched Rowdy Pritchard's vehicle continue down to the end of the block, then turn into a driveway.

She headed in that direction, slowing down and pulling to the curb when Rowdy and No-Neck got out and walked up the driveway, disappearing from view. Bridget drove forward and slowed as she approached the house, for once disappointed that she'd gone with the distinctive red sports car and not a nondescript sedan.

As she passed the house, she looked over in time to see the two men walk into the side door off the driveway—ushered inside by Mayor Dale Strong.

CHAPTER TWENTY

Ethan parked the SUV in his reserved space and stared at the back door to the police department. Walking into his office didn't have quite the same pull when he knew that Bridget wasn't going to be waiting there for him. Finding her there yesterday had been a surprise, and he'd been completely unprepared for the impact it had. The mere sight of her took his breath away. Every instinct in him screamed for him to reach for her, pull her close, kiss her, make her see that they should be together.

And instead, he did nothing, and she left.

He walked down the hall toward his office. But instead of the usual early morning quiet, a small construction crew had set up and was hard at work. Plastic tarps covered several desks and large chunks of drywall lay on the ground. And there was a five-foot-wide hole cut into the wall that separated his office from the rest of the police department.

"What the fuck?"

Karen Merz popped up from the other side of the opening. "Oh, hi, Chief Ford. Lynn said it'd be okay to start on the smaller projects."

One of her workers brushed by him, carrying an armful of building supplies, and Ethan stepped out of the way, his mouth open.

"We'll get the window installed by the afternoon," Karen said. "The blinds won't be in until next week."

Carl walked in and stood next to Ethan. "Huh. Always wondered why there wasn't a window in that office. That will be nice."

Ethan clenched his teeth. The office had been claustrophobic, but it had its advantages. Now he wouldn't be able to roll around with the town's bookie in his office, even if he could convince her to.

"Fuck," he said, shaking his head.

"Swear jar," Carl reminded him, walking toward the break room.

Ethan stalked to the front of the police station, looking for Valerie Childs, but the detective hadn't arrived yet. He turned to the break room to get coffee, and wondered where he'd be working while the contractors took over his office.

"Son of a bitch."

"Swear jar," Georgie said from behind him. "Boy, you're going to buy all the donuts this week."

He pulled a couple dollars from his wallet and dropped them into the jar. "I don't suppose you know who signed off on Karen Merz' construction here?"

Georgie shook her head. "Probably no one did. That Lynn Fitzgerald is a pushy one."

God, she was probably right. Did anyone in this town have any respects for the rules?

He walked back out to the main office with his coffee

and took over a desk near Valerie's. It was within sight of the public counter, and within hours he knew exactly why the last chief never wanted a window into his office. There was no place to hide in the main office, and every citizen quickly escalated their issue to get his attention. By late afternoon, he'd promised to look into whether the dog catcher was selling people's pets on the black market, taken reports on car break-ins, loud neighbors, and unruly children terrorizing old people at the park, and along the way, contributed another ten dollars to the swear jar.

Valerie dropped a sandwich on his desk. "You should eat something. If your blood sugar keeps dropping, you'll have to take out a loan."

He smiled and unwrapped the sandwich. "Thanks. Sorry if I've been difficult. I don't know what to do about Lynn Fitzgerald."

Valerie sat at her desk and started to close up her files for the day. "Hey, on the plus side, it's a small job. It lets Lynn show off for her younger girlfriend, and the work needs to get done anyway."

"I guess so," he said.

"I was quoting you. That's what you told me in your email last week."

Ethan looked down. "I should probably be less open in my email correspondence."

"Yeah, probably," Valerie said, then nodded toward the counter. "I have a feeling this one is for you."

Ethan glanced at the public counter and saw Mayor Dale Strong standing with his hands on the counter, staring directly at him. Three down, two to go. Though he really didn't expect Grace Ransom to hit him up for a favor before the vote. The newest member of the council struck him as too honest to resort to that.

"Mayor Strong, how can I help you?" Ethan asked, joining the mayor at the counter.

"I would like to talk with you," he said, then looked around. "In private."

"Of course," he said. "My office is under construction. Do you mind meeting in the break room?"

"As long as it's private."

Strong followed him to the break room and Ethan closed the door behind them. "There is a matter of utmost importance."

Of course, Ethan thought, but gave the mayor a thoughtful nod.

"I would like to file a police report," he said. "A complaint against Bridget Donnelly, for running an illegal gambling operation."

The exact same words as in the anonymous police report, Ethan recalled.

"I can take that report," he said, studying the man's expression. "You do understand that if you're saying that you know about the illegal gambling operation because you participated in it, that is also a crime?"

The mayor blanched slightly, but nodded. His eyes shifted around the empty room. "I was hoping I could get immunity from prosecution in return for my cooperation with law enforcement."

Someone had been watching too much TV.

"That isn't my call. You'd need to talk with the prosecutor

about that. I can talk with Will Patton over at the district attorney's office, but getting an immunity deal can take some time."

"We don't have time," Strong said. "I want her shut down now."

Ethan's shoulders tensed and he struggled to keep his emotions in check. "Why now?"

"Because this is when she does most of her business. If you wait too long, you won't be able to catch her until the next big prize fight or the World Series."

"I'll get a complaint form for you and you can start writing out your statement," Ethan said, standing.

The mayor stood, also. "Chief Ford, wait."

Ethan turned back. "Yes?"

It was probably too much to hope that the mayor had changed his mind.

"The vote on your contract," he said, and Ethan's stomach clenched again. "It's coming up shortly."

"Yes."

"I want this taken care of before then."

"Or what? Are you threatening me?"

"If you want this job, then you'll put Bridget Donnelly out of business before the next council meeting."

"You're only one vote, Mayor Strong," Ethan reminded him.

Strong smirked. "I'm a very influential vote. And I only need to sway one more council member, since Snell is going to lose his fucking mind when he finds out you approved Ivy Montgomery's liquor license."

The mayor drew himself up to his full five-foot-eight-inches and then walked out of the break room, and out of the police station, without filling out the report. Ethan stood in the middle of the empty room, his fists clenched at his sides and his mind racing.

What in the hell was he doing here?

He was being blackmailed by the mayor, and three other elected officials had at least attempted to bribe him. He'd had to remind his own police force to not engage in illegal activities. Hell, even the woman he loved was an unrepentant criminal.

And that was the kicker—he'd fallen hard for Bridget Donnelly. That hadn't been his plan. He'd been blindsided by her. Knocked flat. And it wasn't something he was going to get over any time soon, if ever.

His plan—start over, clean up this corrupt little town on the edge of the world, put down roots here—that wasn't happening. He had failed. He was not cut out to be the chief of police, to restore the department and the town. God knows someone needed to do that, but it wasn't going to be Ethan Ford. At this point, he'd recommend a priest versed in exorcisms, because no mere law enforcement official was going to cut it.

He left the break room and stormed back to his office, which now felt like a fishbowl. Through the window, he watched the day shift leave and the few officers on the night shift check in, but his mind was still replaying the conversation with Mayor Strong.

There was no way in hell he was going to arrest Bridget— damn it, he'd probably let her walk under pretty much any circumstances. He wasn't that strong of a man to resist her charms. But he especially wouldn't arrest her on the mayor's say-so.

Which left him only one option.

He reached into the bottom drawer and found a piece of stationery. Before he could change his mind, he wrote out his letter of resignation, signed and dated it, and dropped the keys to his department-issued SUV on top of it.

He stood and reached for his jacket. He'd walk back to the rental house, load up his truck and be gone by tonight. It wouldn't be the first time he'd had to leave town in a hurry.

The phone on his desk rang and he answered it out of habit.

"Chief, I have your brother on the line," the dispatcher said.

"What?"

The phone switched over to a staticky line. "Ethan?"

At the sound of Trevor's voice, he sank back into the chair, preparing for bad news. "What is it? Are you okay?"

"Yeah, well…I know I said I could handle this, but turns out, I need your help," his brother said. "I got in a little over my head."

Yeah, me, too. It was almost a relief, falling back into this rut. Whatever mess Trevor had gotten himself into, it was something Ethan could fix.

"What can I do?"

The poor connection picked up Trevor's sigh of relief.

"How soon can you get to Barstow?"

Chapter Twenty-One

It had taken even less time than he'd thought to pack his truck, and it was getting dark by the time he was driving out of Lost Coast Harbor. Lights flickered on the houses as people returned home from work, giving him a voyeur's view of families inside their homes before they closed the curtains.

He'd left the keys and the letter on his desk, then turned off the lights and closed the door to his office. By morning, someone would realize that he was gone. His former supervisor had told him that the Bakersfield Police Department would always have a spot for him, and Ethan hoped that was true. But even if it wasn't, he had to admit defeat.

The tiny picturesque town on the coast had beaten him. For all his good intentions, and talk of doing the right thing, he wasn't any better than the con artists who'd raised him and that knowledge gnawed at his guts.

This path was at least familiar—his brother needed him, and though Trevor would probably be fine on his own, it felt nice knowing that he was needed and would be able to help him. Unlike in his own town, where he couldn't fix a damn thing.

The truck rolled through the last stop sign in Lost Coast Harbor where the city street turned into a long and empty two-lane road out of town, and Ethan's heart grew heavier with each rotation of the tires.

It wasn't just the professional defeat wearing at him. It was the personal one. Trevor was never going to change, and neither was Bridget. The first, he could accept. This was how his brother was raised—no respect for the law, recklessly doing what he pleased, heedless of the consequences. When he asked Trevor to give up his lifestyle, he knew that the odds were virtually nonexistent.

But Bridget was different. Despite her family's reputation, the Donnelly Devils weren't raised by criminals. And all he wanted Bridget to do was…give up the plans she'd carefully put in place and delay her dream of building something on her own. All for a guy who she'd known just shy of a month, and who had offered nothing in return.

Ethan hit the brakes and pulled over to the side of the road, his hands gripping the steering wheel.

What the fuck was he doing?

If he left now, without a fight, he'd regret it immediately and forever. His stomach twisted at the thought of not seeing her again. No one had ever fascinated him like Bridget, made him feel like he could spend a lifetime learning what made her tick. And not for any purpose other than to figure out how to make her happy.

"Damn it," he whispered.

He spun the steering wheel and made a U-turn on the two-road lane, heading back to Lost Coast Harbor. He wasn't giving up that easily.

Trevor was going to have to wait.

BRIDGET WAITED IN THE SHADOWS, LISTENING TO THE occasional sound of tires on wet pavement, the patter of moisture falling from leaf to leaf in the trees, and the steady beat of her own heart. She could have easily picked the lock, let herself in to the house, and waited for her prey. In dark jeans, and black sweater and coat, she was already dressed like a burglar. But she had no idea if Mayor Strong had an alarm system, or if he carried a gun.

When she thought about it, she didn't really know much about Mayor Strong at all. He sold insurance and she'd had her house and car policies through his office for years. That was going to change. She'd be damned if she was going to give him her money after he tried to put her out of business.

It was still hard to wrap her mind around that. Dale Strong was a cautious gambler, which might be an oxymoron, but did describe him well. He studied stats and teams and followed trades closely, then bet small amounts. She would have never guessed he wanted to be a bookie. The job took a certain level of risk tolerance that he didn't appear to have.

Car headlights glinted off the mailbox at the end of the driveway. Bridget stepped back behind a tall, thick shrub between the mayor's house and his garage. The garage door rumbled open and Bridget's pulse picked up. Her breath quickened, and her palms tingled. The car rolled in and then the door closed behind it. She stepped to one side of the path and waited.

A moment later, Mayor Strong walked out of the side door and toward his house and Bridget stepped out of the darkness.

"Eeep!" Dale Strong jumped and clutched his briefcase to his chest.

"Mr. Mayor," Bridget said. She parked her herself on the path, feet apart, looking him right in the eye.

He gasped, his mouth opening and closing like a fish, and then slowly released his grip on the briefcase. "Bridget. What—what are you doing here?"

"I have a business proposal for you."

Even in the dark, she saw his face pale.

"I, uh, you can reach me at the office—"

"You want to talk business at your office? Should I bring Rowdy and Martin, oh, I mean Fury, with me?"

Strong moved forward as if he would walk right through her, but she planted her feet and stood her ground, staring him down. He stopped short of running into her.

"What do you want?"

"You sent Rowdy to talk to me?"

He paused, then nodded. "Maybe."

She rolled her eyes. "Yes or no."

"Yes."

"You need better enforcers. No one takes Rowdy seriously, and where the hell did you find Martin?"

"He's my wife's nephew. He used to be a body builder."

"Great, use him for lifting heavy objects. But you're going to have to collect from people, and those two do not inspire timely payments."

"Why are you telling me this?" The mayor looked around

nervously, peering into the darkened backyard and then down the driveway. "Is someone else out there?"

Bridget sighed. "I came alone. You wanted to talk business, right?"

"You didn't show up."

She frowned. "I was detained, but I'm here now."

"Maybe we should go inside," Strong said.

"No, I won't keep you long," Bridget said. "You want to jump into sports betting in this town and split it up, but I have a better idea."

He tilted his head.

"You buy me out," she said.

His head tilted even farther. "Buy you out?"

"It's easier, because you get a readymade client base," she said. "It's cleaner, because having two bookies means competition, and that can lead to, shall we say, territorial disputes. Those can attract the wrong kind of attention. You know, like, the cops?"

He nodded quickly and looked around again.

"I bought out Oscar Pimentel five years ago and I'll make you the same deal he made me. And I've got to tell you, I've improved on his business. With my database, you won't have to start from scratch."

"Database?"

Strong raised an eyebrow. He was nibbling around the hook that she'd baited.

"I have spreadsheets going back five years that show betting patterns for all my customers, win-loss ratios, who is betting on home games, who is a dead bang loser, you name it."

The mayor licked his lips. "Spreadsheets?"

The hook was set. She had him.

"How much are we talking?"

A slow smile crossed her face and she began to slowly reel him in.

"There are a couple of conditions, but I'm sure you'll find my terms favorable."

CHAPTER TWENTY-TWO

Ethan let himself in the back door of the police department. He'd rather not run into the night dispatcher, who might ask questions about why the police chief had returned for another shift.

He hung up his jacket and then he took the coward's way out and sent his brother a text message that he wasn't on his way. He dialed Bridget, but his call went to her voicemail.

Fine, he'd go in person. At this hour, she might still be at her office. If not, he'd track her down at home. It wasn't a very large town, and he was a trained investigator.

He reached again for his jacket, but the sound of a door crashing open drew his attention. Through the new window, he saw Georgie running out of the dispatch office.

"Chief!"

"What's going on?"

"There's a fire—up on Townes Valley Road."

He raced toward the dispatch office to see the computer log. Bridget's address. Structure fire.

"Can you get McBride on the phone?"

The dispatcher hit a few keys and handed Ethan a headset.

The call connected and Ethan heard sirens in the background.

"Chief, I'm heading there now," Curt said.

"Call me when you get there. I'm on my way."

"Can you try and reach Ms. Donnelly? If she's not there, tell her to stay in town. We're preparing to go on to the neighbor's parcel at first light with a warrant."

Ethan's heart dropped at the words and he exited the dispatch office quickly, running smack into Dylan Jencks and knocking him over with a loud clatter from the buckets and brushes he was carrying.

"Jesus, Dylan," he said, lifting the kid up. "You all right?"

Dylan's eyes were wide as he nodded. "What's going on?"

"Can't talk now. I've got to get up to Townes Valley Road," Ethan said, hurrying into his office. He picked up the cell phone and searched his desk for his keys. "Fuck. Damn it."

"We're gonna need a bigger swear jar," Dylan said.

Ethan looked up, surprised the kid was still there, hovering in the doorway, looking worried.

"Whatever it is, Dylan, it's got to wait until tomorrow. Where are my damn keys?"

"Uh, I know where they are," Dylan said, shuffling in the doorway of the office. "I took them, so I could move your vehicle to the washing bay and, well, I dropped them."

Dylan's face was paper-white as he confessed. Ethan swallowed hard and tried to keep his voice from rising. "You dropped them?"

"In the storm drain."

He opened his mouth to respond, but saw how sick Dylan looked. "I'm really sorry, Chief. I think I can get them out."

Those keys were halfway to the Pacific Ocean. Exhaling a long breath, Ethan nodded. "Okay. You work on that. In the meantime, I've got to find another car."

"Take mine," Dylan said, his face lighting up. "You won't get there faster in anything else."

The Lost Coast Harbor Police Department didn't have a fleet of cars. His night crew was out on patrol and his day shift drove their cars home. With one squad car out for a repair, that left his SUV—which now had no keys. His own truck would get him there, but it was packed with all his belongings and not as fast as Dylan's Camaro. Ethan hesitated only a moment, and then nodded and pulled Dylan's keys out of his desk, grabbed his phone and ushered the kid out of his office.

"It's got an LS9 under the hood, about 638 horsepower. It can get away from you if you're not careful," Dylan said, running along next to him. "In fact, maybe I should drive you. I know that car. The roads are a little wet, too. The engine's too powerful for the wheelbase and if you don't—"

"Shut up and drive," Ethan said, throwing Dylan the keys. He needed to reach Bridget and McBride was going to be calling him and he didn't want to be on the phone while wrestling a muscle car up unfamiliar mountain roads in the rain.

"Cool, thanks!"

Minutes later, Ethan was gripping the armrest with one hand and waiting for Bridget to pick up her cell phone. The call went to her voicemail and he left a terse message for her to call. Then he typed in a text and sent that as Dylan gunned the accelerator and the car lunged forward on a straight stretch of country road.

"Jesus, Dylan. Where'd you learn to drive?"

"I taught myself. Lots of practice. Trial and error."

The error part of that explanation didn't help Ethan's nerves. The car slowed slightly for a curve and out of instinct, Ethan tried to put his foot through the floor, certain they were going way too fast to make the corner. But the car hit the apex of the curve and accelerated out of it, graceful and smooth. He let out a relieved breath.

"Don't worry, Chief. I know these roads," Dylan said.

The headlights flashed off the guardrails as the road climbed up and away from Lost Coast Harbor. Every minute that he didn't get a response back from Bridget felt like a month, and he had to resist the urge to send her repeated text messages.

Dylan slowed the car as they approached the turnoff to Bridget's house. A sheriff's cruiser was parked at the road, lights flashing, and he could smell the smoke. Ethan leaned forward, his heart slamming against his ribs.

Smoke drifted up the driveway and was lit from behind by the flashing lights on the top of the cruisers. Even without opening the door, he could smell the smoke, but as soon as he stepped out of the car, he could taste it. A soft orange glow in the distance made his heart thud.

A deputy with a thick shock of brown hair strode toward him.

"Chief Ford?"

"Deputy McBride," Ethan said, shaking the hand of the man he'd been talking to on a nearly daily basis.

"You reach Ms. Donnelly?" Curt asked.

Ethan shook his head. "No, not yet. What happened?"

Curt frowned. "The fire guys can walk you through what they think, but I called for the arson investigator and he'll be here in the morning."

The sheriff's deputy glanced over at Dylan and did a double-take. "I know you."

"I'm the intern," Dylan said, his face serious.

Curt squinted at him. "You're Dylan Jencks. I've given you three tickets for speeding."

Dylan nodded. "Yeah, I thought you looked familiar."

Curt looked back at Ethan with a skeptical expression, then shrugged.

"You're going to freeze your ass off, Intern Jencks," he said, eyeing the young man's thin T-shirt and jeans. He pulled a sheriff's department windbreaker from the trunk of his car and tossed it to Dylan. "Here. Put this on, and then help me put out traffic cones."

McBride and Dylan walked off and the fire captain motioned for Ethan.

"Chief Ford, I'm Captain Davis," he said. "I'll take you to the house."

The gravel driveway was nearly a half-mile long, and as they drew closer to the house, the smell of smoke grew stronger. His eyes stung by the time they reached the farmhouse. A fire tank truck sat in front of Bridget's house and several firefighters were still dousing the smoldering garage.

"The pump house is a complete loss," Davis said. "Some of the garage may be salvaged, but the contents are probably gone."

"The house wasn't burned?"

"Come over here," Davis said, and led Ethan to the side of the house. He pointed to the siding with his flashlight, and the light reflected off shards of glass on the ground. "Molotov cocktail, but one that didn't ignite for some reason."

All the air left Ethan's lungs in a rush. Bridget could have been home. She could have been hurt. Or worse.

"I'll let the arson investigator handle the official report, but I think it's safe to say this was not an accidental ignition," he said. "We'll stick around tonight to keep an eye out for sparks. And to make sure someone doesn't come back to finish their job."

That thought made him ill. He walked around to the front porch and sat on the steps, watching the smoke and ash rise in the dark. At least she wasn't here, wasn't in the house when someone tried to light it on fire.

But where in the hell was she?

BRIDGET BLEW OUT A LONG BREATH AND TRIED TO CALM her nerves, but her hands still trembled from the adrenaline rush of confronting Mayor Strong. She gripped the steering wheel and turned off the main road, Lost Coast Harbor sparkling in her rear view mirror.

If this worked, and she was fairly sure it would, it could solve her dilemma. She just needed to tell Ethan, without exactly telling him. Selling an illegal business was probably also illegal. Maybe. Anyway, she would rather not be the test case on that.

Her euphoria lessened when she thought of Ethan, especially how sad he'd looked in his office. How hollowed out she'd felt since then. If she could just convince him that she was going legit. Not like his brother, but actually going legit. She hoped she got the chance to explain that to him and it wasn't too late.

Her car zipped around a corner and she slowed, spotting a row of orange traffic cones ahead. As she neared them, she saw flashing lights and two cruisers blocking her driveway.

"Oh, damn it," she whispered. Her stomach dropped as she smelled smoke. She parked on the shoulder and jumped out of the car, a uniformed sheriff's deputy walking briskly toward her.

"Ms. Donnelly?"

She nodded, looking past him at the smoke pouring out of her driveway. Her grandmother's house. Her home. The vineyard. Her entire future. She blinked the tears away and focused on the words the deputy was saying, but had to shake her head. "I'm sorry. Can you repeat that?"

"Bridget!"

Ethan walked out of the smoky darkness, his eyes focused on her, and her stomach jumped. His jacket flapped open as he walked toward her with long strides. His eyes were on her, and his mouth set in a firm line. Relief flooded her. It was going to be okay. Ethan was there and—

"Where the hell have you been?" he shouted.

And he was angry with her.

"What?" She shook her head and glared at him. Her house burned down, and he was yelling at her?

"I've been trying to reach you. Deputy McBride tried to call you," he snapped. "No one could find you."

He stepped up to her and before she could answer, he reached for her, cupping the back of her neck and kissed her.

Really kissed her, with a passion and a fervor that made her body ignite.

"I'm really mad at you," he whispered, when they came up for air.

"Well, I'm mad at you, too," she said, raising her face to look him in the eye. She was holding onto him with both hands curled tight into the fabric of his jacket. "It's my house that burned down. You don't get to yell at me."

The tears that had been threatening since Sunday started to flow and she squeezed her eyes shut. God, she didn't want to cry in front of him.

"Come here, Irish," he said, his voice suddenly low and gentle. "Your house is fine. I'm sorry, baby. Don't cry."

His arms wrapped tight around her, pressing her against his chest. She exhaled, her breath catching.

"My house is fine?"

"The pump house is gone," he said. "The garage isn't looking too good."

She exhaled, letting herself sink into his arms and against his chest, her tears dampening his shirt.

"When I couldn't find you—" His voice was low in her ear, a slight tremble to it.

The fear in his voice hit her and relief swept through her. If that was it, maybe there was a chance.

"Ford!"

Deputy Curt McBride ran toward them, with a tall young man following him. "We got permission to enter the property from the Andersons, and the DEA team is on its way. From what we can tell, the guys who have been setting up the grow site are gone, but we're expecting that they'll return and when they see the presence here, well—" He nodded at the line of sheriff's cars and fire engines. "Dylan and Ms. Donnelly need to be out of here."

Ethan nodded, his face grim. "Right. Bridget, you and Dylan go back to the police station, okay?"

Curt handed Ethan a black object. "If you stay, you'll need this."

"Thanks," Ethan said, stripping off his coat to reveal his holster. He slipped on the vest and fastened it, then adjusted the weapon on his belt. "I'll meet you back at the station."

He brushed a kiss across Bridget's mouth, seeming distracted now by the activity going on around them. It was the first time she'd seen him doing his job—not the glad-handing that his title required him to do, not the budget balancing, the human resources duties, the politics involved with being chief of police. But being a law enforcement officer, responding to a threatening situation.

She swallowed hard at the reality of what he did and the sort of danger that put him in. And why he might need that flak jacket. Fear churned in her stomach at the thought.

"Ethan?" she whispered.

He glanced over at her. "Are you okay driving Dylan back to town?"

"Sure, yeah," she said, her voice weak.

He walked into the dark and the chaos and Bridget leaned back against the car. Her heart pounded and she was having a hard time catching her breath. Behind the car, she heard people running—backup arriving from Lost Coast Harbor, racing toward the trouble.

"Ms. Donnelly, I can drive if you'd like." She nodded at

the young man in the sheriff's windbreaker and handed him her keys, then followed him to the convertible, her mind still racing.

Dylan, the intern who had made himself Ethan's sidekick, seemed to enjoy driving the sports car back down the windy road to Lost Coast Harbor. He chatted away about suspension and horsepower and torque, while Bridget stared out the window at the passing scenery and tried to sound interested in his running commentary. But her thoughts were still back on Townes Valley Road, on the tall and brooding man in the bullet-proof vest who kissed her like he was saving her life, even after she had completely betrayed him.

God, she didn't deserve someone like that. She tried to be good, and granted she was new to it, but even her attempt to go legit involved some criminal activity.

Dylan parked her car in the spot next to the chief's truck and then let her into the back door of the police station. Ethan's office was unlocked and she let herself in, staring in dismay at the newly installed window that opened his office up to the rest of the police department.

She sat in Ethan's chair and leaned back and stared at the ceiling. Her phone buzzed and she reached for her purse, but her gaze fell first on a handwritten letter on the desk.

It was addressed to the town council and she read through it several times, her mind absorbing bits and pieces each time, but still refusing to accept it.

I regret to inform the council that I must tender my resignation...

Her breath caught in her chest.

...cannot be effective at my job...

The words blurred in front of her.

...effective immediately.

The hurt was a physical pain, something that she hadn't experienced before. A deep ache, simply from learning that she had driven away the man she loved. And she did love him. So much it scared her.

Chapter Twenty-Three

Ethan gripped the steering wheel and hit the apex of the curve, accelerating out of it onto the straight length of road that would lead to Lost Coast Harbor. He couldn't help but smile when the car responded to his subtle pressure on the accelerator. Now he understood why Dylan had racked up so many speeding tickets and found himself in indentured servitude.

He parked Dylan's car in the locked parking lot behind the police station, then let himself into the building. His office was dark, and he let himself in, expecting to find Bridget.

Instead, the long legs flopping over the end of the couch belonged to Dylan Jencks, who woke with a start when Ethan turned on the lights.

"Oh, hey, Chief," he said, sitting up and rubbing his eyes. "I was just waiting to see what happened."

He was still wearing the windbreaker that Curt McBride had given him earlier, and Ethan wondered if he was going to ever take it off.

"The sheriff's office took two men into custody when they returned to the grow site," he said, looking back out in the main office. "Where is Bridget?"

"She left a while ago," Dylan said.

"Did she say where she was going?"

Ethan took his jacket off and caught a hint of wood smoke from the fire.

"No. She was in here for a few minutes, then she was gone," Dylan said, unfolding his body from the couch. "Guess I'll go home. Thanks for letting me go tonight."

"Sure, no problem," he said. "Thanks for helping McBride out at the scene."

Dylan grinned and wheeled his bike down the short hall to the back door, and Ethan stood alone in his office. He reached for his office phone to call Bridget. The keys to the SUV, coated in a thin layer of muck from the storm drain, lay on the desk blotter and he picked them up and slipped them into his pocket.

Then his eyes scanned the desk for the resignation letter. It was gone. He looked on the floor, in the waste basket, and in the top drawer of his desk—no letter.

Oh, Christ. He couldn't imagine another police officer coming into the office and taking it off his desk. But if Bridget saw that… He dialed her phone and got her voicemail again.

Goddamn it. Now he had to see her, had to explain.

He stalked down to the dispatch office and greeted the dispatcher. "Who is on patrol right now?"

"Officer Hollis," she said.

"Can you get him for me?"

"Sure thing, Chief."

Seconds later, the young officer was on the line. "Hollis,

I need to track down Bridget Donnelly, she's driving a red Thunderbird—"

"Sure, I know the car."

"You might try her parents' house, maybe do a drive-by of Grace Ransom's address. If not—"

"I saw her earlier," Hollis said. "Give me five minutes."

The line went dead and Ethan thanked the dispatcher and returned to his office. He ran a hand through his hair. He needed to explain that letter, not just why he wrote it, but why he wasn't going to submit it.

His phone rang, but it was the cell phone in his pocket and not the desk phone, where Hollis would likely call.

"Trevor," he said, answering the phone.

"Hey, got your message," Trevor said. "You're not coming."

It wasn't a question.

"No. I'm not. Something came up."

There was a long pause. "Good."

"Good?"

"I shouldn't have asked." Trevor's voice was quiet, and there was something in his tone that Ethan hadn't heard before.

"Look, Ethan. I appreciate everything you've done for me, but you're right. I need to handle this on my own," Trevor said.

Damn, was that maturity he heard in his brother's voice?

"Are you in trouble?"

He heard the sharp exhale of Trevor's laugh. "Yeah, a little. I've just never been on this side of a con before, you know?"

Ethan blew out a breath. "What's going on?"

"One day, brother, I'll fill you in on all the details," he said. "But right now, I gotta run."

"Stay in touch."

The desk phone rang and he reached for it.

"I will," Trevor said, and the line went dead.

Ethan answered the phone and Hollis greeted him. "Found your girl."

"Great. Where?"

He reached for a pen on his desk, but Hollis' answer cut him short.

"At your house."

Ethan was silent for a long minute. Bridget went to his house.

"Chief, did you hear me?"

"Yeah, thanks, Hollis." He hung up and ran for the door.

Five minutes later, he parked his truck behind the red convertible in his driveway, then let himself in the front door of his house. It was dark and quiet, but he knew she was here. No lock would keep her out. And as he walked through the living room he detected a hint of her perfume. It was from her coat, laying over the chair. He stripped off his jacket and piled it on top, then made his way down the hall to the bedroom.

Bridget was stretched out sideways on his bed, her long dark hair spilling onto the white comforter. In the moonlight, her skin was porcelain, against which her full lips stood out, beckoning him.

"Ah, Irish," he sighed, climbing onto the bed and lying next to her.

That was when he saw it, the paper gripped in her hand.

He reached down to take it, but Bridget's fist tightened around it. He looked into her wide and wet blue eyes.

"You're leaving," she said, her voice low and pained.

"No, I'm not going anywhere." Ethan reached up and stroked her hair, smoothing it away from her face.

Her brow furrowed. "You resigned."

"I'm not resigning."

"Your closets are empty."

She was a better detective than he was a liar, apparently. Ethan reached up and brushed her hair back from her face, letting his fingers trace along her smooth cheek and down her neck.

"Bridget, please understand," he said, leaning closer and lowering his voice. "I was hurt, and I was angry. I would have regretted this decision immediately, and every day after."

"Then, why?"

"I don't know, I've never been in love before. I have no idea what to do with that," he said, his voice raw.

He didn't know how to convince her. For the first time in his life, he didn't have an angle to play, or a way to manipulate her—and he didn't want that. But mere words were never going to capture how he felt about her. How he wanted her, needed her.

"I made it to the city limit, and then I turned around. I couldn't do it. I couldn't leave you," he whispered.

"I love you, too," she said. Her voice sounded forlorn and her eyes filled with tears.

"Could you say it so it doesn't sound like a cancer diagnosis?"

She shook her head and her breath hiccuped. "No. It

scares the hell out of me."

He leaned in and pressed his lips against her forehead. "I love you, Bridget Donnelly. And I'm not going anywhere. Now come here. I have a very strong need to show you how much I love you."

She trembled under his kiss and his heart leapt at the response. He'd do whatever it took to be with her, and if that meant that Mayor Strong was going to torpedo the vote on his permanent contract, then fine. Bridget would just have to learn how to love an unemployed cop.

But instead of kissing him, Bridget sat up on the bed. She shook her head.

"No, I can't. I have to tell you something."

IN THE DARK BEDROOM, WITH ETHAN IN FRONT OF HER, looking so strong and true it took her breath away, she was losing her nerve. She moved, putting a little distance between them.

"You were right."

Ethan sat up and waited for her to continue.

"I'm keeping you from doing your job, aren't I?" she said. "I mean, I was."

"Bridget, I promise, I'm not resigning," he said, taking her hand.

"No, I mean… I can't do that anymore. So, I quit."

He leaned in and slipped a warm hand behind her neck and she met his eyes. Her stomach trembled at his soft gaze. "What do you mean you quit? Quit us? This?"

Her heart stopped at that thought and at the serious tone in Ethan's voice, the pain on his face. "No, never that. The business."

His eyes softened and he sighed. "I don't care about that. Honestly, I'm willing to look the other way if that's what it takes. God, I don't want you to change for me. I love all of you, Bridget. Even that you're impossible and impulsive and that you have no respect for the law."

A bubble of hope inside her rose. "You don't have to do that."

His fingers stroked the nape of her neck and her body reacted—heat swirling through her, a tingle that started under his touch and radiated out.

"What about your plans?"

She blew out a breath. "I'm not going to have the cushion I wanted, and I may have to delay my plans a little bit. Or— God." Her voice broke a little. "Or I may have to borrow some money from my father."

The thought still made her tense and it was hard to get the words out.

"I know, it's not the end of the world to ask for help from a rich relative. I just never wanted to do that. I feel like they gave me a great start in life, and I should be able to do it on my own."

"Not completely on your own," he said, his eyes on hers, a slow smile spreading across his face. "What if I want to help?"

"Oh," she said, a frisson of joy shimmering inside her. "Oh, I'd like that."

The thought of building something with Ethan, something they grew together from the soil up—that sounded nicer than she could have ever imagined.

"How did your clients take the news that you were quitting before the championship games?" he asked, staring into her eyes.

Bridget bit her lip and Ethan's breathing picked up. "Don't be mad," she whispered.

He shook his head. "No, I won't be."

"I sold it."

Ethan didn't say anything for the longest time, but then he exhaled and gave a short nod. "You sold your illegal business?"

She nodded. "Is that illegal?"

"I know I just said—" He looked down and pressed his lips together.

"Should I not tell you the rest?"

With a short laugh and a shake of his head, he pulled her toward him. "You're no longer a bookie?"

"Right." She moved so she was straddling him. Ethan eased an arm around her waist and pinned her to him, then wrapped his fist in her hair and tugged gently, tilting her head back. He pressed his warm lips against her neck, his beard leaving a delicious rough thrill in its wake.

"So I don't have to cuff you?"

She shivered as his lips traveled lower, her breath coming faster at the thought of being restrained while Ethan had his way with her. "Well…"

One hand slid under her shirt, stroking her back. Her heart raced.

"Kiss me, Bridget," he whispered, cupping her face, so his lips nearly touched hers. So close, so tantalizingly close.

The sound of her name on his lips sent a deep, delicious

throb through her body, through her sex. A tight fist of sweet tension that had begun building as soon as he'd touched her. She didn't even have to lean in to kiss him, and as soon as their lips met, that throb grew into a consuming ache. When his tongue swept through her mouth, the ache became unbearable.

"Is that what you needed to tell me—that you sold out?" he asked.

She nodded, her head spinning from the kiss.

"Let's just leave it at that," he said. "I don't think I need to know anything more than that."

"Good," she whispered. "Now come here. I have a strong urge to show you how much I love you, too, Ethan Ford."

With a growl, he rolled them back onto the bed and kissed her again. "Did you get a good price?"

She smiled and nodded. "I got the price and terms I wanted."

There was something in his eyes that looked an awful lot like pride. "I do not doubt that."

"You're not going to ask who bought me out?" she asked, as he worked her sweater up over her head.

"Is it a member of the police force?" he asked, and then bent to kiss her exposed skin. He cupped a breast in his hand and traced the edge of the lace bra, sending another shiver through her.

"No-o-o, God, Ethan, that feels so good," she said, as his mouth sucked gently at her nipple through the fabric.

"As long as it's not my officers, I don't care," he said, unfastening her bra.

Bridget pulled his shirt off, eager to feel his skin against hers. She pressed her hands against his chest, kissing his hot skin and feeling his heart beat under her lips, her fingers. Ethan's hands roamed down her body, undressing her slowly, as if they had all the time in the world.

She arched and moaned, her hand grasped his hair, her body impatient for his touch.

"Shh, love," he whispered. "I'm taking my time tonight."

"But, I need—"

"I know what you need." He brushed a finger across her sensitive folds, then deeper, stroking her. His lips and tongue followed and the sensation shot through her body, lighting up her nerves. Tension built inside her as his tongue flicked against her clit, teasing her, driving her toward the edge.

"I need you inside me," Bridget gasped, and he answered with a thrust of his hand against her sex, finding the spot that made her fall apart with a cry, and her vision went dark but for dancing colors and lights behind her eyelids. "God, oh, God, Ethan."

His tongue swept across her nerves again and her body shook with the force of her orgasm. "I love watching you come undone," he whispered, kissing the inside of her thigh.

Bridget's breath was ragged and her heart pounded. Ethan kissed his way up her stomach, his hands stroking her body, leaving a trail of tingles. He made his way up the length of her, kissing her, tracing her bottom lip with his tongue and her body came alive again, the need for him growing. Her hands found the button of his jeans, pushing the pants off him. She brushed against his hard length. His breath quickened as she held him, stroked him, and then ran her finger through the bead of moisture at the tip.

"Need you, now," he gasped, pulling her up.

He fumbled with the drawer of the nightstand, returning with a packet that he ripped open. She pushed him down again, rolled the condom on his cock, and eased onto him.

The sensation of him filling her fired her nerves and she tipped her head back and closed her eyes. Ethan's hands were on her hips, holding her as he thrust into her. The sensation of him inside her, becoming a part of her—this was all she needed.

"Come here, Irish," he gasped, pulling her down. "I need to kiss you."

She smiled and lay on him, his hands stroking her back, bodies sliding together. He gripped her hips and that tight ball of delicious tension grew with each thrust.

"I love you, Ethan," she whispered, just before their lips met.

The answering groan from him reverberated through her body, and her sex clenched around him. "Oh, God, Bridget," he gasped, his body shuddering. "I love you, Irish."

His hands gripped her tight, tension burst inside her, and she cried out as the orgasm overtook her. She collapsed against his chest, breathing heavily, wrapped in his arms.

Ethan kissed her head, his breath stirring her hair. "Thank you for stealing that letter from my desk."

His voice was low and serious and roused her from the blissful haze.

"You're glad I broke into your office?"

His arms tightened around her. "I've never been more grateful for anything in my life."

She smiled against his chest. "Maybe I won't retire the

lock picks just yet."

His laugh rumbled through his chest. "How about I give you a key to the house instead?"

"Not the office?"

"No, I'm not giving you a key to the police department," he said, the smile evident in his voice. "I thought you were giving up your life of crime."

She trailed her fingers across his skin. "I am, but I'm new to it. It may take me a while to adjust."

"Take all the time you need, beautiful," he murmured. "I'm not going anywhere."

CHAPTER TWENTY-FOUR

Ethan closed the blinds on his office window, locked the door, and took off his pants. He was getting used to the window in the office. Being able to see what was going on in the main room made him feel like he was more a part of the daily operations of the police department, and it made the office look twice as large. But he missed the idea that he could have some privacy.

The doorknob rattled. "Just a minute," he called out, reaching for the dark gray suit.

The door jostled again, and then opened a few inches. "You decent?"

"No, not remotely." He unbuttoned his uniform shirt and slipped it off as Bridget walked in. Her long black hair flowed loose down her back, and she wore a slim skirt and blouse that he thought of as her sexy accountant outfit. He grinned and winked at her as she leaned against the door and watched him change into his suit.

"Good. I like it when you're not decent," she said. "By the way, I do not like this window."

"Neither do I, Irish."

"Are you ready for tonight?"

"It will be nice to get it over with."

His contract hadn't been moved off the agenda, which surprised him. He figured he had two council members' votes—Grace Ransom and Marlene Dewey. Since he was helping Dylan apply to the police academy, Marlene Dewey would probably vote for him twice if she could, and he wouldn't put past her to try. Grace was either too new to be corrupted yet, or a genuinely ethical person. That would be a refreshing change in Lost Coast Harbor.

He wasn't sure if Lynn Fitzgerald had been sufficiently mollified with the work he'd allowed Karen Merz to do without bids. She had been right that some of the projects didn't require a bid, but he stood his ground on the rest. He also told Lynn that if her girlfriend ever again demolished anything in the police station without express, written permission, he'd arrest her for vandalism. That may have cost him a vote.

Snell would probably vote against him, if he knew about Ivy Montgomery's liquor license. And he wasn't sure what the Mayor Strong would do, but he hadn't come back to fill out any paperwork on his complaint about illegal sports betting, so Ethan hadn't felt obligated to do anything on his end.

He buttoned his shirt and started to work on the tie, but Bridget stood in front of him and took over. A hint of her perfume drifted around them and his body reacted. Too soon, she was done tying the knot and adjusting his collar for him.

"You look so handsome," she said. "I'm looking forward

to doing this in reverse."

"Too bad it's not a beauty pageant," he said, dropping a kiss on her lips. "What are my odds?"

Her eyes sparkled. "I've got a hundred that you'll get approved on a four-to-one vote."

"Is that the long-shot?"

"No, it's even money."

He kissed her again, lingering over her lips. "You don't have to come, you know. The vote's in a closed session."

"I'll be there for moral support."

He slipped his suit jacket on and took Bridget's hand for the walk to City Hall. The outcome of the vote didn't matter nearly as much now. He wanted to keep his job, and he could see plenty of things that needed to be improved, and they were things he could do. But it was a job. What he wanted now was a life, one that he and Bridget built together.

"So if the council rejects my contract, think I'd make a good bookie?" he asked, as they walked through the fog toward the city building.

"Are you good with math?"

"Nah, not really."

"You might want to try something else," she said.

"I hear there's an opening for laborer at a new vineyard outside of town."

"Not for another few weeks, when the vines arrive. However, then there will be eight acres of vines to plant," she said. If she was disappointed that she'd had to halve her first planting of pinot noir vines, he couldn't hear it in her voice.

She squeezed his hand. "I wouldn't worry too much. I have a good feeling about this."

So did he. And that feeling grew when he walked into the council chamber and saw his officers lined up against the back wall. Carl and Valerie stepped forward, looking sharp in their dress uniforms. Ethan gave them a nod.

"Thank you."

"It's our pleasure," Carl said. "The kid's having a problem with his tie. You might want to help him."

He nodded toward Dylan, whose tie looked like a badly wrapped gift.

"I got this," Bridget said, and pulled Dylan out to the lobby to fix his tie.

The crowd was thin in the council chambers, with fewer than a third of the seats filled, and the meeting scheduled to start in a few minutes. The closed session was up first, and would take place in a conference room behind the public chamber. The council members were likely already gathering, he thought. But then he saw Kenneth Snell wander into the chambers. His eyes lit on Ethan and narrowed in rage. The councilman crooked a finger at him.

"You gonna take that, Chief?" Carl asked.

"You gonna back me up?" he asked with a grin.

"Say the word."

Ethan laughed and walked toward the front of the chamber, then followed Snell out of a side door and into the empty hall.

"You son of a bitch," Snell hissed. "You signed off on that liquor license."

"Yes."

"I warned you," he said, shaking his head. His mouth contorted with anger. "You won't get my vote, and I'll take the rest of the council with me."

"What you asked me to do was an illegal bribe, a *quid pro quo*. I won't do that," Ethan said, keeping his voice level.

Mayor Dale Strong walked out of an office and toward them. It was the first time Ethan had seen the mayor since the day a couple of weeks earlier when he'd demanded Bridget's arrest. Then, the man had been uncomfortable and nervous. Tonight, the mayor had a calm about him, a confidence that Ethan hadn't seen before.

Snell didn't seem to care whether the mayor heard him yelling at Ethan. He looked back at Strong with a nod. "Hey, Dale."

"Kenneth," the mayor said. "Everything okay?"

"No. Everything is not okay. I'm afraid that I won't be able to vote in favor of Chief Ford's contract. He's having an affair with Bridget Donnelly. Everyone knows it."

The mayor shrugged. "I don't think that's grounds to vote against the chief's contract."

Snell glared at the mayor and then turned back to Ethan. "You look the other way when she's breaking the law, so don't act like you're ethical."

Ethan's temper rose. He knew Snell would go after him, but he had not expected Bridget to be collateral damage. He started to object, but Mayor Strong raised a hand.

"Kenneth, Ms. Donnelly is a respected member of this community. She'll likely be taking over Donnelly Lumber when her father retires, which will make her one of the largest employers in town, and she has never been on the wrong side of the law," Strong said.

His words were unexpected, and not at all true. Ethan's

mind immediately went to what the mayor's angle was—the long con he could be playing—and he came up empty. Was the earlier demand for Bridget's arrest a way to get something from him? If so, the mayor forgot to make the second half of the play.

"I'm sure Ms. Donnelly's family would not take this sort of accusation lightly, Kenneth," Strong said.

Ethan glanced between the two men, but kept his mouth shut, still trying to interpret the mayor's sudden change of heart.

"Kenneth, you're free to vote your conscience," Strong said. "But we're voting now. Get in there."

He opened the door to the conference room and shoved the councilman through. Then the mayor stepped back into the hall, shook Ethan's hand, and gave him a smile. "Looks like it's going to be a four-to-one vote. Congratulations, Chief Ford."

THE CROWD AT DONNELLY'S PUB WAS IN A MOOD TO CELE-brate. The NBA finals were wrapping up and the back room was packed. The pub, in the front of the building, was more subdued, except for the rambunctious group in the corner that kept insisting on toasting the new police chief.

Bridget leaned back and watched her brothers try and out-do each other with toasts. Under the table, Ethan squeezed her hand. His touch sent warm shivers through her.

"*Sláinte*."

Bridget raised her glass and clinked it against Ethan's, which was nearly empty. She kissed his cheek, then slipped away from the table to get him a fresh beer.

Gavin smiled as she approached the bar. "Another stout for the police chief?"

"Yes, please."

"I'm happy to buy a beer for the man who makes you smile like that," Gavin said, giving her a wink.

"He won't accept gratuities. He's like, honest, or something," Bridget said, and for the first time ever, slipped a five-dollar bill across the bar. Gavin stared it in mock amazement.

"A public servant who pays his tab? Now I like him even better."

Her gaze returned to Ethan, watching him interact with her family, as if he'd always been a part of it. He was chatting with Annabel, who hopefully was giving him tips on navigating the Donnelly clan, while Grace listened and nodded in agreement. She was another honorary family member who would help him learn the ropes. At the other end of the table, her father was laughing with Valerie Childs, who was halfway through her pint and looking more relaxed than Bridget had ever seen. The detective was probably thrilled that Ethan's job was secure and she wouldn't have to be interim police chief again.

The handsome bearded man with the amber eyes glanced up and caught her staring at him, and her heart flipped. Ethan smiled and heat swirled low in her stomach.

"Stop mooning around and deliver this beer," Gavin said, sliding a fresh pint toward her. "I swear, Bridget, you're the worst waitress I've ever had."

"That's because you never pay me."

She picked up the beer and walked back to the table, setting it in front of Ethan. He dropped an arm around her shoulder and she nestled in next to him, close enough that she could hear his whispered promise about tipping his waitress later.

A crowd walked through to the back room, and one of the young men waved at her, and then walked to the table.

"Hi, Bridget," Owen said, approaching the table. "How have you been?"

"Never better," she said with a smile. "You remember Chief Ford, right?"

He nodded and shook Ethan's hand, then glanced around the bar and dropped his voice. "So, uh, is the mayor around tonight?"

Bridget shook her head. "Haven't seen him. I hear he hangs out more at the Vista del Mar."

Owen wrinkled his noise. "The VD? Really?"

She shrugged. "Good luck."

Owen wandered off and Ethan pulled her closer to whisper in her ear. "Why would the mayor be at the Vista del Mar?"

Bridget picked up Ethan's pint and took a sip, stalling while she wondered how much to share with him. He did ask, and she wanted to be honest with him—as much as she could, at least. After a moment, she smiled, licked her lips, and leaned toward him.

"He's there because my brother runs a respectable establishment and won't risk his pub by permitting gambling here."

Ethan looked down and shook his head, and picked up the beer. "Was that one of your conditions for the sale?"

She raised an eyebrow. "Maybe."

"And the vote?"

She shook her head. "You got those four votes on your own." Then she thought about a moment and corrected herself. "Well, maybe I had some influence with Grace. She is my best friend."

When the party finally broke up, after Molly insisted that Ethan had a standing invitation to Sunday dinner, Bridget drove Ethan back to his house.

"Thanks for being my designated driver," he said, nuzzling her hair while she parked the car in front of his house.

"You're welcome," she said. "Can't have the new police chief setting a poor example."

She unlocked the front door of his house with the key he'd given her, an act that gave her a happy thrill each time she did it. It was a small thing, but she liked that she could now surprise him any time without having to break out the lock picks.

"Come to bed, Irish," he growled, grabbing her around the waist. His warm breath brushed her neck, making her heart skip. "I need you."

She laughed and turned and wrapped her arms around his neck, kissing him. "I'll be right there. I just need to check my email."

Ethan pulled back and his warm eyes studied her carefully, a hint of concern clouding his expression.

"Not taking up gambling are you?"

"No way, that's for suckers." Bridget kept her arms around his neck and smiled until the doubts vanished from his eyes and a slow grin cross his face.

"Good girl," he said. "Plug my phone into the charger for me?"

She kissed him again, took his phone, and pushed him down the hall. Getting his phone from him turned out to be easier than she thought it would be.

The sound of the shower turning on meant she had a window of opportunity, and she quickly tapped in the lock code on Ethan's phone and brought up the text message program. She found the number she was looking for and typed in a message, deleted it, then tried again. She bit her lip, reread it one more time, and hoped she was doing the right thing.

Hope you're okay. You should come visit Lost Coast Harbor.

She hit send before she could change her mind. She'd been thinking about it a lot in the last couple of weeks. Family was important. Too important to throw away, and Trevor was Ethan's only sibling, his only family. This would be a good thing for both of them.

Bridget smiled to herself and deleted the outgoing message, erasing the evidence from Ethan's phone. She reached for the charger and the phone in her hand beeped with an incoming message, startling her.

Thanks. I'd like that.

With a small smile, she nodded and deleted that message, as well. Yes, this would be a very good thing for Ethan. He'd thank her for this. Eventually.

"Hey, where'd you go, Irish?" he shouted from the master bathroom.

She walked down the hall, stripping off her clothes as she went. "Hang on, Sheriff. I'm not going anywhere."

Acknowledgments

Again, my long list of people who deserve my undying gratitude starts with Lily Danes, my co-conspirator and co-creator of Lost Coast Harbor. She always sets the bar high with each book she writes, which gives me something to strive for. Though we don't write our books together, I have learned so much from working with Lily and am a better writer because of her input, support, and friendship.

Thanks to developmental editor Jodi Henley, for her expertise and insight into my characters. Much gratitude, also, to Kaari Busick, who always makes my writing shine, and Kerri Nelson, for your amazing proofreading skillz!

Many thanks to Debra Sennefelder, my amazing critique partner. She's the first person to read my words and the truth is, I write to amuse and entertain her.

And, as ever, a huge shout out to the community of Divas, for being so generous with your knowledge and support!

About the Author

Eve Kincaid is a lapsed lawyer who decided that fictional crime was more fun than the real deal. When she's not writing about mysterious women and the men who love them, she's probably shopping for books, lipstick, or imported cheeses to complement a nice California pinot noir.

You can keep up with Eve's new releases by signing up for her reader newsletter at evekincaid.com. She'd love to hear from you. Just don't be creepy about it.